THE RED RAVEN

is a play within a play. It is the diary of a woman who, in reading another woman's diary, finds this mirror-image of her memories revealing more of her old love affair than she guessed and more of herself than she knew. Questions that have haunted her for years find answers: How could she have so innocently pushed her lover into her best friend's arms? How could two people who loved her betray her? What is the meaning of love?

This "fresh and very vivid account of a loss of innocence ... acutely observed" is "the work of a skilled and confident novelist ... the novel is informed by the same taste and grace that distinguished Miss Palmer's autobiography."
> —*The New York Times*

"A jewel!"
—*San Jose Mercury News*

"A stunning creation!"
—*Birmingham News*

"Impressive!"
—*Detroit News*

Other Books by Lilli Palmer

Change Lobsters and Dance

Published by WARNER BOOKS

THE
RED
RAVEN

A NOVEL

LILLI
PALMER

WARNER BOOKS

A Warner Communications Company

THE
RED
RAVEN

PART ONE

1

It began with the bronze head on the studio mantelpiece. I hadn't noticed it before, although I had been posing for several weeks.

"Break," said the painter, stuck her paintbrush in a mason jar, wiped her hands on a rag and disappeared into the kitchen.

For the last fifteen minutes I had been staring fixedly at the mantelpiece, for that was part of my pose. I knew it by heart, the old vase next to the two sculptured frogs, the empty wine bottle and the potted azalea with no flowers. But I had never noticed the bronze head before, probably because it was hidden by the vase (Greek? Flea market?).

I lifted the little piece of sculpture out into the light. A girl's head, no more than four inches high. I held it up, turned it sideways to study the profile, but I couldn't see it clearly, my hand was shaking so badly.

The painter came back from the kitchen with the coffee tray.

"Is this a portrait?" I asked. "Is it anyone in particular?"

She glanced at me over the top of her glasses and poured the coffee.

"Why?"

"I think I know her. Is she—could she by any chance be a French girl?"

"Yes," said the painter. "The coffee is nice and hot." I sat down on the hassock beside the easel, taking the bronze head with me.

"Anabel Maclean?" I pronounced the name as casually as I could.

The painter looked up from her coffee cup, took off her glasses, tilted her head sideways as if she were hard of hearing, put the glasses back on again and looked at me intently.

"Do you know her?"

I turned the sculpture from side to side as if I were interested in the technical details.

"The forehead," I said. "I recognized her by the forehead—that triangle above the nose. Like a bird's . . ."

I stopped.

"Yes?"

"That's really the only interesting thing about the face," I said, putting it on the floor.

"You think," said the painter, passing judgment.

This was something new. As partners in a joint enterprise, we had hardly talked before.

My job was to hold the pose, sitting in a chair, relaxed, hands limp, head slightly angled; her job was to struggle with the canvas. This she did in silence, except for occasional angry growls. We fortified ourselves with background music on the radio or the record player. When things got really tough, she would play Mozart. On the very first day she had laid down the ground rules: no talking, just music; during breaks still no talking, just coffee.

She poured herself a second cup, threw her head back and swallowed it in one gulp like a shot of cognac. Then she bent over, lifted the sculpture off the floor and dusted it off with her sleeve. She rubbed the nostrils and ears roughly with a turpentine rag, as if to humiliate the model in absentia, took off her glasses and held the bust right in front of her nearsighted eyes, almost touching it with her nose.

"Yes," she said. "The forehead was good. Very high, very broad. Almost as if she were intelligent."

"She wasn't?"

"No. She had intuition—that's already a good deal. I'd have recognized her by the mouth, myself."

"Really?"

"Tight-mouthed. A mean mouth."

"Anabel wasn't mean," I said firmly.

"No?" She put her glasses back on and studied me. "When did *you* know her?"

"Before the war."

"When, before the war?"

I thought back, forced myself to make an effort and get things straight.

"Two or three years before."

"I'd lost touch with her by then," said the painter, putting the head back on the floor. I couldn't stop myself from picking it up, turning it this way and that. I felt that she was watching me and put it down again.

"You can take it home with you—on loan."

"What would I do with it?" I said hastily, got up and looked at my watch. Although I studied both hands intently, I couldn't make out what time it was. I just stood there foolishly in the middle of the room. The painter watched me in silence and waited. I took two steps away from her, then turned back again.

"When did you know her?"

"When her name was still Anabel Beauregard. We lived together."

"Lived together . . ." I repeated, staring at her. She nodded. I walked slowly back to the hassock, playing for time, sitting down carefully, smoothing my skirt, clasping my hands around my knees.

"What do you mean, you lived together?"

"In my studio in Paris, Rue Vineuse," she said quietly.

"I never knew that Anabel was . . ."

"Yes, she was. She played it both ways. I've always stuck to women myself. But that's a matter of taste, not virtue."

Slowly, casually, and without any special intention—I thought—I folded my arms across my chest. She watched me and laughed.

"Go ahead and cross your legs too! What a prissy little thing you are! How old are you, for God's sake? Thirty? You're not in any danger. You ought to know that."

I got up, looked toward the door, looked at my watch once again, murmured.

"And—you did this head?"

"Who else? It's not very good, but it's like her."

"Very like her," I said.

She was still studying me through her glasses, neutrally, without smiling.

"I think that's enough for today. You're sure you don't want to take it home with you?"

"Quite sure."

"All right. Eleven o'clock on Friday."

2

Did I say it all began in the painter's studio? Mistake. That's where it ended. My discovery of the bronze head was the epilogue.

In one of my suitcases was a cardboard box tied up with string. It stayed there permanently, in the same corner, right down at the bottom. I never left it behind, but I never unpacked it either. I just needed to know it was there, first, so that nobody could open it—this was the only suitcase I always kept locked—and second, in case some day I decided to undo the string.

I knew what was in the box: a diary and a letter. I had never opened either of them. I didn't want to. I couldn't. Whenever I opened the suitcase to pack and saw the box in the bottom corner, looking more ominous and threatening every year, I would pile underwear and sweaters over it. But I never left it behind.

•

The incident with the bronze head occurred toward the end of 1947. I'm sure of that because I happened to be in London at the time, although we had already been living in Hollywood for two years. In 1947 my former husband was filming on location in England and I found myself living in a hotel; I was neither actress nor housewife and woke up in the morning without a schedule to meet, feeling free but lazy. So I was quite pleased to be posing for a painter; it gave me something definite to do twice a week.

I hadn't known her long. Someone had taken me to the gallery where she had a one-woman show. The exhibition had been on for weeks, and nearly all the paintings had little red "Sold" labels stuck to the bottom right-hand corner of the frame. Twenty or thirty people, catalogues in hand, were wandering about the two large rooms, in the usual solemn, vaguely embarrassed way.

Suddenly the street door burst open. In the entrance stood a small, stocky woman of about fifty in trousers and poncho, a sort of Venetian Doge's cap on her head. A flat, angular face, a child's turned-up nose, and a wide, thin-lipped mouth—the painter, no doubt, although there was only a slight resemblance to the photograph in the catalogue. She stood still for a moment, as though refueling, then marched diagonally across the room toward the office door, closing it behind her. A second later it flew open and she reappeared, flanked by the owner of the gallery, a bespectacled bald-headed giant, and a young man, flapping helplessly around both of them.

"This one and that one over there," she said in a loud voice, pointing to two paintings with red dots on the frames.

"Out of the question. They're sold." The giant's voice was brusque though subdued, yet people in both rooms began to gather around; no one wanted to miss what was going on. Neither the giant nor the painter, engrossed in their anger, saw or heard us.

"Take them down," said the painter curtly. "I have to make some changes. I told you to hold them in reserve, not to hang them. You can have them back by the end of the week."

The gallery owner glared at her over the top of his glasses as we waited expectantly, then turned and went back to his office without a word.

The painter pursed her child's mouth, folded her arms and watched the young man struggle with the hooks on the wall. Looking around, she noticed us for the first time. As she glanced at me, something caught her eye and she stared fixedly, without embarrassment.

The young man stood panting, waiting and silently beseeching, balancing the two paintings in their heavy carved frames.

"Put them into my station wagon."

She marched to the door, held it open for him, then turned back. Planting herself in front of me, she said, "I'd like to do a sketch of you. Maybe even a portrait. How about it?"

•

At the first sitting she put the charcoal down after ten minutes.

"Take that thing off. Here!" She walked over to a chest and took out a light poncho with a fringe of llama hair.

"From Cuzco. Genuine."

"Did you paint in Peru?"

"For many years. I was going to stay there."

"Why didn't you?"

"I'm too old. Or not old enough." She laughed and pointed to a chest of drawers in the corner on which stood a grinning mummified Peruvian head with shaggy black hair, the Venetian Doge's cap perched on top. It looked not unlike her.

In the gypsy-camp bathroom where she washed her brushes and which stank of turpentine, I changed into the poncho. I didn't think it suited me, but she gave a satisfied nod, made three or four sketches and started to paint. That was three weeks ago. We never spoke, just listened to music, drank coffee and said, "Goodbye then."

I had tried to find out something about her at the gallery. "A difficult person. Tricky." That didn't bother me; it applied to most people who wanted to achieve something. No one knew her personally. I didn't either, although I spent an hour and a half in her studio twice a week.

17

Slowly the colors on the canvas began to merge into a dense texture. Not that she ever said, "Would you like to look at it?" She probably guessed that I did anyway during breaks, as soon as she disappeared into the kitchen.

•

On that ominous day—a foggy, wet, English afternoon—I had walked all the way from her studio back to my hotel. I needed time. I couldn't get rid of a tingling, prickly feeling, the kind you get from an electric shock, although it was over an hour since I had held the bronze head in my hands, Anabel's head, shrunken, the way the Jivaro Indians preserve the heads of their enemies.

I knew perfectly well what I had to do as soon as I got back to my hotel room. It wasn't to be put off any longer.

Upstairs, I stood by the window for a while. The fog outside did me good, it left no view to look at, just a gently drifting, shapeless mass. From time to time it parted and for a moment there was a glimpse of the Thames far below, slate-gray and sullen-looking. Then the river disappeared again behind the quilt of fog.

Not that I wanted to put it off one last time. On the contrary, now that the time had come, I felt almost impatient. But I refused to comply right away with this sudden urge. A few minutes of torturous suspense was the least I deserved after so many years of procrastination and excuses. Besides, I wanted to make sure that I knew what I was going to let myself in for, once I descended to the hotel's luggage room.

Slowly I walked down the long corridor, spent some time chatting with the porter, forbade the page to accompany me, selected the suitcase and lugged it all the way back to my room.

I set it on the bed and looked at it. It had been light enough to carry; it was empty, after all. Except for the cardboard box.

My keys. A light, tentative touch, and the locks snapped open almost of their own accord. There it was.

I took a pair of scissors, cut the heavy string and lifted the lid. The diary. Brown leather with an elaborate lock, probably real gold. Lying beside it, the key, also gold. Everything Anabel owned was real. And the letter.

I opened the book. On the blank title page was a scrap of torn-off paper with a message printed in pencil in capital letters: "NO! FIRST THE LETTER!"

I tore up the scrap paper. No, first the diary.

The careful, round, even handwriting was as familiar to me as my own. And yet there had been few letters from her; we had nearly always been in the same city, in London. Obviously this diary was one of a series, because it didn't explain anything but started right in the middle of a Mediterranean trip in the summer of 1935. That was before I knew her.

But, judging by what the painter had said,

I didn't know her later either. I had no idea she kept a diary, and a pitiless, hate-filled one too, as a glance at the first page told me. Hatred for her husband Bill, for her daughter Nina, most of all for herself. So she had hated herself even in those days, before she ever met Jerome and me.

The first entry was dated October 10:

I always leave the lunch table now before B.
helps himself to fruit. I can't stand the way he
bites into an apple, making the juice spurt
in all directions.

Right hook at her husband, Bill Maclean. Bill. Slowly he came into view, in a tweed jacket, deliberately and expensively old-fashioned with two nineteenth-century slits at the back, a stiff very high shirt collar, his wavy hair and freckles. Once—when could it have been?—I watched him holding Anabel's fur coat for her, but, instead of letting go, he threw both his arms around her from behind, pressing his face into her hair and murmuring: "Oh, that feels good!" He had forgotten I was there. She held still, but I was glad he couldn't see her face.

Next entry, October 11. A slap in the face for her daughter Nina, who must have been fourteen at the time:

We finally arrived in Genoa yesterday and
I put her on the train. She took it for
motherly solicitude.

I stopped reading and thought: Never! Never at any time did Nina credit her mother with solicitude toward her.

Actually I just wanted to make sure I'm rid of her until the Christmas holidays. As the train pulled out, I blew a kiss after it. What I really felt like doing was throwing myself on the tracks in front of it. Like Anna Karenina. Tolstoy knew. This longing to be annihilated, crushed to a pulp . . .

It had grown even darker. I was having trouble deciphering the words. I went back over the last phrase: ". . . annihilated, crushed to a pulp . . ." The writing was careful, relaxed and rounded, the dots meticulously placed above the *i*'s.

I closed the book.

3

I lay in the dark for a long time, trying to get my mind off the diary, but it clung like a tarantula. In the end, dead tired but still wide awake, I remembered my old childhood remedy. "Think of Charlemagne," my father used to say when I was too excited to fall asleep the night before some great event. Why Charlemagne? My father would smile mysteriously and say, "You'll see. It helps." Charlemagne under his jagged crown never failed me. It always took some initial effort to make him appear—he was so very gray— but once I got him into focus he stopped the merry-go-round in my brain, even if he only stayed enthroned in my mind for a few seconds.

Okay, Charlemagne. Bring him on! There he was, carved in stone, sitting large and squat on a very small horse—face like a pancake—nose worn off—gone again. But I could hear surging, splashing sounds all around me, as though I were surrounded by water. Whenever I thought myself back into the past, I would "go under," faces and events would come swimming toward me, others lay darkly at the bottom or drifted about like seaweed, eluding capture.

Except for anything to do with Jerome. All that was lying just below the surface, crystal-clear, outlines and background floodlit. I could hear his voice and those of the people around him, and my own voice too, as distinctly as if I had taped them.

•

We first met Anabel just after we moved into our little apartment in Hampstead. That was the end of our nightly sneaking into the house in Parsifal Road, where I lived with my mother and my two sisters. If my mother ever heard us, she never let me know it. The house was also home to a few boarders, whose private lives were strictly their own affair, and in this respect my mother treated her grown-up daughters as boarders.

Up to that time, during the day, if I wasn't filming or rehearsing and if it wasn't pouring rain, we used to wander about in Hyde Park. We loved Hyde Park. It had brought us luck; ever since the afternoon when I first laid eyes on Jerome, it had been our refuge.

April 2, 1936! That was the right date, the day it all began. Lyon's Corner House at Marble

Arch. Not very chic, but at the time I was only playing small parts and had to look twice at every shilling. Early afternoon, the café was empty. I was waiting for my agent, who was supposed to bring me a film script—unless they'd decided once again that they wanted an English girl for the part.

The agent hadn't shown up. I'd give him another ten minutes, then take the bus home. My mother would guess by my face what had happened. By tomorrow I'd have forgotten all about it and be off eagerly pursuing other possibilities. As I turned the pages of my newspaper I suddenly felt a pair of eyes on me, burning through my beret and my mop of hair. Diagonally across from me sat a young man, drinking his tea. The chair next to him was tipped against the table to show that it was reserved. Somebody had stood him up too. Dark complexion, dark hair, dark eyes that quickly frisked me—obviously not an Englishman. When I looked at him, the eyes stopped investigating and he smiled. I turned back to my newspaper but remained conscious of his gaze, which never left my yellow mane. At that time I was a flaxen blonde, convinced that this would help me become a film star. A few minutes later he deposited his cup of cold tea beside mine, sat down on the empty chair and suggested that we might go for a walk, since it had stopped raining.

Crossing Oxford Street, he put his hand under my elbow, a touch that has always ignited a response in me, out of all proportion to the purpose intended. (I once happened to glance through the window of my taxicab and see a man I loved accompany a strange woman down the road. I bade my driver to stop for a moment. I wanted to see if he would put his hand under her elbow while crossing the street. He did. I drove on.)

As if prearranged, we walked briskly into Hyde Park. He knew a corner, he said, where one could get a deck chair without paying sixpence an hour. I knew all about that corner. The summer before—my first summer in London—it had been my luncheon restaurant. Day after day, I had sat there eating my unbuttered crispbread and slice of ham that was supposed to shrink my stomach and end its craving for milk chocolate, for on camera I looked like a full moon. That was a year before. In the meantime I had lost ten pounds as well as my fond belief in an immediate and meteoric career in England.

Way ahead, not far from the Serpentine, there was a stretch of grass so remote that the park keeper hardly ever came around to collect the money for the chairs. We walked in silence. Now and then I glanced at him surreptitiously. He sensed it every time and smiled back at me. Out in the daylight his complexion and hair looked darker than ever, the upper part of the face almost sinister, with a low forehead and heavy eyebrows which nearly met above the nose, and slanting eyes, set a little too close together. The lower part, the nose, mouth and chin, were so delicately chiseled that they might have belonged to a girl.

I noticed of course that he, too, was taking an occasional glance at me, appraising, perhaps even approving, though I wasn't quite sure about that. I wasn't very sure of myself at all, didn't know how much of the odor of sensible shoes, bobby sox, and ink-stained fingers still clung to me from the happy years I'd spent— not that long ago!—hiking under a heavy rucksack along the Rhine and the Mosel rivers together with my classmates, boys and girls. Aggressively healthy, noisy and indefatigable, we climbed trees, walked twenty miles a day and slept in youth hostels or barns, closely supervised by our teachers. No hanky-panky of any sort.

The result was that I displayed a hearty jocularity toward boys or, even worse, my behavior would be that of a possible competitor on any project they might propose. I knew I had to get rid of that penetrating girl-scout smell but found for a couple of years nothing to replace it with except embarrassed silence. Gradually a sort of tentative flirtatiousness developed, awkward and immature and at first quite ineffective. My girl friends seemed to have no difficulties in changing texture, but I remained strangely retarded in some areas.

Take dancing, for example. Mortified, I watched other girls executing the most complicated steps and turns in their partner's arms. How on earth did they guess what the fellow was going to do next?

I confessed to my mother that if a boy asked me to dance I would always plead a terrible headache. So one day at lunch my father surprised me by announcing, straightfaced, that he had arranged for me to take private lessons

in the foxtrot, the English waltz and the tango.
A young lady of good family would be my
teacher.

The young lady of good family was called
Fraulein Wassermann. She was about twenty,
four years older than I. She had a wind-up
phonograph, a stack of records, and a huge bust.
The latter was a drawback because it got in
the way when she clasped me tight (for purely
pedagogical purposes), especially in the tango
with its convulsive movements. She would hold
me elegantly by one hand as we swayed leg
to leg in dips and kneebends, but a second later,
when she clutched me to her with a typical
tango jerk, I would bounce against those huge
boobs, out of breath and out of step.

The first time I came up against a hard
masculine chest instead of those bouncy boobs
turned out to be an anticlimax, for the owner of
the hard masculine chest wasn't nearly as pro-
ficient in the steps as I was. I therefore clutched
him in an iron vise and manipulated him back
and forth and up and down, the way Fraulein
Wassermann had ordered.

I still remember the expression on his face
as he hurriedly escorted me back to my table.

•

The young man and I found two deck chairs
under an ancient beech tree, pulled them
close together and stretched out. In the distance
children played and their nannies on the benches
watched them, chatting and knitting. Occasionally a dog came and sniffed at us but soon went

off again in response to a whistle from an invisible master.

I decided to put order into the situation.

"What is your name?" I asked severely.

The young man hastily came up with his personal data. His name was Jerome. His father's name was Simon Lorrimer, his mother's Garibalda Pampanini.

I heard no more. Garibalda Pampanini! Twice I had stood in line for the third gallery at Covent Garden to hear her in *Turandot* and *Carmen*. Pampanini's son! His mother was from Sardinia, wasn't she? Yes, from Olbia. The youngest of fourteen children. "My grandfather was in jail at the time. He worshipped Garibaldi. My mother was the second daughter he named after him; the elder one was already married and he had to have someone at home who would answer whenever he yelled, 'Garibalda!'" From early childhood on she had sung the solo parts in the local church choir until, inevitably, somebody heard her and had her trained by somebody else. The rest followed just as inevitably: The great soprano Adelina Patti found herself indisposed one evening, and eighteen-year-old Garibalda made her début at the Paris Opéra as Aïda. The tenor's name was Caruso.

"And your father?"

Jerome plucked two blades of grass, pressed them flat between his thumbs and blew, producing a strident sound.

"My father? He's away at the moment."

"Where is he?"

"Somewhere. My parents have been separated for years. They may even be divorced for all I know. My mother paid for new uniforms for the Papal Guards year after year, trying to get a civil divorce recognized. You see, she's a good Catholic. On Catholic holidays we have a procession through the apartment, Mamma in front, I follow with the incense, then the cook, then the chauffeur—he doesn't like it, he is Church of England—and finally Benito, the dachshund. Every corner of every room has to be cleansed and sanctified with incense. That's how good a Catholic she is."

I dropped any semblance of polite restraint, and asked eagerly for more information on Garibalda—what she was like to live with ("Not exactly dull"), whether one could talk to her ("Sometimes—then she sounds like a wise old peasant woman"), whether she was a good mother.

"A good mother? She's a singer. I was one of her least remunerative guest appearances."

"*Was?* You're not anymore?"

"The other day she tried to auction me off. She had a suitable candidate in mind, so she looked me critically up and down and decided my body was too long for my legs and I'd have to propose sitting down. But I didn't want to get married, either sitting down or standing up. So she cut the cord."

"You must have had a hard time when you were a child."

"Only when I came home from boarding school at the beginning of the holidays. She would draw me a bath and give me a spoonful of castor oil before she would let me embrace her, 'because a son must be clean inside and outside to greet his mother.' "

I stared at him. He laughed.

"She was much more amusing than other mothers, I can assure you. Now what about you? Where are you from? What do you do?"

"I'm from Berlin."

"Refugee. I knew it. You live in Hampstead."

"How did you know?"

"All refugees live in Hampstead."

True. The first German émigrés chose the suburb of Hampstead because the solid Victorian houses with the maple trees in front reminded them of respectable German streets.

"I'm an actress."

"I know."

"How could you know?"

"By the color of your hair. Do you have a lover?"

Outraged, I stared at him without answering. What a cocky little bastard! He took my hand.

"Chapped," he said, stroking it. I snatched it away and hid it in my sleeve, yet could not stop myself in time from explaining, even apologizing.

"The water at home is hard. I always forget to buy hand lotion."

"Glycerine jelly," he said. "The best and the cheapest. Everything else is scented trash. I know—I'm a painter, the turpentine lacerates my skin. I'll bring you some tomorrow. Where do you live?"

That's how it began. With glycerine jelly for chapped hands.

The grass in Hyde Park began to flicker . . . our deck chairs floated away . . . I tried to bring Jerome back into focus . . . there he was . . . next day, at our garden gate in Hampstead, carrying a package . . . I was watching him from the window . . . the picture grew blurred and fuzzy . . . dissolved and faded out.

4

Next day the telephone woke me up.

"Where are you?" The painter's voice.

Where was I? I had to switch on the light before I knew.

"At the hotel. Why?"

"It's eleven o'clock," she snarled and hung up.

Half an hour later, when I arrived at her studio, panting and without breakfast, she was sitting at the easel muttering something without looking up, absorbed in background shading. I hastily pulled on the poncho and assumed the pose, hands clasped, head turned to the left, toward the mantelpiece.

There it was, the little head, slightly more

forward, in full view now. Perhaps she had been looking at it again.

She turned her eyes, those concentrated, absent, painter's eyes, on me.

"You look tense. Think about something."

"For instance?"

"It doesn't matter. But think about something definite, an experience of some kind. It will show in your face, but that doesn't bother me because I'm working on your knee. Your body will relax and you won't be conscious of holding a pose."

Think about something definite. My mother waved in the distance . . . Charlemagne galloped past without a word . . . Jerome appeared . . . and stayed. Jerome. That first beautiful year, when neither of us had a penny, when we could afford a movie only every second Saturday, upstairs in the balcony.

One memorable Saturday we were sitting up there, though not for the sake of the movie.

"You've got to meet my mother," Jerome had said several times. "Then I won't always have to be explaining things to you."

Why couldn't I go to her place and say hello? Out of the question. Garibalda didn't allow her son to bring a girl to the apartment. Why not? Garibalda never gave reasons.

Well then, how could it be arranged? "By accident," said Jerome, and that's why we happened to be at the Carlton Cinema for a movie premiere. Garibalda had promised to appear.

Jerome had the use of her Bentley for the evening. She would occasionally lend it to him, without chauffeur, of course. And without gas. Garibalda felt "the girl" should contribute that, a full tank if possible. The inside of the car smelled of tuberoses. I was wearing a new dress; Jerome for the first time was in a dark suit.

From the bacony we watched the theater fill up. "There she is," said Jerome. Quite unnecessarily, because no one could have failed to notice her entrance. White ermine from head to toe, diamond earrings, orchids in her hand— a bird of paradise followed by three penguins, immaculately attired gentlemen of suitable age. She walked slowly down the center aisle, smiling right and left, displaying two rows of very white teeth. She was recognized, there was some restrained applause, and she sat down.

Having seen her on the Covent Garden stage, I knew what was underneath the ermine: the ample body of an Italian prima donna crammed into a corset, but saved by an unexpectedly long neck which supported the dark head with the splendid blackberry eyes like the stem of an exotic jungle fruit. When the lights went out, I could still see the gleam of the white fur and the sparkle of the diamonds.

After the movie we fought our way into the foyer and watched Garibalda slowly and regally descending the wide staircase. Jerome pushed me forward, and the lady in white stopped in surprise.

"*Mio figlio,*" she explained to her penguin escort; it sounded like a Verdi recitative. Jerome nudged me another step toward her and she extended a white kid glove, which I held gingerly while making my curtsy. "Ah," she said graciously, "so this is the little girl. Charrrming." Turning to Jerome, she added something in Italian, smiling like a Christmas angel. Jerome translated it for me later. What she'd said was: "If I find one scratch on the Bentley, I'll beat the living Jesus out of you."

"*Naturalmente*, Mamma," said Jerome gratefully, kissing the white glove. Then she glided away from us.

●

"Break," said the painter and disappeared into the kitchen.

When the first swallow of hot coffee had gone down, I made a bold decision.

"Couldn't you move that head?"

"Which head? Oh yes, of course. If it bothers you."

But she didn't get up. She kept right on drinking and smoking and looking at me with a smile.

"Does it upset you?"

I didn't answer. She got up and hid the sculpture behind a book on the shelves.

"I need a quiet, relaxed model," she said, sitting down again.

"Sorry."

"If I were Cézanne, I'd send you home and say, come back tomorrow. But I'm not Cézanne."

"Maybe I wouldn't come back."

"Quite. I can't afford to take a chance, with a painting half finished. Okay, no more work today. Tell me about it."

"About what?"

"About Anabel. All I know is that she went to England and got married. What happened to her?"

I poured myself a second cup of coffee but remained unable to answer. I decided to go over to the attack.

"You tell *me* about Anabel."

She leaned back in her chair and took off her glasses, stretched like an old tomcat and replied in a surprisingly civil tone, "What would you like to know?"

"What was it like, living with Anabel?"

"Just as bad as living with a man."

"Was she your model?"

"No, but she would have liked to be. I had advertised for one and already interviewed a few. Too thin, all of them. It was soon after the war and there wasn't much to eat. Then the doorbell rang and there she stood. In a raincoat, belted too tight to show off her waist. I didn't give a damn about her waist—"

"What were you looking for?"

"The right proportions, of course, and hers were all wrong. Shoulders too wide, legs too long and too thin. But I liked her. I liked her enough to make coffee. She slithered about among my canvases like a canned sardine, a cup of coffee in her hand, smacking her lips, and said all in one breath: 'I don't enjoy coffee if I can't make a noise—I like it here.' Then she put her cup down and started to take her clothes off, unhurriedly, relaxed, exactly as if she were about to take a bath at home. She folded each piece of clothing neatly and laid it on the hassock, the one you're sitting on now—"

I jumped up. She stopped speaking and tilted her head sideways as if I'd said something she hadn't quite understood.

I sat down again. Quietly she resumed, ". . . laid it neatly on the hassock and stood up. 'Well?' she said. 'Beautiful?' 'No,' I said. 'Like a picked chicken bone. Try a fashion magazine. Maybe they can use you.' 'Are you sure you can't use me?' she asked. And stayed. That's how it began."

She stopped speaking and reached for a Gauloise. "I made a big mistake, and I should have known better. After all, I was ten years older and a hundred years wiser. But I fell for her, and when I realized it, it was too late."

She lighted the new cigarette from the old one. "I mistook her passion for warmth, had to pay a pretty stiff price—considering my resources."

"What were your resources?"

"A skin as thick as a rhinoceros's. You needed that in Paris in those days if you came from the provinces. I didn't know a soul when I arrived but I knew I had talent. And I knew that men weren't attracted to me. Probably because I wasn't attracted to them. Sometimes I got fond of a woman, but most of the time I lived alone. Anabel was an exception. She got under my skin, perhaps because she was both lover and child to me. She couldn't have been more than eighteen. I educated her, taught her, she knew absolutely nothing and was proud of it. But she gradually caught on to a thing or two."

So this woman with her glasses and her

paint-stained smock, sitting there in a cloud of smoke, had lived with Anabel when I was still at school! Anabel at eighteen, too fragile even then, callow, and shameless. And the other one, the painter, what was she like at that time? She had been much closer to Anabel than I had ever been. Had she been able to get rid of her without getting hurt?

"How did you break with her?"

"Drastically," she said grimly. "I couldn't afford her any longer. Not on account of the money, though that part of it was pretty rough, but because I couldn't paint anymore. I used to stand at the window looking down at the Avenue Kléber instead of sitting at my easel. I'd watch for a taxi stopping in front of the house. Sometimes I'd listen half the night. One evening I caught myself staring down into the dark and wringing my hands like Lillian Gish in a silent film. That's when I realized I had to do something. So I packed her things into three suitcases, tossed them in any old way and threw a few paint rags in between her evening clothes for good measure. You can never completely get rid of that smell. I even topped it off with a few drops of turpentine. Finally I took my big scissors—that pair over there—cut her fur coat into little pieces and arranged them neatly on top. I closed the suitcases and placed them on the landing outside the front door and went to bed. Without a sleeping pill. At some point the door bell rang. I woke up—and remembered. I was afraid I'd back down, so I said to myself in a loud voice, 'Are you a doormat or a painter?' She shouted at me through the door, 'What did you say? Open the door.' I got up and opened it. 'What does this mean?' she asked, pointing to the suitcases. 'It means that I'm a painter,' I said, slapping her face as hard as I could. Then I closed the door."

I sat quite still. This woman had slapped Anabel in the face as hard as she could. She read my eyes and said calmly, "I never regretted it. It had to end like that. It was the only way of breaking with her."

"Was that the end?"

"Just about." She laughed, as if she enjoyed the memory, shook her head (over herself or over Anabel?) and reached for another Gauloise, exhaling the first puff of smoke together with her next words. "A few months later I was sitting in a chair at a vernissage when someone put her hands over my eyes from behind and said, 'Guess who.' I tried to free myself because I'd recognized the voice, of course, but she hung on tooth and nail. 'Smell this,' she said, pressing her hands hard against my nose until I thought I'd suffocate. 'Turpentine!' Then she let go and pushed her way quickly through the crowd and out the door."

"And the bronze head? You said Anabel never . . ."

"She didn't. I modeled the head much later, I don't know why. I'd forgotten all about it until you dug it out yesterday. I'd forgotten Anabel too. I don't even know whether she's still alive."

5

The minute I stepped out of the door I was swallowed up in the thick, blackish-green fog. The famous London pea-soup fog. It would suddenly appear out of the blue and envelop the whole city in less than an hour. There would be no more buses or cars; only the streetcars would keep running, slowly, as in a dream. No traffic lights, instead policemen in white coats waving torches or flashlights at major intersections. Even if you knew your way inside out, you got lost. I stopped several pedestrians who loomed up suddenly like ghosts to ask where I was, but they didn't know either. At last I made out a great *U* flickering in the distance, an entrance to the Underground. I groped my way down a few steps and saw a faint beam of light shining hesitantly at first, then more convincingly, and suddenly, instead of drifting helplessly around in the black of night, I had found my bearings and was safely back in civilization.

My hotel was within sight of an Underground station. I swam through the pea soup the few hundred yards to the entrance and let the revolving door swing me back into the security of its warmth and bright lights.

As I entered my room, the telephone rang. "Are you there?" growled the painter's voice. "Good. That's all I wanted to know." And she hung up.

On days like this, everyone in London either stayed home or stayed put until the fog lifted. Not a soul would expect me or come to see me today. Dead silence outside. Now and then a foghorn on the Thames.

I had intended to visit my mother in Hampstead and return to the hotel late, tired out, too tired to open the diary.

There it was, lying in wait for me, not letting me out of its sight, spying on me. "I don't want to know," I had said at the time. "I don't want to hear her confession." But perhaps it wasn't a confession.

•

Diary. October 1935. Return to London.

Naiveté. It would disarm me if I didn't have such a bad character. After I'd switched the light out in the sleeping car B. confessed that he was terribly disappointed about something but hadn't been able to tell me

until now, in the dark, on our way home.
Paul Mildman had raised his hopes that
"everything would be all right again" once we
got away from that old double bed at home.
"Get into another landscape," he had advised,
preferably on board ship. M. may be a good
friend, even a good doctor, but he's an idiot.
Did he think the rocking of the waves
would throw us on top of each other?

Poor Bill Maclean. Run aground. Still thinking he could win Anabel back by his hungry
serfdom. It never dawned on him that he had
married Diana the huntress and had long ago
become her prey, not even her trophy.

Was he present when we met her for the
first time? A vernissage at the Lafarge Gallery.
Was that really the first time? Strange that I
wasn't quite sure, that the day wasn't etched
on my memory. Did the owner of the gallery
introduce us? Probably. I remember a man with
a mustache, standing beside us. The painter.
Anabel had bought a painting, the most expensive one in the whole show. He kissed her hand.
The gallery owner was sticking the little red
"Sold" dot on the frame. I also remember Jerome's expression while he watched. No one
had so far offered him a show, not even one of
the crummy little galleries in Chelsea.

There she stood. In a red coat. Alone, so
Bill couldn't have been there. She turned away
from the painting she'd just bought without even
glancing at it. She was looking at us, at Jerome
and me. I think she even exchanged a few words
with us. Later, as we walked down the narrow
staircase, she was behind us and tripped, and

Jerome caught her and said something that made her laugh. Then we all went into the Berkeley Bar next door. She must have invited us, for we didn't have the money for such things.

Now at last the whole picture emerged, persons and background stood out, like a photograph under the developing solution, growing more distinct by the minute. Anabel was sitting on a stool at the far end of the bar, wearing something sheer and sleeveless, her coat draped around her shoulders like a red frame. Everything about her was elongated and delicate as eggshell, even the head and straight black hair hanging down over her forehead, hiding part of her face. Thick straight eyelashes strung over her dark eyes like an awning, the nose a bit too long and narrow. She looked like a beautiful sad raven.

That must have been sometime in the summer or fall of 1936, because I could see my white dress with the black dots that I'd bought out of the proceeds of my late lamented play.

Impatiently, I turned the pages. I wanted to know what she had written about me. It must be there somewhere, she couldn't have left that out. I rifled quickly through the winter of 1935–36 . . . the spring . . . the summer . . . wait now, slowly now! July . . . nothing . . . August . . . there it was:

> Vernissage at Lafarge. Bought a painting. It'll go into the attic, but the painter looked hungry. That's why I was invited, after all. Met two young people. Refugees. She, at any rate, he perhaps not.

Was that all? Then why did she invite us to dinner? There must have been something about us that she liked.

•

First evening at the Macleans' home. What food! Served by a butler, followed by a maid in a white cap with the sauces, three different kinds. I didn't know which one to take and got no hint from her expressionless eyes.

Afterward we sat in the drawing room. Eighteenth-century walnut tables, deep armchairs, large modern paintings, flowers everywhere in gigantic pots. And now at last there was Bill, the way I would often see him from then on, shadow-boxing in the farthest corner of the room with his back to me, feinting and ducking and hitting the air to the low murmuring of a radio next to him broadcasting a match. Anabel paid no attention.

The first of countless meals at the Macleans', of countless hours spent in that room. I plunged in headlong, hadn't been aware of how much I needed it. I quickly got used to the weird paintings, stopped praising the flower arrangements and poured out my anxieties, my presumptions, my self-deceptions, my stratagems, my disguises as well as my comforts and my exaltations to Anabel, who sat facing me in a yellow wing chair, her thin fingers spread out on the arm, always on the alert, always passionately involved. Afterward, when I climbed into my little car to drive home, I always felt restored and safe and armed to the teeth. I had a girl friend again.

In my childhood "the girl friends" played an important role. There were quite a lot of them, five at least, including one "best friend," and over the years I was absolutely loyal to them. They were of special importance to me because even as a child I was obsessed by an urgent need to confide and share. I simply had to communicate everything I thought and felt to somebody, preferably to several people at once. Nothing seemed to me worth doing if I couldn't tell someone about it. Unlike Oscar Wilde, according to whom even the dullest thing becomes exciting if one makes a secret of it. Not to me.

It was different when other people confided in me. Then I could keep a secret. After all, it wasn't *my* secret, so it wasn't important and was soon forgotten.

When emigration separated me from my friends, some of them left behind in Germany, others scattered to the four corners of the earth, I was forced to keep to myself, something the English appreciate anyway. My need to communicate dried up. Now at last it could blossom again.

Anabel's diary began to mention me right after that first dinner at her house, first in monosyllables, then, all of a sudden, possessively.

L. for lunch.

And a week later:

L. for supper.

45

Then, soon after that:

L. all afternoon, until Nina came home.
She refuses to go to her room when L.'s here.
Won't leave her alone. Hangs around,
always wants to "listen," sticks like glue.
Spoils everything for me.

So it had become important to her. *I* had
become important to her.

The only thing that rubbed me the wrong
way was her manner of bringing Nina up. But
I kept my mouth shut, I didn't feel sure enough
of myself to raise objections. At the Macleans'
things were not the way they were at home,
and "at home" was my only guideline. We had
been kept on a short, tight rein held by such
careful, loving hands that they maintained their
grip even when the walls came crashing down.
At the Macleans' they used reins of a different
kind. Some of them were slack and worn out,
and the one they kept Nina on seemed to be
hopelessly twisted, probably right from the start,
because, according to Anabel, Nina had come
into the world "by mistake." She was short-
necked, plump and—perhaps because of that—
resentful.

"She has pimples on her face," said Anabel.
"Why does she have pimples? I never did."

Nina was being brought up in the "modern"
fashion. By the time she was ten, Anabel was
reading Shakespeare aloud to her. She said the
child preferred it to *Babar* and *Peter Rabbit*.
Nina was not supposed to be afraid of anything,
so from time to time her parents would go out

at night on their couple's day off, leaving Nina alone in the house. Sometimes, when I got home from the theater, my telephone would ring and a piping, childish voice would say, "I can't sleep —I'm scared—don't tell Mother." Then I would remind her of Georgie, the German shepherd, keeping guard in the hall, ". . . and if you can't sleep, recite very slowly 'The quality of mercy is not strained . . .' And if you're still awake, try 'O, what a rogue and peasant slave am I . . .' And if that doesn't work either—call me back."

She never called back.

Who knows, it may have been good for Nina to confront life unafraid and well versed in Shakespeare. Although Anabel had been educated in France, she was a walking Shakespeare lexicon. And lion-hearted. One night there was a fire next door. While the house's owners stood in the street wringing their hands and counting the treasures they had thrown out of the windows, Anabel tied a wet cloth around her mouth, forced her way through the back door and into the smoke-filled kitchen and rescued the cat.

It was Nina who told me that, not Anabel.

•

Throughout the first year of our friendship I was appearing either in bad plays on the legitimate stage or in bad films in the movie studios. I remained, however, obstinate and blind, confidently expecting the big breakthrough, telling myself at the mere sight of a new script: this is it! In all my hopes, forebodings and inevitable catastrophes, Anabel was with me every step of the way:

> L. for tea after her matinee. Told me all about the bloody mess. They are all on half-salary since yesterday! If the producer were not such a crook, I'd pump some money into the thing to see if it doesn't catch on. Behind her back, of course.

She hardly every spoke about herself. All I knew was that she had been born in Paris, that her mother had died early on, that she hated her father and stepmother and had used her first passport to get out of France. But why had she married Bill? Bill, of all people? Because he reminded her of her father, she said once. Of the father she hated! (But who had left his considerable fortune to her, not to her stepmother.) Like Bill, he had been a stockbroker, an occupation she detested. Then why? "To get my own back." (On whom? On her father? On Bill?) "I'm a vindictive person. Didn't you know that?"

No, I didn't know that, and it wasn't true. She said it because she liked to see me baffled, chewing my fingernails. Then she would laugh and say I shouldn't believe everything she said. But what was I to believe? Gradually I gave up asking questions and hardly noticed that I was the one who did all the talking, while she listened. And what a listener she was! I could even tell her everything about Jerome, all the things I didn't tell my mother. Though my mother too, and no less intensely, shared all my daily triumphs and defeats, everything except my "private life." There she was strangely embarrassed. So was I. I told her only what was strictly necessary.

Diary:

> L. has a mother. A mother who is important
> to her. Odd! The whole relationship is odd.
> At home L. is the head of the family—
> and at the same time "the child." The mother
> speaks bad English, smiling disarmingly.
> Still has all her own teeth.

Her own teeth! Of course. That was something unusual in England. "No one should have teeth. Teeth are unhealthy," people used to say, and even young girls and boys would grin cheerfully at you with chalk-white china choppers.

> The mother rents rooms to other refugees.
> This is a help to L. All the same, L. ought
> to get away. She shouldn't keep on being
> Mummy's goldilocks forever. But she can't
> bring herself to do it. At present she's living
> half with J. in a tatty little apartment, and
> half at her mother's, eating her dinner with
> meat and vegetables and pudding like a good
> girl. And next morning, at the studio, she's
> supposed to ooze sex appeal. Makeup alone
> won't do it.

On the nose!

> The mother was an actress before she married.
> You'd never guess. Or maybe you would.
> Sometimes, when she gives you a searching
> glance, she looks anything but bourgeois.
> I don't think she likes me. Doesn't trust me.
> Maybe she's jealous.

Way off the mark! My mother wasn't jealous. She was watchful.

> Yesterday I called for L. at her house. J. was there too. He loves that mother.
> He'd move right in if she'd let him.

But she wouldn't let him. After my father's death she had accepted the fact that her three daughters had boy friends, something unknown in her day. She invited the young men to the house, offered them tea and was glad to bid them goodbye again. If asked, she'd give her opinion. She found Jerome "interesting" but still not the right man for me. She wanted her three future sons-in-law to be like my father. She wanted three replicas of the man who had made her a happy woman for twenty-four years until the day he died.

●

Jerome accompanied me only rarely when I went to the Macleans'. Now and then he would come to supper. With the help of a glass of wine and a good cigar he could even get along with Bill. He wasn't particularly interested in Anabel; he said she was too thin, she ought to wear a brooch to show which was the front.

The diary rarely mentions him.

> L. and J. for supper. L. follows him with her eyes wherever he goes.

Did I?

> J. is a mixture of decadent gypsy and randy intellectual.

And:

> If J. ever pats me on the head as if I were a
> dog again, I'm going to tell him I know
> he's a shit.

When was that? When was Jerome a shit? In November 1936, pretty early on. No, they didn't like each other, argued a lot. Anabel would get nasty when she thought he wasn't sufficiently attentive or affectionate with me. I was both the link and the buffer, so I was sometimes quite glad not to have Jerome around. "You're spoiled," I used to tell Anabel. "Bill spoils you because you don't love him. That's the difference."

When I talked to Jerome about her, I didn't get very far. "Stop singing her praises. And stop being so eternally grateful. We don't *owe* her anything. We give her as much as she gives us."

"What do we give her?"

"Color. That's worth more than good food."

I saw it differently. Anabel gave *us* color, exquisite, expensive color, something I was very keen on. When I wasn't working, we used to go to concerts with her, sit in her box at the opera, go driving in her Rolls Royce on Sundays. Once we went to *Così fan tutte* at Glyndebourne. That time Bill came along too, sitting in front next to the chauffeur, fumbling with the car radio in order to catch a boxing match somewhere. After that we gave up music and concentrated on old towns, castles and churches, leaving Bill to his Sunday golf. Until then all I had seen of England was the film studios and the stage doors; now I began to get to know it for the first time. Jerome would sit next to me, hand on my knee, the Rolls would glide soundlessly along, through Tudor villages with thatched roofs and duck ponds. Those were the best Sundays; I was sitting between the man I loved and the friend I loved.

Anabel's diary reads like a Baedeker:

Chester. Bought Sheraton table for the guest room. Restored, of course. L. doesn't have a clue about such things. Showed her where it had been repaired. She's learning. Found a bracelet for her, old paste, very beautifully set. She didn't really appreciate it, but she acted pleased so as not to hurt my feelings.

Or:

Winchester. L. sat in the cathedral for hours in rapt silence. I froze. How she can enjoy herself!

That I could. Right from the start. If I concentrate, I can even now capture a tiny whiff of the physical joy I experienced when, at the age of about twelve, I'd bring my bicycle up from the cellar on a warm summer morning and climb on the saddle, my head high, my eyes half closed, my feet so full of pent-up energy that they barely needed to touch the pedals— and I'm off, on my way to school again, past the Reichskanzlerplatz, down the gentle slope of the Heerstrasse, where you could take your hands off the handlebars and raise both arms sideways, not just to show off but to expose as much of your body as possible to the rush of warm air—and so I would streak along in the sunshine, perfectly and deliriously happy.

Years later, when I tried to imagine what it must be like to lie in a man's arms, I would always think of those summer-morning bicycle rides as the very essence of bliss and of ultimate rapture.

6

When I rang the studio doorbell at twelve o'clock, she made me wait a long time before she opened the door. In spite of the warm weather, she was wrapped up in something thick and shapeless ending in trousers tucked in galoshes.

"Got a cold," she croaked. "Can't work to-day. You can go home."

I hung my coat on the hook.

"Shall I make you some hot tea with lemon?"

"I hate tea," she muttered, waddling into the studio ahead of me. "I'll make coffee."

Strange silence in the studio. For the first time there was no music. The painter appeared with the tray, panting and wheezing behind the thermos and the cups. We drank without talking.

"Isn't there anybody in your life . . ." I ventured, surprised at my courage.

"What do you mean?"

"Somebody to look after you?"

"Can't stand being looked after. I can doctor myself. I studied medicine for a few terms." She coughed and clutched her throat.

"You shouldn't talk," I said.

"All right. *You* talk."

She looked at me expectantly, having set the trap. My turn now.

"What would you like to hear?"

"About Anabel. What else?"

"There's not much to tell. We were friends, just . . . friends."

She grinned.

"You don't have to spell it out."

"Well, we were friends."

"I know that already. Anything else?"

She coughed violently, almost choked. I poured her some more hot coffee. When the spasm had passed, she opened her mouth like a bird, perhaps because she couldn't breathe or because she wanted to be fed.

"It just occurred to me that I first met Anabel in the same setting in which you saw her for the last time, at a vernissage. Strange, isn't it?"

She showed no surprise, muttered, "What were you doing there? Buying?"

"No. We had no money."

"Who's *we?*"

"My boy friend and I. He was a painter."

"Here in London? What was his name?"

"Jerome Lorrimer."

"Lorrimer? Graphics?"

"No, a painter."

"He does graphics now," she whispered. "Quite good ones. Didn't you know?"

I shook my head. She gave me a serious, almost shocked look.

"Did Anabel break it up?"

"No."

Under her gaze, I stared out of the window.

"When she was living with me," she whispered hoarsely, "she was still practically a child. Innocent, with a sort of animal meanness, the way children are."

"Anabel wasn't mean."

"You said that before. Maybe she grew tamer over the years, that's all. It wasn't a question of being immoral, she *had* no morals. Helped herself and never paid up. She was a tramp. And a predator."

I stared stubbornly at her.

"I know a different side of her."

"Which side?"

"She was my friend."

"Not anymore?"

"No."

"Why not?"

"Circumstances. I live in America."

She looked cross and coughed hoarsely.

"You were going to tell me something, but it's like getting blood out of a stone. Go on home. I'll call you when we can work again."

I left.

7

A diary entry in September 1936 says:

J.'s father iş back.

That's all.

Yes, he was back, but he remained invisible. And my acquaintance with Garibalda hadn't grown any closer since the Carlton Cinema. I had seen her once more, but only from a distance: at Covent Garden as Tosca. She had given Jerome two tickets, a rare treat, and we sat in the stage box.

Garibalda was slightly past her prime. She carried herself more majestically than ever, but it was obvious that she was making a great effort. Jerome, in the chair next to me, lived with her through every sound she made. Before a high note he ducked, as if somebody were about to hit him. During the third act, when she reached the dreaded *"Vissi d'arte . . . ,"* he closed his eyes, slid deeper and deeper into his seat and whimpered soundlessly until she landed—not altogether victoriously—on the high C. After which she relaxed, resting lovingly though a little too long on the following lower notes. Jerome relaxed too. He sat up straight and dabbed at his face with his handkerchief. Gently, because he'd had a hard day. On days when she was going to sing at night, Garibalda used to throw things. That day she'd thrown a jar of her special face cream at him, which may have contributed to her beauty but not to his, for it left him with a large blue bump on his forehead.

And now his father was back.

"Can you remember the time when your parents were still living together?"

"Vaguely. The only thing I remember clearly is one day hearing a loud bang. A very loud bang. In fact, that may be my earliest memory." He frowned, knitting his thick eyebrows into an unbroken black stripe. "It was early in the morning, the sun was shining and I was wearing a sailor suit—for the first time, I think. That's why I was so excited. I was hopping about the apartment on one leg, and finally I hopped into the living room, where my father was sitting. Probably working on his mathematical problems even then. Anyway I refused to stop hopping, although he firmly told me to. I remember him trying to grab my collar, which I thought was a lot of fun, and I crept under the piano and crowed like a cockerel. Whereupon he fired his pistol at me. He was in uniform, so he had it handy. That was the bang I remember. The bullet lodged in La Pampanini's piano, which was unfortunate."

"For your father?"

"No, for the piano."

•

He rarely spoke about his father. All I knew was that he was a physicist and lived in Chelsea. Jerome lived there too, part of the time. Or he slept at Garibalda's. A Bohemian existence. I put an end to it when I found the two rooms in Hampstead, but his most precious possession, his easel, remained at his father's place. This made me jealous. But there was "more atmosphere" at his father's.

"Perhaps it would be a good idea for you to meet him," said Jerome hesitantly.

"Aren't you allowed to take me to his place either?"

"On the contrary, I'll have to."

It was a Sunday and Jerome was still in bed, although it was already twelve o'clock. Sometimes he didn't even get dressed on Sunday. I disapproved. (My father would have, too.) Either one was up and dressed or one was sick.

I tidied up the room, hung his things in the closet. He sat up, caught hold of me and pulled me down beside him on the bed. Stroking my arm, he looked at me dubiously.

"I'll have to," he repeated.

"Have to what?"

"Take you to his apartment. It's really only one big room. He's there now and he won't go out again until next May."

"Why not?"

"Because during the months with an *r* in them he stays home. He's done it for years. He hasn't even got a winter coat."

"Why not?"

He let go of my arm and took my hand instead. He stroked it—it wasn't chapped anymore—remembered, laughed and kissed it, then turned it over and began to study my palm.

"Hardly any lines at all. Barely the major ones," he said, wrinkling his forehead. "Like a chimpanzee. How can I explain my father to a chimpanzee?"

He sighed and shook his head. "You see, everybody—you and me included—is always worrying about what we are. My father decided to concentrate on what he's *not*. And there he found his vocation. Do you understand what I mean?"

"No."

He smiled patiently.

"Think of shellfish, oysters for instance. You don't eat oysters in months without an *r* in them, do you?"

"Does your father think he's an oyster? Is he afraid of being caught and eaten?"

"It's not quite as bad as that. He knows he's not an oyster, but he loves them and the *r* business suits him nicely. He is available between September 1 and April 30. Then a four-month closed season. He's not completely normal, of course, but what does 'normal' mean anyway? The people Simon works for at Kodak—"

"You call your father Simon?"

"That's his name. The Kodak people consider him completely normal. They gave him a job here in England years ago. He developed two camera lenses for them, which bring in a lot of money. Not that they ever offered to raise his salary. Neither did he ask them to. He's always broke, but as long as he has his eyrie and as long as no one makes any demands on him, he's quite happy."

"And he just sits there in one room for months? Like in prison?"

"Prison wouldn't worry him as long as he could have his books. You'll see, the walls are lined with books on math and physics. Nothing else interests him. No, that's not quite true, food interests him—and sex."

"You talk about him as if he weren't your father."

"He's not. Or only by accident. You'll know from the physical resemblance that he sired me, but that's the extent of his fatherhood. He only lived with Garibalda for a few years."

"How did they ever get together?"

"By mistake, I suppose. She was quite famous already and he was a lieutenant. In those days he was very good-looking. Now he's like a barrel. Some time ago I was rummaging in old suitcases in the attic and I found his uniform. I couldn't button the tunic! She must have been in love with him, because apart from the uniform he had nothing to offer. He belonged to a distinguished regiment, though. If it hadn't been for that business with the horse . . ."

"What horse?"

"His horse. He could never remember which was his horse, and that won't do in a cavalry regiment, where horse and rider are supposed to be indivisible. Simon's problem was that he couldn't distinguish one horse from another. Finally he tied a red ribbon to the tail of his horse. That worked for a time. But then came the day of the parade, general on the grandstand, military band, dress uniforms, medals, rows and rows of black horses' noses, and black horses' tails—and one red ribbon rippling in the breeze. The general was not amused. End of a military career."

"And of Garibalda too?"

"I wonder." He leaned back, clasped his hands behind his head and considered the question as if it had never occurred to him before.

"It's still not entirely at an end between those two. I think they just happened to wake up in separate places one day. From the very start he had affairs with her girl friends, because it was more restful that way, he didn't have to go hunting around. But absentmindedly —he has been absentminded all his life—he would call Garibalda by one of her girl friends' names, and she didn't like that one bit. Once he even escorted the wrong woman home after a party. That did it, I believe. Maybe they would have stayed together longer if he'd tied a red ribbon in Garibalda's hair."

•

A few days later, on a Sunday evening, we took

the bus to Chelsea, the part of London that's been the favorite haunt of artists, scholars and madmen for centuries. I was given some last-minute instructions.

"We mustn't stay long. When the boy brings his dinner, we must leave at once. He has room service like in a hotel. His—his current female sends it up. He keeps some kind of emotional life going, and he's very choosy. He confines himself exclusively to restaurant owners. During the months without an r, he systematically works his way through all the restaurants in the neighborhood, and he has an eagle eye for sex-starved restaurant owners. There are hundreds of eating places in Chelsea, so he's never at a loss and gets first-class meals sent up to his room. He must have some very special aces up his sleeve, for he always gets away with two conditions: First, an affair is strictly limited to one season, for by the end he is sick of the menu; second, she is not allowed to bring the food up herself. He eats alone. He only enjoys his meals if he can concentrate on every bite, without having to talk. I'm not allowed to be there either. Except occasionally when he happens to be "between restaurant owners" and no one is feeding him. Then he lets me stay and share his dry bread."

We were hanging on to the straps in a crowded bus and I gave him a quick kiss, without anyone noticing.

"Literally dry bread?"

"He's quite fond of dry bread. It's indispensable to fill his stomach, otherwise the red wine doesn't taste good."

The bus stopped. We jumped off.

"That's where he lives, up there on the fifth floor. Let's take it slowly."

There was no elevator in the house, one of the many tall eighteenth-century buildings that line the banks of the Thames. Slowly we climbed the narrow, dark stairs, switching the electric light on again at every landing. When we reached the fourth floor, Jerome said, "Let's sit down. There's something else I must tell you."

We sat down on the stairs, panting.

"I would like it if you two—" He broke off. "Well, anyway—don't be surprised at the entrance ritual. Simon has a pet fly which he loves and which he doesn't want to escape." A look at my face, and he continued hastily, "He's always loved flies, and you'd be surprised how long they last with him. He gives them names, usually after popes. He's had whole dynasties of them. The present one's called Leo. Leo VII. You'll see little bowls of sugar water all over the place. And when the fly settles on his bald head and buzzes, he's happy."

"Jerome—he's nuts!"

"Why is it all right to like a goldfish but not a fly? Just wait. You've never seen such a fine black specimen."

"Is it some special kind?"

"No, just a regular fly. But his are always extra-fat and black."

We climbed the last flight and Jerome knocked: one knock, then three rapid ones. From inside a deep voice called, "Okay," at which Jerome sat down again on the top step, pulling me with him.

"He said 'Okay,'" I whispered.

"That means he's looking for it, on the lamp, on the table, under the table, on the bookshelves . . ."

"But it takes hours to find a fly."

"No, it doesn't. He has his own methods, he knows where they hang out. For the books he uses a feather duster."

A gruff voice from inside the room growled, "Now!"

The door opened a crack. Jerome sprang to his feet, jumped across the threshold, pulling me after him, and slammed the door behind us.

At first I saw nothing but a broad back making for the desk and paying no attention to us.

"Come, take your coat off," said Jerome casually. "Give it to me. The chap over there behind the desk is Simon. Simon, this is the girl I've been telling you about."

"Evening," said the fat man, putting on his glasses. "Watch out, son, he's on your sleeve."

"Is it the same one as last week?"

"You have no eye for detail. Strange in a painter, I must say. Leo VII died on Monday night. I found him on the windowsill, all rolled up and shriveled. This is Leo VIII. Much smaller. Bluish wings. Can't you tell?"

"Let me take a closer look," said Jerome, picking up a ruler from the table.

"Don't you dare!" exclaimed the fat man. "You wouldn't get him in any case—he's far too intelligent for you. In a single morning I taught him where all his sugar-water bowls are, and he buzzes like a lawnmower."

"Well, kindly teach him to buzz strictly in your domain," said Jerome, taking me over to the other side of the room. There stood the easel, in front of a big slanted window offering a view of treetops and, below them, the Thames. It certainly had more atmosphere than our flat in Hampstead, whose window looked out at the back of a warehouse.

"This is my studio. Up to that white chalk mark. When Simon is here I remain strictly within my borders while I'm working and pay him ten bob a week."

Each side had an armchair, a big table and a couch. Simon's walls were hidden by bookshelves, Jerome's were covered with canvases and drawings. The white chalkline on the floor ran diagonally through the middle of the room.

"Won't you sit down?" said the fat man, beckoning.

I moved over to his side. Jerome sat down on the floor beside me. Above us hung a birdcage with the door wide open. Inside cowered a moth-eaten old canary.

"Does the bird fly around in the room too?" I asked.

"Several times a day," said Jerome, "as you can see from the white splotches on my canvases. Sometimes I just leave them. That damned bird has a good feeling for composition."

"And what happens when it sees the fly?"

"Nothing happens," growled the old man. "They're scared of each other."

I took my first close look at him. He was

fat but not flabby, the face was round, the features sharp as if carved with a chisel. Wide, dark eyes, without bags or wrinkles, the eyes of a young man. Two fleshy cheeks pressed from each side against a small, delicately carved nose and a pointed mouth. All of it framed by an ample double chin at least two inches in depth, like a separate, folded white collar.

"I'm sorry I can't offer you a drink," he said. "I haven't stocked up yet. I only just got back. But perhaps Jerome . . ."

Jerome laughed, got up and strolled over to his side. In one corner stood a small refrigerator and a stove. He opened the refrigerator with a key he took out of his pocket and removed half a bottle of white wine and the remains of a loaf of bread. Two glasses appeared from somewhere and a third from the bathroom. Simon began to look very cheerful and promptly reached for the bread, then for the bottle.

"Cheers, little lady," he said, emptying his glass. "So you're an actress. What are you appearing in right now? Do I have to come and see it?"

"No," I said hastily. "It's not a good play."

"Are you well paid?"

"No, she isn't," said Jerome darkly, knitting his eyebrows. "There's no point in getting your hopes up."

"Pity. I wouldn't mind being kept by a young actress. I'd even be prepared to do something for her in return. Oh well. Cheers! Better luck next time. Speaking of money, I hear your mother's getting married again."

"First I've heard of it," said Jerome, "but it's possible. She narrowed it down to two candidates some time ago."

"Which one's got more money?"

"The one she'll be bringing to see you." Jerome turned to me and added, "She always drags her candidates up here to be looked over by Simon first. That's her Italian family sense."

"Up to now I've always talked her out of it. After all, she's still doing all right on her own. But perhaps the time has come. How old is she exactly?"

"How should I know? Can't you remember?"

Simon shook his head.

"Even in the old days you couldn't believe a word she said."

He extended his head gently toward the lamp and Leo VIII actually emerged from his dark hiding place and settled on the bald surface, buzzing contentedly. Simon closed his eyes.

"Is he rubbing his forelegs together?" he asked, as if in a trance.

"Yes," I exclaimed. "He's rubbing them. Look, Jerome."

But Jerome, who was standing by the window, was unimpressed and went to get my coat.

"They all rub their legs together. Rub and buzz, that's all they do. We must be off. Here comes the boy, Simon, with a huge tray."

"Time to go, children, time to go. Now's the moment. When he's grooming he doesn't like to interrupt himself to take off. Still—be careful!"

The last thing I glimpsed from the doorway was a motionless shape at the desk, a bulky colossus, its eyes closed like the Golem, on the softly gleaming bald head a black speck, gorged and glossy.

•

Hard to imagine that this man, with his papal flies, and Dame Garibalda had ever dropped anchor next to each other long enough to bring my Jerome into the world!

I glanced stealthily at Garibalda, lying in a deck chair under a big umbrella. We were in Eastbourne, an expensive old-fashioned seaside resort on the English Channel. In a second deck chair next to her, a young man with a bronze tan lay asleep: Federigo, a pilot in an Italian air force unit. I was glad he was asleep. When he was awake, his black eyes glowed too fiercely and the tips of his mustache twitched with desire.

Garibalda was a health fetishist. Cold seawater, uncooked fruit and vegetables and morning exercises were indispensable for good skin, teeth and vocal cords. She went to Eastbourne twice a year and swam in the sea every day. Usually she was accompanied by a Scottish laird of ancient family who had worshipped her all his life. When he couldn't be at her side—he had a bony, stern wife at his ancestral seat— she received a letter from him every day. This daily letter was important to her; it was her rod and staff, even—or especially—when she was being unfaithful to her Scotsman, which happened occasionally.

Early October 1936 was one of those occasions. Her saltwater cure was due, but the laird, to his chagrin, could not get away. On the spur of the moment Garibalda yielded to the passionate entreaties of a young Italian, who until then had been spending his leave in vain on his knees in her dressing room at Covent Garden. He had a lot to offer. He was young and handsome and he was there. Unfortunately he was pathologically jealous and apt to be savage. Garibalda was reduced to tipping a bellboy in order to smuggle her daily letter from the post office into her bedroom.

She had ordered Jerome to Eastbourne for a week, possibly to protect her from physical assault by her passionate troubadour. Jerome, however, declared that he didn't want to be away from me for so long, and so she lowered her Sardinian eyelids in resignation and announced that I was included in the order. But we were not to stay at the Grand Hotel with her and her flying ace but would have to make do with a modest boardinghouse outside Eastbourne. It didn't matter to me. I was used to modest boardinghouses, and the thought of finally getting to know Garibalda, perhaps even making friends with her, was exciting.

The first two days offered little opportunity to remind her of my presence. She ignored me in the friendliest possible way. Early in the morning Jerome and I would already be out on the beach, lying in the two deck chairs she had rented for herself and Federigo. We would jump up respectfully when she approached, wearing an enormous straw hat and a chiffon beach wrap over a bathing suit with pleated shirt.

The bronzed pilot in his white trunks was displayed to full advantage at her side. They would smile graciously in our direction and stretch out in the chairs. "The children" sat beside them on the cold sand.

We were glum. The modest boardinghouse was modest indeed. For the first time in my life I discovered that a mattress can be important. Mine felt as if it were stuffed with potatoes. The food was inedible and the sea was icy. Instead of swimming, Jerome and I jumped and splashed around and turned blue after five minutes. Garibalda and her escort, however, seemed to find a warm Gulf Stream current and swam with graceful, leisurely strokes.

After the second "modest" dinner we decided to leave the next day, whatever happened. We packed our things and spent a better night on the potatoes for knowing that it was the last one. The next morning we marched to the beach to await the right moment for telling Garibalda we were off.

She was already lying in her deck chair, wrapped in chiffon scarfs. Federigo said the air was cool and he was going swimming right away.

"I'll be right with you," said Garibalda, amiably, following him with her eyes as he trudged down to the water.

As soon as he had disappeared into the surf, she extracted a letter from her handbag and immersed herself.

We exchanged glances. Was this the right moment? Yes, Jerome signaled, as soon as she stopped reading.

It was a long letter, four closely written pages. She took her time, oblivious of our presence, occasionally chuckling to herself with her eyes closed, like a young girl.

Suddenly a shadow fell on the page. The troubadour was standing before her, dripping and threatening.

"Who's that letter from?"

Garibalda batted her eyelashes.

"This letter?" She stared at the pages as if she couldn't imagine how they had gotten into her fingers. Federigo's hand shot out to grab it, but she was even faster and tossed it boldly into my lap. "This letter is from her dear mother," she said, smiling gently into his blazing black eyes, and turning to me she added tenderly, "Thank you, my child, for letting me read it."

I automatically picked up the letter and clutched it in a daze. The blackberry eyes were still fixed on mine, but the smile was no longer tender, it was imperious. I hastily stuffed the letter into our beach bag.

Federigo, forsaking his role of troubadour in favor of Othello, looked suspiciously from one to the other, the damp tips of his mustache twitching ominously. He took a step toward me, but didn't quite dare to grab my beach bag, so he remained standing in front of us, glowering and covered in goose pimples from the cold.

"I'm ready to go swimming with you now, dearest. Come along," announced Garibalda, peeling off the chiffon and pulling the reluctant Federigo toward the water.

"Well," said Jerome, "let's see what your dear mother has to say," and retrieved the letter from the depths of the beach bag.

Dear mother had an ardent love letter from Scotland. Jerome grew happier with every page. Finally he folded it up small and stuck it under the sole of his right sandal.

"We're going to make a little deal with Garibalda. She'll get the letter back only if she lets us move into the Grand Hotel. Otherwise your dear mother's letter will be handed over to Federigo. Go back to the boardinghouse and wait for me. You're not up to the kind of storm that's about to break."

I left in a hurry.

Half an hour later Jerome appeared in our room, disheveled but cheerful. He reported that Garibalda had cut short her health-giving dip, leaving her Othello to brave the waves alone. She had returned to the deck chairs, out of breath and hand outstretched.

Jerome, still squatting in the sand, had looked up politely and attentively.

"Where's the letter?" she began majestically, every inch Aïda, and the battle began. It had to be fought with restraint on account of the neighboring deck chairs, but the sand flew in all directions. Jerome proved himself a worthy son of his mother, squatting stolidly in his sandals, fending off his mother's slaps and pinches and smiling inscrutably, his strongest weapon.

Not until she saw Federigo heading for shore did Garibalda give up. Gnashing her teeth, she signed a check, which her son held up to the light before putting it away.

Then he took off his right sandal.

At noon that day, we were standing with our suitcases in the Grand Hotel lobby when Garibalda and Federigo returned from the beach.

"Mamma," announced Jerome happily, "imagine! We've got a double room exactly like yours on the same floor."

While Federigo was getting the keys from the desk, Garibalda turned on Jerome. "Haven't you got any shame, you misbegotten pup? Appearing publicly in the Grand Hotel with a girl you're not married to!"

"But Mamma," said Jerome innocently, "you and Federigo—isn't that the same thing?"

Garibalda raised her right hand in a solemn gesture of benediction *cum* traffic policeman and turned her blackberry eyes heavenward. "Leave your sacred mother out of this," she intoned and disappeared into the elevator.

We never found out how she explained our sudden presence to Federigo. But from then on both behaved as if they didn't know us.

We didn't mind. Restored by soft mattresses and splendid meals, we spent four unforgettable days at the Grand Hotel in Eastbourne.

8

No sign of life from the painter. I called the studio. No answer. Strange—she hardly ever went out.

I went over and rang the doorbell long and stubbornly until, finally, I heard footsteps. "It's me." Silence. Obviously she was making up her mind. Then the door opened a crack and she pointed to her throat without speaking.

"I thought so," I said and pushed the door open. She looked like an old Eskimo woman left out in the snow to die. A woolen scarf covered her head, two sweaters full of paint stains and moth holes were tucked into crumpled pajama pants. On top was an old sheepskin rug tied up with string.

"You can't talk?" No answer. I pushed her aside and marched to the telephone.

There was plenty to do while we waited for my doctor. The heater in her bedroom wasn't working, hence her extraordinary outfit. I dragged her mattress and bedclothes, covered with coffee stains, into the warm studio, while she sat silently on the hassock, watching, sweat pouring down her face.

"You ought to be ashamed of yourself," I yelled, as I ran back and forth looking for clean sheets and not finding any, putting water on to boil and turning the pantry upside down in a vain search for tea and lemons.

I pulled her up from the hassock and untied the string. The sheepskin fell to the floor and I pushed her ahead of me and then down on the mattress. She put up no resistance when I dragged the two sweaters over her head, taking the scarf with them, and bundled her up under the blanket. She lay quite still, staring straight ahead. Maybe she wanted to die.

"Do you want to die?"

She shook her head.

"Well then."

•

My doctor came—a pasty-faced, overworked, impatient young man with bitten fingernails. He wasn't happy in his profession, and his patients got on his nerves. Sometimes his eyes would narrow as if he couldn't take anymore, and he would start talking about his own stomach symptoms. But he was a good doctor. No professional bedside manner, no miracle worker, but prepared, if necessary, to make a house call at three o'clock in the morning.

While he was examining her, I went into the kitchen and tidied up and washed some dishes. Then he called me in. The best thing would be to take her at once to the hospital. A glance and a gesture from her cut him short. Well, then, could I take care of her? I heaved a deep sigh, making sure she heard it. Cheerful self-sacrifice would have been the last thing she needed.

He left, leaving prescriptions and instructions. I got my coat, took the key out of the lock and departed.

When I returned a little while later with fresh linen and medicines, she was lying there on the mattress as if she were dead. I pulled her up by the hair—she offered no resistance—held the pills and then a glass of water to her lips, and burst out laughing. That furious face under my fistful of hair! She glared at me and for a moment there was murder in the air. Then her face crumpled up as if she were about to burst out laughing herself, but all she could produce was a hoarse, barking growl. She drank and swallowed painfully. I let go of her hair and she dropped back on the pillow and immediately fell asleep.

I left again to find an electrician to repair the bedroom heater, had to be satisfied with vague promises, and returned. She was still asleep. I wandered quietly about the studio, examining the canvases, looking over her books —and suddenly came face to face with the

bronze head again. A glance at the mattress—
she was sleeping quietly, her mouth neatly
closed.

I carried the little bust to the window. At
last I was able to examine it at leisure. The
narrow, Egyptian-looking skull, the hair around
neck and cheeks like a thin silk scarf, the "mean
mouth"—a sullen mouth, a taciturn mouth, but
mean? Never. I'd often seen her sitting by the
window with exactly that expression on her
face, severe, concentrated, turned off. She
worked several hours a day, brailling books and
delivering them to the home of the blind. Doz-
ens of its rooms were fitted out with armchairs
and radios she had supplied, and she liked to
spend whole afternoons there talking to the
residents, many of whom she knew well. Sometimes she would make Nina accompany her. Not
a good idea. Nina would stand by in silence
while the blind people crowded around her
mother. Nina had nothing to contribute, remained literally invisible.

The painter hadn't moved, but I felt her
eyes on me. She was watching me with apparent
indifference, as I stood by the window with the
bronze head in my hand.

I put the sculpture down on the window-
sill. Time for her pill. I refilled the glass and held
it threateningly under her nose. She struggled
upright by herself, swallowed and took a drink
of water. Victory.

Before lying down again, she made a sign
that she wanted something to write with. Maybe she was in pain and had decided to go to
the hospital after all. I found a sketchbook and

a piece of charcoal by the easel. And her glasses. Slowly and painfully she wrote something, tossed it over to me and watched with indifference as I picked up the charcoal and angrily rubbed at the black mark on my fresh white sheet. Impatiently she pointed to the sketchbook and closed her eyes. I deciphered the shaky, smudged letters printed in charcoal: "YOU CAN HAVE IT."

I seized the charcoal and printed underneath: "NO THANKS"—and realized that I was behaving like most of Beethoven's visitors, who used to push a notebook under his nose expecting him to write an answer to their written questions. Which made him angry every time.

"No thanks," I said in a loud voice. She opened her eyes and barked—or perhaps it was a laugh—until she choked.

I stuck a throat lozenge in her mouth. "Don't forget to take your pills, every three hours. The lozenges are to stop the coughing. Try to sleep. If you feel bad, call me. You don't have to speak—I'll know. I'll be back tomorrow to get your breakfast."

She stared at me, nodded imperceptibly and closed her eyes.

9

On the way back to the hotel I thought about Nina, couldn't get her out of my head. Plump little Nina, who had inherited nothing from her mother except her black eyes, those watchful black raven's eyes that missed nothing. Those eyes had watched her mother leave the door of that house in St. James's Street, hail a taxi and drive away. Those eyes, those raven eyes, obeying some raven instinct, had continued to watch that same door until they were rewarded by the sight of a man coming out into the street: Jerome.

What date was that? (Why was I so keen on getting the dates straight? What did it matter exactly when it all happened? It did matter. Once I had finally decided to open those locked doors I might as well let it all stream out in the right order, like a parade, events following events according to their marching orders. I might even feel some sort of painful satisfaction at having to rethink and relive methodically through the memories of those years, one by one, continually coming to a stop and exclaiming: Ah! So *that* is why we did this or that! Or: Ah! *That* explains why such and such took place! And in spite of the pain there was the clean surgical satisfaction of "knowing at long last" and a feeling of liberation.)

Years later, when Nina told me about it, she couldn't remember exactly what date it had been. All she knew was that the tulips were in bloom because that afternoon her class had taken a course in botany in St. James's Park.

If the tulips were blooming, it must have been April or May. And it was probably a Thursday. On Thursdays I had a matinee. Who had made the first move? One or the other always takes the initiative, gives the first signal. Which of them had it been? Jerome?

The diary hardly mentions him in January 1937; in February it ignores him altogether. She wrote only about me, about my interminable, tiresome worries which never seemed to tire her, my pipe dreams, my new winter coat. Then suddenly in March:

Called J.

So it was Anabel. Yet, who knows, perhaps in response to a word or a look from Jerome . . .

No entry in the diary for three days. On the fourth day, at last, the whole story.

Called J. again. Asked for L. He laughed and
said didn't I know she was at the theater.
I told him I had to talk to him. Important.
For all three of us. He laughed again. I said,
"Three o'clock at the boat house in Regent's
Park," and hung up. He kept me waiting but
he came. Strolled up as if he were out for a
walk. I was wearing my red coat. He told me
I looked like a red raven. Too cold to hire
a boat. We walked over the little bridge into
Queen Mary's rose garden. Nobody about,
the benches still wet. We wandered around.
I told him everything. Of course he knew
but he was surprised that it dated back to
the Berkeley Bar. I went too far and told
him I had felt an electric shock as I sat next
to him and our knees touched for a split
second. He laughed again. Probably thinks
I'm crazy. Am I? I don't think so. I've never
felt like this before. But I shouldn't have told
him, you don't tell things like that. But that's
why I've ever since avoided all physical
contact with him, as far as I possibly could.
   I never mentioned L. Neither did he.
Gave me a few sidelong glances. Why is he
always smiling? Self-defense? Then he said he
wouldn't mind stepping out of line a bit, but
not too far and with small steps only. He
wasn't geared for "passion." As he said that,
he even dropped that damned smile. Then
he strolled calmly out of the rose garden,
toward a taxi rank. With me beside him.
He gave the address of his apartment, opened
the door, got in and didn't seem to notice
that I got in too.

I had to stop reading for a moment, although only the details were news to me. But

I hadn't known before—and it brought back at once all the old hurt, all the old feeling of impoverishment—that it had been in our apartment, our cheap little apartment, in the cheap little bed with the cheap chenille bedspread . . .

Wouldn't it be wiser to skip a couple of pages? Did I really have to know the details? And the details are always the things that get stuck in one's mind. Could it be that I was actually enjoying them? No, goddammit, it was plain necessity to read every line or I would once again invent a taboo-territory around which my thoughts would circle and snarl.

It was exactly as I had imagined it hundreds of times. But exactly. My eyes were closed tight. I was functioning only inside myself. At one point the telephone rang. J. let it ring but finally picked it up. We both knew who it was. L.'s matinee was over. She just wanted to say hello before lying down for her hour's nap in the dressing room. She didn't notice anything.

Correct. I have no memory of that conversation.

I quickly left. J. made no effort to stop me or to see me home or get me a taxi. It was raining. I got soaked, had to walk a long way before I found one. I rolled down the window to let the rain continue wetting my face. I needed the rain. I needed to come to my senses.

The next day she wrote only one sentence:

No word from J.

Same thing on the following day. On the third day:

Is he doing it on purpose? Surely he knows
that one needs some word—some sign.
Everytime the doorbell rings, I think:
Here it is. Perhaps a single rose! How corny
can you get? I can't see her now. Don't know
what excuse to make. She thinks I'm sick and
insists on coming over. Why doesn't he call?
Bad conscience? Was he bored? Or—on the
contrary—did I take him too far out of line?
Anything's possible. I need some word
from him. He'll *have* to let me hear from him.
He owes me that much. At least *that* much.

Next day:

I would like to kill myself. In some
repulsive way. Cut my throat. With Bill's
razor. I'm ashamed of myself. Ashamed.
Ashamed. Ashamed.

No entry for two days. Then:

L. came bringing flowers. She thinks I'm upset
about something she has said or done. She
stayed for ages, is convinced I'm sick. She's
right in thinking she's done something to
upset me. I hate her for knowing nothing.
She has no right not to be suspicious, not to
sense anything. She has no antenna to tell
her what's going on inside the people she
loves. She has no right to trust J., and if she
trusts me, she's a blockhead. If she'd given
me one suspicious look, I'd have hugged her
like a sister. But she's a cow. I threw
her flowers into the garbage can.

I had to get up, I had to move my head
from side to side, up and down, around and
around. My neck was rigid, it felt as if it might
break off. It had to get unstuck before I could

read any more. Perhaps I would then get some
more air into my lungs and breathe normally.
In and out. And in and out.

The next day:

> A ray of hope. Next Monday is J.'s birthday.
> Bill wants to celebrate at the Savoy Grill.
> I'll see him! I'll be able to tell from his face
> why I haven't heard from him. I'm eating
> again, I'm stuffing myself. Bought a white
> evening dress. White makes you look fatter.

I can still see that white evening dress. She
looked like a calla lily. I was happy because it
was Jerome's birthday, because we were at the
Savoy, drinking champagne, and because Anabel
was her old self. Or almost. She tried to light
a cigarette with Jerome's lighter, but her hand
was shaking so hard that he placed his hand
over hers to steady it.

"You're trembling," I exclaimed anxiously.

It's the champagne," said Jerome. "It sometimes affects me that way too."

Why do I remember that? His hand on
hers . . . Was the cow beginning to catch on
after all? Not perhaps in the top layer of my
conscious mind but somewhere in the one right
underneath.

> He placed his hand over mine, otherwise I
> could never have lighted my cigarette. In full
> view of everybody he placed his hand over
> mine. I knew then I could call him up again.
> Had to wait until the next evening, until L.
> was at the theater.
>   "Jerome," I said, "I'm sorry. I wish it had
> never happened. I must have lost my mind.
> Forgive me. Help me!"

85

"Of course," he said. "How?"

"I must explain to you. Come to the boat house on Saturday afternoon. That will be the last time."

On Saturday I had another matinee. And it wasn't the last time. But at least she never went to our apartment again. She rented one in St. James's street under a false name. Nobody knew about it, nobody recognized her. Except Nina.

•

The entries for the next two months record happiness, intact, flawless, no hint of even a faint shadow of guilt feelings. One short sentence brought back a long-forgotten incident. Immediately after the evening at the Savoy, Anabel told me she was going to order an evening dress for me, from her own couturier— Hartnell! Hartnell dressed the royal family! I had never owned a couture evening dress. I was to choose it myself. Mannequins paraded for me alone, presenting models, turning this way and that, smiling a sterile smile and withdrawing. Anabel selected the most beautiful dress of all, probably the most expensive one too. I threw my arms around her neck. Nobody had ever given me such a present.

All the diary says is:

Ordered an evening dress for L.

•

They were leading a separate, independent life, those two, but it was I who called their tune. As long as I was working, they had nothing to fear, it was child's play. But if my film came to an end or my play closed, I cut their lifeline and the apartment in St. James's Street remained unused.

In the summer of 1937 it stood empty for two months.

On July 1 he's going away. With L. To stay with friends in the south of France. Vacation. Only one more week and he'll be gone. Two months! How am I to live through those two months? I'm making all kinds of plans, all dangerous. Like taking Nina to some place nearby. But she doesn't want to go and it's too risky without her. Two months! I'll have to talk her into it.

But apparently Nina wasn't to be talked into it, because Jerome and I left on July 1—it was a real wrench for me to leave Anabel behind—and we didn't see her again until the end of August.

10

July 1, 1937. My first vacation since I left
school, the very first with Jerome. Our final
destination was Grasse, where Jerome's friend
Peter Gurnemantz owned a peach farm. But
first we were going to Paris; we had saved
enough money to be able to stop over for a day.
At the Hotel de la Muette, for old time's sake.

The Hotel de la Muette had been my first
harbor when I arrived in Paris late in 1933 at
the age of eighteen, ready to remake my life
in French, to conquer the film studios and the
legitimate stage and start a "world career." I
didn't even get my nose inside a film studio and
had to admit total defeat one year later.

That was a bad year, 1934. In January my

father had died in Berlin and the two of us who had managed to get out, my sister Irene and I, knew that we must get the rest of the family, our mother and younger sister Hilde, out of Berlin as quickly as possible. We sold everything we possessed. With the proceeds I went to London in January 1935 to try my luck in English. Slowly, very slowly, I gained a foothold and at the end of that year a shout of joy: a contract with a London film company. Irene came over from Paris, my mother and Hilde and some furniture from Berlin. We were a family again.

And now Paris, for the first time after three years. Three years is a long time when you're twenty-one. An eternity since I'd boarded the London train at the Gare du Nord, grimly determined, nodding an indifferent goodbye to the city rushing past outside my compartment. It was a completely different person who now sat in the taxi, looking out the window at the familiar streets, squares and buildings. Now I asked nothing of the city, didn't want to belong to it, struggle with it, conquer it. I was a tourist, I belonged somewhere else and had a return ticket in my purse. Thus for the first time I appreciated Paris and cried out with delight at the sight of the Champs Elysées and the Arc de Triomphe.

"I thought you'd lived here," said Jerome. "You act as if you were seeing it for the first time."

"I am seeing it for the first time."

Arrival at the Hotel de la Muette.

I recognized the concierge; he did not recognize me. I shook his reluctant hand just the same.

"Don't you remember the two sisters who lived here three years ago? Up on the top floor? The ones who always saved German stamps for you. Remember?"

Something began to dawn on the walrus face with the stiff, bristly mustache.

"The ones who always kept salami and cheese on the window ledge?"

"That's right. They send their regards."

"Merci," he said in bewilderment and escorted us to the elevator.

A nice room, even a private bath, very different from the hole Irene and I had lived in. I stepped out onto the terrace and looked down over the treetops at the Bois de Boulogne, the same treetops that had so often comforted me, except that now, from the elegant balcony on the first floor, they were closer and even more friendly. For the first time in my life I felt a sense of achievement and the span as well as the end of an era.

●

While I was meditating, Jerome was speaking into the telephone. He was calling Babs, so I quickly stepped back into the room. Babs, Babs Siodmak. High time I introduced her—after all, she played a role in the story, wove a few essential threads and decisively though unintentionally influenced the course of events.

Babs had once been my "predecessor." One

day Jerome happened to mention her name and was surprised and amused by my reaction. "But I know her!" I exclaimed excitedly. "I knew her in Paris! That is—well, I saw her once through the window of the Café Colisée," I concluded lamely.

"You sound like the poor little girl with the matches," said Jerome. "Why through the window?"

"I didn't go to cafés in those days."

"Pity. Yes, the Colisée, that's where she still holds court. She has to have a regular café in every city, where she holds her levees. When we were living together in Berlin while I was studying at the academy, it was the Continental on the Kurfürstendamm. It has to be a café, there have to be masses of people coming and going, getting up, sitting down, waiters rushing around, and it has to have the smell of cigarette smoke, coffee and coats. Only there does she feel really comfortable. Once I dreamed that she had died and been buried, but I dug her up again and she opened her eyes and sat up in her coffin. 'Come along, Babs,' I said. 'Go on home and lie down and rest.' 'I've rested enough,' she said, putting on her hat. 'I'm going to the Continental!'"

She was so much talked about in refugee circles in those desperate days in Paris that she became a kind of mythological figure in my imagination, floating about in delicate colors and fluttering her famous hands, "which Botticelli might have painted." And then, one day, on the Champs Elysées, somebody pointed her out to me through the window. There she sat, enthroned inside her Café Colisée, serene and elegant, dressed, however, not in delicate colors, but strictly in black and white, Paris fashion. Thereafter she stopped floating about in my mind and remained firmly anchored inside the Colisée—but still way beyond my reach.

Now, however, via Jerome, I felt myself suddenly catapulted through the window and sitting right next to her, one of the family, so to speak. She was a good ten years older than Jerome but that was an advantage, he said, he was always eager to learn. When Robert Siodmak, the director, appeared on the scene in Berlin, he yielded gracefully to him, and they parted on the most affectionate terms. Robert and Babs emigrated to Paris, but she and Jerome still kept in touch by letter.

And now he was actually talking to my mythological figure on the telephone, laughing and making a date. Six o'clock at the Café Colisée. Where else?

Babs, in black and white, tanned, beaming, and surrounded by her court, recognized Jerome as soon as he came through the door and called out, as if she were in her own living room:

"Sherome! Feins ici!"

My Botticelli came from Stuttgart and had a Swabian accent!

"Carçon, teux chaises!" The others were drinking coffee, but they ordered ice cream for me as if I were a child and gave me an extra-large spoon and a waffle to keep me quiet. I was excluded from their conversation, which dwelt on memories of Berlin, and was tempted to bang my spoon against the plate. Once she

did turn to me, gave me a candid, friendly look and said that Jerome and I made a charming young couple.

"You talk as if you were my aunt," said Jerome.

"That's the way I feel," she replied, stroking my cheek.

•

That night the sleeping car left for Nice and our destination—the "Gurnemantz holiday."

The transformation of the German sculptor Peter Gurnemantz into a French fruit farmer had taken place in 1934. In pre-Hitler days he had married the eldest daughter of a Jewish banker in Berlin and had refused to divorce her despite considerable pressure from Goebbels's Ministry of Propaganda. Instead he emigrated, along with his whole clan, his wife Ursula, his five-year-old son, and Ursula's younger sister, Eva.

Gurnemantz, a burly, blond fellow from Schleswig-Holstein, had little to say during the day; at night, after two glasses of Pernod, he became a bit more talkative, but not much. He lived chiefly through his downward-slanting eyes, which seemed unwilling to leave whatever they were resting on at the moment. Nervousness, not to speak of panic, was outside his experience. When, for the first time in his life, he had to say to someone in Paris, "Could you lend me a hundred francs?" he realized as the words came out of his mouth that his career as a sculptor was over. At that very moment he made up his mind to start a new life, preferably one in which he could use his huge, square peasant hands.

His banker father-in-law appeared on the train from Berlin, a small, gray and nervous man. He carefully took his pajamas, slippers and a heavy woolen dressing gown out of his meticulously packed suitcase. Equally carefully he removed from inside the lining of his dressing gown a canvas whose ecstatic colors sparkled with glee over the inefficiency of the German customs officials: a Renoir landscape which had once hung in a magnificent golden frame in his dining room.

The next day he boarded the train back to Berlin. He had no intention of emigrating. "I'll be on the last train to leave Germany," he told his two daughters as they stood on the platform in tears. And he was. Destination: Auschwitz.

•

Gurnemantz sold the Renoir and with the proceeds bought a hillside in the south of France. On the sunny side he planted hundreds of peach trees. On the very top he built a house, built it with his own hands and without ever having learned how. During the day he planted and watered his young trees, and in the evening he studied textbooks to learn how to mix cement and control tree diseases.

Now, three years later, he had invited us to visit him in Grasse and help with the harvest. Our first Gurnemantz vacation.

11

Ten years later, while I was sitting for the painter, Peter Gurnemantz the sculptor popped up out of the past.

She was up and about again, though still a bit shaky. Her voice had come back. Every day I brought her a fresh vegetable soup, which she could warm up. She wouldn't accept any help. "This is *my* kitchen. Out!"

I wandered around the studio, stopped in front of the bookshelf and took out a large art book, *Twentieth Century Sculpture*.

She carried the tray in from the kitchen and set it down on the table. breathing heavily, glancing over my shoulder at the massive bronze figure of a woman I was studying.

"Maillol," she said. "I worked in his studio

in Marly-le-Roi for a few months. There were no fine tools—he had deliberately blunted them all because he thought he was getting too persnickety, too wrapped up in detail. That gave me something to think about. I blunted myself too, concentrated on the large issues, on the essential way things hang together. Helped me a lot. Very important."

"Did you happen to know a pupil of his by the name of Gurnemantz?"

"Peter? He was just a beginner at that time. I lost trace of him, but I remember his work. Talented. I don't know what became of him."

"A fruit farmer."

"What?" She laughed, reaching for her Gauloises and her glasses. "Why?"

"Hitler."

"Pity. He'd have made it. Did he give it up entirely?"

"Just about," I replied. "When I knew him, just before the war, he'd done one last sculpture fifteen feet high and sixty feet long."

"There's no such thing," she said crossly.

"Well, it's there, and as far as I know, it's still standing. It's a house! He built himself a house like a huge sculpture, like a human body resting on its side."

"A house like a sculpture! Have you seen it?"

"I've even lived in it, three times, for three summer vacations. It was built on a hillside, not far from Grasse, strung out and undulating in large curves. The belly was the living room, the head the library, the two guest rooms the thighs.

Around the belly, like an apron, a wide terrace. The rainwater cistern was also the swimming pool, shaped like a peanut and icy-cold. The whole thing stood amid olive trees, and there were olive trees right in the middle of the living room; Gurnemantz had built the walls around them."

The painter stared at me with her mouth open, yapping softly like a bloodhound.

"Actually it was very practical. It didn't collapse in storms or leak when it poured with rain. It was also ridiculously cheap. That was the main thing. He had planted peach trees and had to wait three years for his first crop. We lived in one of the thighs and helped with the harvesting. The only other help he could afford was Aesculapius, the donkey, who carried the baskets back to the house when they were full."

She stretched out in her armchair and stared at the ceiling, as she always did when she wanted to get a clear picture of something.

"A donkey carried the fruit back to the house," she repeated slowly. "Paradise! Picking peaches..."

"Not till the sun started to go down—otherwise it was too hot. We all slept all morning, Gurnemantz, his wife, Ursula, her sister, Eva, their little son, Jean-Pierre, and Jerome and I."

"How do you pick peaches? With a knife? With clippers?"

"By hand. It's not as easy as it sounds. You have to take them by surprise. Peaches are tricky, they know that you have to handle them like Christmas-tree decorations. If you press too

97

hard, you leave bruises. The trick is to give them a quick twist and snap them off before they have time to adjust to the new position."

"Tricky fruit!" she said pensively. "I'm not surprised, they're so round and smooth and sweet. Tell me more about the donkey."

"When you'd filled two baskets, you whistled, and he'd come trotting up, God knows where from. A beautiful animal, light-gray and very intelligent. First you gave him a bruised peach and then he trotted up the hill to the terrace. There Ursula would be waiting with the most important job of all, the sorting. On the terrace wall stood the wooden crates and stacks of green pleated paper cups. There were three grades. Number one: large peaches with rosy cheeks. Number two: small peaches with rosy cheeks. Aesculapius used to hang around while we were sorting. Number three belonged to him. He nodded his head and opened his mouth whenever a scruffy one turned up."

"Paradise!" murmured the painter with her eyes closed. "And then?"

"Then we fitted the peaches into the paper cups, packed them, marked the price on them, loaded the crates into an ancient pickup truck . . ."

"Paradise!" she repeated almost inaudibly.

"We ate supper late, trying to stay awake as long as possible because we had to leave at three in the morning. We sneaked out of the house, trying not to wake up the little boy, crowded into the truck and roared down to Nice."

"Nice!" she exclaimed, sitting up straight.

"To the market? I've been there to buy flowers many a time."

"We sold our peaches there twice a week. At four o'clock in the morning."

She stood up and paced excitedly about the studio, smoking.

"And you helped sell them? Shouting and haggling?"

I laughed. "I'd have liked to, but the men wouldn't let us. 'Women bring the price down,' they said. We had to sit in the truck and watch, but that was fun too."

"I bet it was," she exclaimed, combing her shaggy black hair with her fingers. "I always got there too late, about eight o'clock, and by that time everything was calm and orderly, the fun was all over. But sometimes my friends would get up early, or stay up. They said at four o'clock it was exciting, a real witches' sabbath."

"Yes, the entire square was in an uproar. Booths were erected, roofed with sheet metal or tarpaulins. A primitive little village would spring up before our eyes, with fancy 'buildings' or slum ones. And the noise! The yelling would even drown out the hammering. Everyone shouted at the top of his voice to no one in particular until finally the hammering and the pushing and shoving came to an end and fruit, vegetables and flowers were all neatly arranged and everybody would collapse behind his counter, exhausted and silent. Then they'd make coffee and eat pancakes."

The painter sat down again and looked at me, fascinated.

"And you watched it all? Jesus! I made up

my mind to see it hundreds of times, but I was always either too drunk or too disorganized. I always overslept."

I patted her hard painter's hand and poured her another cup of coffee.

"And then? You waited until the cafés opened and ate breakfast?"

"No, something much better. When the men came back with their empty crates and full purses, smelling of Pernod—"

"Pernod!" she cried and her eyes were suddenly full of tears.

"—we'd roar off in the old truck to the Hotel Negresco. In those days that was the most elegant beach on the coast, but at five o'clock in the morning there wasn't a soul around. We'd always find a couple of cabins open and we'd change into our swim suits and run into the warm sea. An hour later we'd be on our way back to Grasse in the early-morning light, so sleepy that we had to take turns driving, because no one could stay awake longer than fifteen minutes."

She sat there in silence, smoking and brooding.

"Anabel?" she finally asked. "Was Anabel ever with you?"

"Twice."

"Did she pick peaches?"

I nodded.

"And swim in the sea?"

I nodded again.

"Strange," she said.

12

Diary, November 1937:

Catastrophe. I was sitting on the floor in the
living room, wrapping Christmas presents.
Suddenly I began to cry. Couldn't stop.
A real crying jag. Sat there among piles of
shiny paper, sprigs of fir and gold ribbons,
and howled. Don't know why it hit me just
then, why among the pretty Christmas paper
and packages, why at all. Was it because
there was so much heavenly blue about
me, with little gold angels? Lately I've been
unusually touchy, as if someone had peeled
off the top layer of skin. Can't listen to music,
can't bear Bill anywhere near me. Told him so.
He didn't say anything but now he does his
boxing in his bedroom. I'm ruining his life,
that's crystal clear. But I don't care. I've

lost all touch with myself, have hidden myself somewhere and mopped up all traces. Perhaps that's why I cried. Lovely floods of tears. I felt relaxed and quite happy crying away— when suddenly L. walked into the room. I hadn't heard the bell, I wasn't expecting anyone. I was simply exercising my privilege of sobbing contentedly in my own living room. And she had to burst in! Fell upon me, took me completely by surprise. Catastrophe.

It certainly was. She was sitting on the floor amid rolls of paper, ribbons and packages. I had to kick it all out of the way to get to her— after all, I couldn't just stand there and watch her sitting on the floor, crying. The least I could do was sit down beside her, ask questions, take her hand, comfort her. Although I felt more like getting out as quickly as possible. When grown-ups cry, I've always wanted to run and hide, but never before so urgently. Anabel in tears! There was something obscene about it. She cried without making a sound, the tears streaming quietly down her face, but her whole body shook with her sobs. It must have come on quite suddenly; she didn't even have a handkerchief.

Sure enough, she wanted me to "tell her all about it." I cried into her handkerchief, stalling, trying desperately to invent something. Couldn't think of anything to save my life. I kept repeating stupidly: "Nothing—it's nothing—really, there's nothing the matter with me—" but she said no one sits on the floor alone crying over nothing. She wasn't going to leave until I told her. Told her what?

I forced myself to sit down beside her on the floor and put my arm around her shoulders. I don't know why it was so hard for me to do it. Her shoulders jerked convulsively when I touched her. I stroked her hair, wet with tears, made soothing noises to show I loved her. Finally I asked her quite sternly what in God's name was the matter. She kept on shaking her head, as if flies were bothering her.

Finally I gave up. Simply let things take their course. Told her point-blank I have a lover. She wasn't as surprised as I'd expected. Nor shocked.

I stopped reading for a moment. Shocked? Was I a prude in those days?

She probably has a pretty good idea of what goes on, as far as Bill and I are concerned.

Naturally. The only thing I didn't know was that there actually was somebody else.

Of course she wanted to know who it is. And I suddenly came to my senses. Could have kicked myself. From one minute to the next I became completely clear-headed and stopped crying. Invented all sorts of reasons why I couldn't tell her who it is. None of them made sense and she wouldn't buy them. Then it occurred to me to give my "lover" a name, at least a first name. I'd been reading Molnar, so I named him Ferencsi. I could read her eyes as she racked her brain, trying to remember if she'd ever met anyone by the name of Ferencsi. And all the time she was patting my hand or stroking my head, smiling and eager to show me that she didn't disapprove. I suddenly felt like hugging her. Instead, I babbled on and invented all kinds of rubbish about Ferencsi. What if I don't remember it all? I think I said he's half French, half Hungarian, Catholic, married, two children—that's important so that she won't drive me insane with bright suggestions about divorcing Bill and living happily ever after with Ferencsi. He lives in Paris and I knew him "way back." Very plausible. He only occasionally comes to London on business. A good touch, it explains why she never meets him. And so—sob—the situation is completely hopeless. She nodded sympathetically and then came out with the inevitable question: "Does he love you?" "I don't know," I replied. "I don't see him often enough." At that she protested indignantly, "What does that fellow think he's doing? He's cheating on his wife and he's making you unhappy. Where's this going to get you? Are you sure you can't tear him out—by the roots?"

She gave me a long look. Her eyes were still red and her eyelashes damp and stuck together. I thought she was never going to answer, but finally she whispered: "I was trying to. When you came in, I was trying to."

•

That was all I could get out of her. She wouldn't say any more. Did Bill suspect anything? I only saw him at meals now; he didn't do his shadow-boxing in the living room anymore. And Nina? Maybe she knew, maybe that's why she hunched her shoulders whenever she caught sight of her mother, as if to protect herself from something. Perhaps she knew Ferencsi.

I sat in my car in front of the house for a while before I felt able to drive off. What a mess. I could still feel her shoulders shaking in my arms. How strange. This was a new Anabel. Gone the aristocratic, splendid bearing, the unshakable poise. In their place a fragile, trembling little heap of misery, sitting there among the Christmas wrappings. Ferencsi. What sort of fellow could that be, what did he look like, how on earth had he managed to . . . ?.

I started up the car and drove slowly away in the direction of Chelsea. One didn't visit Jerome in his "studio" at Simon's except in an emergency, and they had no telephone. Today was an emergency, Anabel needed help. Immediately. I wasn't free, I had to be at the theater by seven at the latest. But there was Jerome, after all. Unsentimental, unprejudiced, discreet, wise, accustomed to shipwreck and disaster since early childhood, he'd probably just smile. The only hurdle was that he didn't really like her.

Simon muttered something uncomplimentary when I came in. Jerome, paintbrush in his mouth, palette in one hand, closed the door behind me, signaling something. Pius III was dying on the windowsill; his successor had not yet been named. Silence in the studio except for the frantic buzzing of the fly's death rattle. Simon rose, walked over to the window and watched the six legs twitching convulsively. Pius was already on his back, yet his twitching managed to propel him sideways for a fraction of an inch. Abrupt silence. Pius lay still and started gently to shrivel up. Simon went back to his desk in silence.

Jerome raised his eyebrows inquiringly. I motioned to him to step into the tiny bathroom. We closed the door. In a whisper I told him, a bit too excitedly, what had just happened at the Macleans'.

He showed no surprise, kept chewing the end of his paintbrush thoughtfully but didn't speak. I hesitated, sensing his resistance. "Jerome—won't you call her up? Take her to a movie. She needs it, she shouldn't be alone today, she's canceled all invitations, doesn't want to see anyone. But she mustn't stay home with just Bill and Nina. I could meet you somewhere after the show, when your movie is over. Take care of her a bit, will you?"

Jerome considered, then nodded. All right, he'd take care of her, but only this once. No permanent caretaking. "She gets on my nerves."

•

Diary:

> Now I've really done it. Missed my chance.
> For months I've been putting it off from one
> day to the next. And yet I knew all the
> time it was urgent!
>   What prevented me from saying to her
> yesterday: "I'm crying because I hate myself.
> I hate myself because day in and day out
> I'm deceiving you, because I love you and
> betray you every second. It's no good telling

myself that I'm not robbing you of anything
that belongs to you. You wouldn't understand.
You'd see nothing but theft and treachery.
You only recognize black and white and you
think you can distinguish between right and
wrong. I have some kind of cancer. I've always
had it. Perhaps something could have been
done about it when Maman died. She would
often put her arms around me and say, "It's
not enough for us to love you, you must love
us in return!" She knew about those bad
cells inside me. It was probably frightening
to her, a child that can't love, a child that
doesn't really want anything. And yet I did
love her, but I never knew it until she died.
Died so quickly that I was hardly aware of
it. How old was I? Twelve. Old enough.
But I had paid no attention, never asked
why she was getting so thin. She had cancer
too. A different kind.

A few weeks after her death I was sitting
on my swing in the garden and swinging so
wildly and so high that the posts shook. But
now there was no voice calling from the
window, "Anabel! Not so high, child, you'll go
right over!"

I let the swing die down. My arms and
legs went limp with the first and overwhelming
feeling of loneliness. How I had resented
that voice! And how desperately I wished I
could hear it again. When the swing stopped,
I didn't jump off, I sat there, hating my dead
mother for abandoning me.

Yesterday, when L. sat down beside me
on the floor and stared at me with her large
round cow's eyes, I felt I was back on the
swing and I could hear the voice from the
window calling, "Anabel! Not so high, child,

you'll go right over!" So I howled a bit longer to gain time, let the swing die down—and invented Ferencsi.

Suppose I'd told her the truth, how would those big cow's eyes have looked at me? I've imagined it hundreds of times. And not without a certain amount of pleasure. It's a pleasure to feel that you can destroy someone, especially when you're the weaker one. Because she's the stronger. Only she doesn't know it yet.

13

How very kind of Jerome to take Anabel out twice a week while I was at the theater. I was deeply touched. He seemed a bit restless at the time, possibly an early symptom of the hepatitis which put him out of action for six weeks a little while later. It wasn't only Anabel who got on his nerves—I did too, though only once, but it upset and confused me for days.

It happened while he was sick and had to remain in bed at our apartment, jaundiced and bloated-looking. I nursed him and spent every free minute away from the theater sitting by his bed. On matinee days I would have liked to ask Anabel to take my place, but he wouldn't let me. She sent her chauffeur over every day with special food, fruit, flowers and magazines, but she never came to see him.

Ours was a two-room apartment, with bath and small kitchen. Only the bedroom was furnished—the bed, bedside table, two chairs and a wardrobe. The second room served as a studio when Simon was being difficult, and as a storeroom for Jerome's finished paintings, for Simon might have been tempted to pawn them occasionally. "If only I could get a few of them framed," Jerome used to say from time to time. "They'd look quite different framed. Then I could show them to a gallery."

I had just made an extra fifty pounds posing for photographs advertising nightgowns and nylon stockings (then brand-new) and felt the moment was propitious. While Jerome was asleep, I sneaked out to a frame shop, carrying three of his largest canvases.

"What kind of frame would you like?"

What kind? At home in Berlin all the pictures had been in carved and curly gold frames, but Jerome hated curls as well as gold. What to do? Helplessly I stared at hundreds of samples, row after row, wide ones, narrow ones, in all colors, materials and profiles.

"Something simple," I said hesitantly. Then, remembering the gallery owners, I added hastily, "But—imposing."

The salesman gave me a look. "I see," he said and selected one. It was certainly simple, and imposing too. It was made of iron and so heavy that I could hardly lift it. I bought three of them, and it took me half an hour to lug them upstairs one by one and stealthily set them up in the studio.

Then, sweating and excited, I sat down on Jerome's bed and confessed what I'd done. He was very touched, eager to see them, and asked me to bring them in right away. Panting, I dragged *Gypsy Mother and Child* into the bedroom. He stared at it, speechless, while I went for the second one, *Foreign Legionnaire*, and then the third, *Olive Trees in Grasse*. I stood the three of them, locked in an iron embrace, at the foot of the bed. Simple but imposing.

Jerome's silence lasted too long for me.

"Don't tell me you don't like them," I bristled. "They cost forty-five pounds."

"Forty-five pounds!" he shouted, and his swollen, jaundiced face turned a dull red. "Are you out of your mind? Are you really blind and dumb? Those aren't frames, they're horseshoes!"

I was already in tears and didn't hear any more, except an order to take "those goddam things" off his canvases immediately because they were suffocating.

"Can't you see that they're not framed? They're murdered."

Sobbing, I carted them back down the stairs. One of them fell on my thumb and squashed it. I drove back to the frame shop and was happy to get twenty pounds back, probably on the strength of my tear-stained face and swollen thumb.

•

Why had he shouted at me? He had been so patient otherwise, all through his long and depressing illness. As if something that had been brewing inside him for a long time had suddenly erupted.

On my return from the frame shop, I found him flat on his back, staring at the ceiling. No music, no book, and his temperature had gone up. I wanted to call the doctor but he wouldn't let me, caught my hand as I reached for the telephone and silently covered his eyes with it.

That was the only quarrel we ever had. Generally his arms were around me. Whenever we were alone somewhere, he'd automatically put his arm around my shoulder, asserting his rights and offering protection. It didn't bother me that other girls always looked at him a bit too long when we went out together; he only had eyes for me. When I had time, he painted me, tenderly, making me look more beautiful. "That's not me," I would say, waiting for the inevitable reply: "Yes, it is. That's you. In my eyes, at least."

●

One afternoon I picked him up at Simon's. The hepatitis was over but he was still too thin and a bit shaky.

I was helping him on with his coat when there was a loud, peremptory knock at the door. A female voice called fortissimo:

"Open the door, Simon, or aren't you alone?"

Simon turned to his son. "Your mother," he

said reproachfully. "Wait," he muttered, searching for the fly. Garibalda's powerful voice came through the keyhole: "The hell with your damned flies or mice or frogs or whatever you've got now, we're freezing out here."

Simon had located the fly and was on his way to the door.

"We?" he exclaimed, appalled, dragging Garibalda into the room, accompanied by a tall, thin man wearing tweeds and a red checkered vest. "Who's this?"

Garibalda acted as though she had had no part in the undignified entrance and made the necessary introductions with a gesture straight out of *Turandot*.

"My ex-husband, my ex-son, his girl friend —Lord Springwell."

"How d'you do," said the thin man, with a slight movement of his head in the appropriate directions.

"Sit down," she continued, taking Jerome's armchair. His lordship sat down cautiously on a hassock, shooing away the fly, which was trying to make friends with him.

"Don't flap at him," warned Simon. "This is Clemens II. He's only one day old and still a little jumpy."

"How d'you do," said Springwell.

Simon picked up a little bowl of sugar water and approached them.

"Here, Clemens, here! There's a good boy. Isn't he incredible?"

Triumphantly he carried the bowl with the small black speck perched on it over to the windowsill.

"Garibalda, you look marvelous. To what do I owe the pleasure—"

"Hugh and I want to get married, and I'd like you to get to know each other."

I looked at Jerome questioningly. The pilot had obviously taken off, but what about her faithful Scotsman? In place of an answer, Jerome drew me down beside him on the floor. No one was paying any attention to us, but we had front-row seats.

"Well, well," said Simon, withdrawing behind his desk. "That certainly is good news—that is, provided . . ."

"Go ahead and ask him," said Garibalda, lighting a cigarette. She was one of the few singers who smoked. On stage too. I'd seen her in *Carmen*, singing the *"Habañera"* with a cigarette dangling from the corner of her mouth. A gasp had run through the house like a gentle breeze; everybody was whispering to his neighbor, "It's lighted!"

"Go ahead and ask," she repeated. "He's prepared."

"Well, well," drawled Simon thoughtfully. "Where do you buy your vests?"

"Fisher and Clogwell," said the thin man. "Thirteen Hanover Square, second floor left. Mr. Whittle."

Simon jotted down something on a scratch pad. He hated vests.

"But watch the back—they never make them long enough to suit me."

"Back," said Simon and scribbled some more. "I'm glad you warned me. Do you pay cash?"

"Of course not," said Springwell, shocked. "He bills me once a year."

"And one pays promptly?"

Springwell looked bewildered. Garibalda may have prepared him for the pet fly but not for such manifest lack of breeding.

"That would be a shock to him," he said icily. "One only pays when one changes tailors."

Simon, blithely unaware of the rebuke, nodded approval.

"Garibalda, you have fallen into the hands of a gentleman. Have you any family?"

"A daughter from my first marriage."

"Pretty?"

"No."

"Then she'll need money."

"Don't worry. Garibalda will be well taken care of."

"How well?"

"Fifty thousand."

Simon stared pensively ahead. "Not good enough. Let's say seventy-five thousand and I'll give my consent."

A pause. Garibalda inhaled, rounded her lips and projected a perfectly rounded capital O into the room.

"Agreed," drawled Springwell.

"Where will you be living?"

"In Canada."

"Good Lord! Garibalda, you're giving up singing?"

"From now on she'll be singing for me alone —in the bathtub," cried the thin chap, bursting into surprisingly noisy laughter.

Garibalda remained silent and continued

filling the room with those splendid smoke rings.

"Excellent," said Simon, standing up. "I herewith bestow my blessing on the happy pair. Er, Jerome—do you happen to have—get a bottle from your refrigerator."

"Very civil of you," said his lordship, visibly moved. "Let's have a drink."

"God forbid!" exclaimed Garibalda, pulling her husband-to-be to his feet. "You don't know the kind of wine he drinks, you'd never survive it. Now that you're friends, we can go. That's really all I wanted. Simon, we're leaving."

"Just a minute!" cried Simon. Then: "Okay, he's still sitting on his bowl. Quick now! All good wishes and *bon voyage!*"

"Goodbye, Mr. Lorrimer, it was a pleasure . . ." said Springwell, trying to shake hands with his host in spite of Garibalda steering him toward the door. She waved in our direction, blew a kiss to Simon and pulled Springwell, who was offering only token resistance, over the threshold. Exit.

"No one could say that you and your mother exactly dote on one another," said Simon after a short pause. "Can't you forgive and forget?"

"I'd be glad to forget her but she keeps getting into my field of vision. And as for forgiving, it's easy enough for you to talk, you only had to put up with her for a few years."

"As far as I remember, you too were parked out fairly early with the hired help."

"Best thing that ever happened to me," said Jerome, opening his refrigerator and taking out a bottle of red wine, ice-cold, but better ice-cold than missing.

Simon was watching him with the eyes of a greedy child, and Jerome smiled and filled two glasses. He handed one to his father and continued his train of thought.

"The going only got rough when she'd suddenly reappear and assert her rightful motherly demands. In her case, quite peculiar ones. For instance, whenever she sang Aïda, I had to appear promptly and shave her armpits. 'One expects a steady hand from a painter. What else is he good for?' she said, threatening me with the razor."

Simon laughed, his double chin wobbling up and down.

"She never wanted you, let's face it. You were a traffic accident. Cheers!"

"She was caught in a trap—she never really wanted a husband, let alone a child. Can you blame her if she's not particularly attached to either of us?"

"You're mellow today because she's going to increase your allowance," said Jerome. And turning to me: "She has now finally received a papal annulment, solemnly proclaiming that her marriage never existed. Yet she knows something the Pope doesn't know, because she's a Sardinian peasant. Simon is and will always be her husband, and if she wants to marry again, she thinks she needs *his* gracious permission."

"And you?" I asked. "Where do you come in? Are you also annulled?"

"No," he said and kissed me. "I'm very much in existence, but I don't 'come in,' I'm not part of the show, I'm kept somewhere in the wings. Occasionally she lets me watch and applaud. The trouble is, I'm getting older as she gets younger. That's hard for her. And yet I know that tonight, for instance, the telephone will ring sometime, summoning me to her apartment. And she'll hug me and kiss me and for an hour she'll be 'Mama.' That's the hardest part."

Simon stared at his son, but before he could say anything there was a single knock followed by three rapid ones. A hurried fly ritual, then he called, "Now!" and opened his desk drawer and extracted a huge, stained napkin, which he tucked into his collar below the double chin.

The door was kicked open, and a boy appeared with a tray, panting, his nose red with cold. He was balancing a steaming chafing dish set on a brass food warmer.

"Lobster thermidor," said Simon. "Jerome, do you happen to have . . ."

Jerome fished in his pocket for a sixpence for the boy, who disappeared in a flash. We too were already at the door.

"Goodbye, children," called Simon. "I deserve your deepest sympathy."

"Whatever for?" I asked, stopping in surprise.

"Because I'm going to have to drink chilled red wine with my lobster," said Simon, waving us on our way.

●

Diary, January 1938:

> I look dreadful. I've lost five pounds. My hair's like straw and it's falling out. My face is so

narrow, I could kiss a goat between its horns.
My body's as thin as a sliver of soap. J.
hates skinny women. "I'm thin myself," he
says. "I want something I can get hold of.
My ideal is a woman who would engulf me
like a wave. Eat!"

That was yesterday afternoon. He was
lying in bed, smoking. He's not really supposed
to since the hepatitis but I didn't want to make
a fuss. Alone with him again at last after
six endless weeks! The flat was shining like a
new pin—not that he'd ever notice! (I've
got a new cleaning woman, Mrs. Cook, fat old
broad, wheezing and snorting, but thorough.
And fresh! When she passed J. on the stairs,
she tapped him on the chest with her
forefinger and said, "Have a good time, son.")

Afterward we talked about L., usually
taboo. "I'm not the faithful type," he said.
"I'm not a good friend or a good son either.
My father thinks faithfulness is either lethargy
or lack of imagination. Fidelity is plain
pigheadedness, he used to tell me, it only
means that you wear blinkers. Be a
Renaissance man, he used to urge me when
I was a child, keep your eyes open, be aware
of everything that's going on around you,
don't miss anything, and above all, never
worry about consequences, just go ahead
and do what you want. There'll always be
somebody to clean up the mess after you're
gone."

I was lying quite still next to him. It's rare
for him to talk about himself. Who knows,
there might be some sort of loophole in his
stronghold where I might slip through—and
stay!

"But . . ." And then came a long pause.

My heart was pounding so hard in my throat
and we were lying so close together that
I was sure he'd feel it. "But what?" I finally
asked. He turned toward me and looked at me
in surprise as though he had waked up to find
a stranger in bed with him. And at once he
smiled that awful, sly, conspiratorial smile of
his. "But what?" I insisted. He stroked my
head and looked for a long time straight into
my eyes. Then he said slowly and deliberately,
"But I'd like to grow old with L. I'd like to
die in her arms. What am I to do to make
sure of that?" He asked *me* that! He expected
an answer. Wanted *my* advice. To grow old
with L.! The words crackled and banged
around in my brain, wouldn't settle. To grow
old with L. Is that a devastating criticism
or is it love?

Both, if you ask me.

I couldn't contain myself any longer or I'd
have suffocated. "And what about me? What's
my place in your design for living?" "You?
You have a very important place, you
represent everything I don't like—and that's
what I do like about myself. Do you
understand what I'm getting at? If you were
a cozy buxom Rubens with four breasts—
like the one in the Louvre I love—instead
of the highly charged electric eel that you are,
it would all be quite commonplace, plain
ordinary wish fulfilment. But the fact that
I'm lying here beside *you* is a triumph for
you. Besides, you're my guardian angel, my
skinny guardian angel. I need you.
You know I do."

The crackling inside my brain sounded as
though a pile of plates had crashed to the

floor. No loophole! Yet: "I need you." That's all I can hold on to. I pulled myself together and said, "Guardian angel is right. I protect you from other women. And I protect L. too." "Against what?" he asked in surprise and sat up. "Against you," I said. He lay down again, and after a while he put his arms around me.

Guardian angel! Did I need a guardian angel? What I needed was glasses!

My mother noticed something, even without glasses. One day she was in the garden of our house in Hampstead watering the wallflowers I had planted to hide the fence.

"What's wrong with your friend Anabel?" she asked, handing me the empty watering can.

"What do you mean, what's wrong with her?" I trotted over to the spigot.

"Something's wrong," she called after me. "Haven't you noticed how ill she looks?"

"She's—thin," I said, letting the water overflow.

"She's thin because some man's making her thin," said my mother with quiet conviction.

I carted the full watering can over to the flower bed, full of admiration for her intuition. When I tried to hand it over to her she didn't take it from me.

"I know who it is, too," she said, folding her arms over her chest. All of a sudden the watering can weighed a ton. I had to set it down. Did my mother know Ferencsi?

"Can't you guess?" she asked, looking me straight in the eye. I consulted my watch, picked up the watering can and waved it back and forth over the wallflowers until it felt lighter.

"You're wrong," I said, handing it to her. "Believe me, you're absolutely wrong. I've got to go or I'll be late to the theater."

"Drive carefully," she said and began to water the wallflowers.

•

Bill noticed something too. Once, after my performance, the four of us had met at the Four Hundred, a nightclub in Leicester Square. He had asked me for a dance, something he didn't often do. He danced well, but always with Anabel.

"Do you happen to know why my wife's so depressed?" he asked as we shuffled about on the tiny, overcrowded floor.

"Is she depressed?"

"Well, look at her." He jerked his chin in the direction of our table. Jerome and Anabel were sitting side by side in silence. Jerome, cigarette in mouth, was a hundred miles away; Anabel was supporting her head on her hand, staring over the heads of the dancing couples with unseeing eyes.

"Is she ill? She doesn't tell me anything. Does she talk to you?"

"Perhaps she's tired," I said. "Maybe she needs a vacation. She ought to come to Grasse with us and stay with our friends the Gurnemantzes at their peach farm. It would be a change for her, out of doors, working in the orchard, swimming in the sea . . ."

•

Take Anabel with us to the Gurnemantzes'! Bill had no objection, made plans to go sailing, and Nina wanted to spend her vacation with friends anyway. Jerome, however, was not enthusiastic. "She won't fit in," he said. "Can you imagine her sorting peaches and trekking to the market at night in that decrepit old buggy? Anabel?"

"You underestimate her," I said. "She's not a hothouse flower. I don't think you really know her."

And so in the summer of 1938 she went with us to Grasse. Peter put her to work without further ado, she was detailed picking peaches, learned to sort them and pack them, waited with us in the truck at the market, loved it all and swam with us in the sea.

Actually it was a good thing she was there, for something was brewing in the Gurnemantz household. Outwardly nothing had changed except that Peter was frantically building a garage (but why? For that ancient truck?), working at it until late at night. Ursula lay under an olive tree, glancing every now and again under half-closed eyelids at the peach orchard, where Eva was picking peaches all alone. In the daytime? In the hot sun?

We speculated about it in our guest room in the "thigh." Something was up—but what, exactly? It was all the more mysterious since there was no tension. On the contrary, the three of them were always throwing an arm around each other's shoulders, making affectionate noises.

Until, a week after our arrival, Ursula summoned us all to a "council meeting." That very evening, please, after supper. Was Anabel to come too? Yes.

We solemnly carried coffee, Pernod and fresh almonds out onto the terrace and lay down on our air mattresses. Ursula blew out the storm lanterns, then jumped up and crouched on the terrace wall, her lean, long body silhouetted jet-black against the star-studded night sky.

We waited, flat on our backs, staring up into the flickering chiaroscuro of the summer night until our tension and expectancy gradually melted away. We dozed. Silence, soft black silence. I fell asleep.

Suddenly somebody was gently tugging my sleeve. Anabel. And from far away, though gradually coming closer, I could hear Ursula's voice.

". . . probably been wondering why I'm loafing around like this. Well, unfortunately I have no other choice. The doctor in Nice says it may take as long as a year to get completely well. Imagine! A full year! He told me something else, too—" She broke off. Then, speaking into the darkness: "My glass is empty."

A large black shape got up—Peter. A gurgling sound from the Pernod bottle, and he lay down again on his mattress.

After a brief pause Ursula's voice resumed, cool and factual. "I've got to give up what the silly old clot referred to as 'marital pleasures,' I'm supposed to rest. *Rester tranquille*. 'Are you out of your mind?' I asked him. 'Okay, suppose I manage to *rester tranquille*, what about my husband? Is he supposed to be *tranquille* for a whole year?' He was embarrassed, said this really wasn't his domain, and—well, there was a certain district in Nice to take care of things of that sort, 'Vous comprenez?' 'Thanks so much, Doctor, how much do I owe you?' That didn't embarrass him at all, that was his domain all right. Well, Peter tried out the certain district. One morning, after the market, he dropped us off at the Negresco and drove on. To a different market. An hour later he picked us up at the beach. We were all pretty grim on the way home, and the first thing Peter did was jump into the water cistern."

She paused. No one said a word.

"That's when I thought of Eva. It's important that you remember that *I* was the one who thought of Eva, no one else. She's always been a part of us, right from the beginning. She's shared everything with us except—well, you know. So why not close the gap? I don't believe anything will change radically. Peter agrees. Tell them, Peter."

Out of the darkness came his deep voice: "I agree."

"It's important to me that you all hear this, so that nobody could later on—" She broke off, couldn't keep up the matter-of-factness, sounded suddenly defenseless, even imploring. After a few seconds she regained control and concluded briefly: "Eva has some reservations. Tell them, Eva."

From the farthest corner of the terrace Eva's chirpy little voice piped up promptly. She had just celebrated her twentieth birthday and greatly enjoyed being the center of attention.

"I have reservations because it's immoral."

"Why?" Jerome's voice, obviously interested.

"Why? Because Peter's my sister's husband. Otherwise I wouldn't have any objection. I'm no virgin, I'm experienced.

Jerome cleared his throat.

"Under ancient Jewish law," said Ursula quietly, "such a thing wouldn't have been immoral at all. In fact, the husband had a sort of first option on the younger sister—"

"Only after his wife was dead," Eva cried heatedly.

"I *am* dead," said Ursula calmly. "And I'll remain dead for a whole year. Then I'll rise again." Silence. "I called you together for a council meeting. You two know us, and that's an advantage. Anabel doesn't know us, and that's an advantage too. What do you think of my proposal?"

Jerome's voice was the first to break through the darkness.

"The most important thing is that Peter shouldn't have to jump into the water cistern anymore. Every situation spells out its morality. Why did the ancient Jews give the widower an option on the sister? Because sisters are often alike, they often have the same kind of skin, similar hair, a similar smell. So if the husband's got himself acclimatized to one sister, he might as well have a go at the other."

"Nonsense," said Ursula. "It was to keep the dowry in the family."

"Both," muttered Peter. "Both solid reasoning."

"Wait a minute!" I exclaimed, sitting up because I couldn't stay down any longer. "Are you all insane? What's going to happen afterward, when Ursula's well again? How can you ever undo that sort of thing?"

"Undo it?" repeated Jerome, trying unsuccessfully to pull me down onto my mattress. "Why on earth should they want to undo it? All this could be a marvelous new source of experience, enrichment . . ."

"Very dangerous!" I shouted a bit too loudly; the darkness intensified every sound.

"Why always play safe?"

Silence again. Sounds of one or the other sitting up. The Pernod bottle gurgled again, and the silhouette on the wall moved too.

"What does our guest have to say?"

Anabel, next to me, had remained quite still on her mattress. Without any hesitation or embarrassment she said quietly, "Playing it safe is never any good. 'Afterward' will bring its own solution. The problem is 'now.' As I see it, the decisive factor is that it's Ursula's idea. You three will never lose each other."

"Cheers!" said Peter.

Ursula climbed down from the wall and lay down by his side. He put his arm around her and gave her a drink of Pernod from his glass.

The council meeting adjourned.

14

She didn't take the diary with her to Grasse. Too dangerous. There were no entries until after we returned.

First entry, September 1938:

Played at being a peasant for six weeks. Close to the soil, the smell of leaves in my nostrils, dirt under my fingernails, my brain gummed up with resin. Gained five pounds. Picking peaches. For hours at a time, until that silly animal came trotting up, gaping at me reproachfully with its big donkey eyes. I'd stick my best peach in his mouth and he'd look amazed and trot off and then I could keep watch through the tangle of branches trying to get a glimpse of Jerome, way off in the distance. Now and then I'd catch sight of a black patch of hair or the tanned arm I knew so well. Meant a great deal to me. Just to feel him close by, to sit opposite him at meals. Better than staying home, crying, like last year. Not once did he come anywhere near me alone. Selected his blasted peach trees rows and rows away from mine.

L. on the other hand would often come and visit with me while we were picking. Helped me fill my baskets. Showed me time and again how to twist the damned things off, declaring passionately, "Just feel how hot they are. You can smell the sun!"

The Gurnemantz threesome—quite interesting! Especially one of the girls, the older one. She is Electra; mourning distinctly becomes her. No fool. Senses everything, catches on at once. I had to watch my step. Had the feeling that she had sniffed the air a couple of times in my direction—and guessed! Was therefore doubly careful with J. The younger sister is nothing much. Just young. Bursting with health. Iphigenia. Even though she is very proud of not being a virgin anymore. That won't save her from being sacrificed, though. First to her dear brother-in-law. Later on—catastrophe. They'll end up loathing each other, all three of them. Of course, what I said aloud was just the opposite. Proclaimed in Delphic tones, "You three will never lose each other." And I have a feeling the process has already begun. Soon they'll be snarling at each other. Perfect harmony *à trois*, the harmony they so bravely dream about, just doesn't hold for any length of time in the cold light of day. Nor in secrecy either—like L. and J. and me.

And now, at long long last, back in London

and back in the old groove. Apartment sparkling clean. Mrs. Cook a jewel.

L. rehearsed a new play. As enthusiastic as ever. Could be this time with some justification. What a blessing a long run would be! For her as well as for us.

The blessing came to pass. My first real success. The play was called *Little Ladyship*. It presented me with a juicy role—and a dislocated shoulder. During the tryout in Edinburgh. On stage. I was running down a flight of stairs, slipped halfway down and banged my elbow against the banister. I didn't fall but remained stiffly upright where I was. My right arm hung limply somewhere behind me, twisted slightly sideways, and refused to obey my command to get back into place forthwith. It seemed to have declared its independence. This surprising fact was the last coherent thought in my mind before I was enveloped in whirling darkness.

When I came to in my dressing room, yelling vigorously, they were cutting my dress off my body and a gentleman I had never seen before was bending over me. Apparently the curtain had been rung down in a hurry and three separate physicians had responded to the stage manager's anxious appeal: "Is there a doctor in the house?" As soon as the strange gentleman had diagnosed a dislocated shoulder, I was rushed to the hospital, put to sleep, and my recalcitrant arm encased in a plaster cast.

Sometimes it popped out again—and back in, and I learned to handle it. Once when I was standing on a chair in the painter's studio, reaching for a bottle of turpentine on a shelf, I fell with the chair and the bottle on top of me. To her astonishment I rolled over on my stomach, howling, and pressed my right shoulder hard against the floor. Crrrack—and it was back in place again.

●

Strange weeks. The same schedule almost every day, as if I were back at school. Now there were daily and regular hours at the painter's to make sure that she took her medicine, to shop for her and see that she ate something. The doctor had made it clear that such were my duties for the time being. She was the only patient he enjoyed, he told me. Actually she was well again, but he kept finding excuses to visit her, though he never sent her a bill. She saw through his "solicitude," went along with it, and gave him a water color.

And every single evening I would reach for the diary, even on the rare occasions when I came home late. I couldn't go to bed until I'd read at least one entry. It had become part of the daily schedule, and I couldn't make up my mind if it was now a sacred duty or a compulsion or even an addiction. At any rate it forced me to relive those three years almost day by day and thus uproot and then liquidate all my previous (and deliberately blinkered) memories of that time. Turning the pages I was either silently nodding in reluctant agreement or shaking my head in furious and belated recognition, until I would close the book for the night and slink

off to bed shaken and undone—and always en-
slaved. I led a double life during those weeks,
my daily prosaic existence and my former one,
the diary one. That one appeared to me some-
what suspended in midair, dislocated, and quite
independent of my will. Like my shoulder. And
as with my shoulder, the first impact had been
devastating, too agonizing to bear without some
kind of painkiller, but gradually I had gotten
used to it, the bits and pieces fell into place—
and now I even had a nightly craving for it.

Every now and again I still felt a twinge of
pain. Then I'd close the book, switch off the
light and have it out with Anabel, with Jerome
and with myself.

•

The painter was sitting at the easel studying my
portrait when I came in with my shopping bag.
"I'm still not up to it," she said, without turning around. "I don't know why. I'm quite well,
but nothing clicks inside."

I took off my coat.

"Shall I take the pose? It might do it."

"I don't think so. I can't see anything except
colors and lines. No patterns, no plan, all running wild."

"Mozart?"

"I'm sick of Mozart."

I took the pot of soup out of the shopping
bag, set it down and reached for my coat. She
turned around.

"I'll make coffee." In other words: I don't
want to be alone.

The kitchen was spotless now, the bedroom heated, and the bedding back on the bed. I had engaged a Spanish cleaning woman who came for two hours a day and cheerfully put up with the painter's grumbling and growling since she couldn't understand her polemics. The only place she wasn't allowed to touch was the studio, and the dust accumulated on the canvases. "That's good, it gives them patina," said the painter.

While she was heating the soup, I took a half-bottle of red wine, a corkscrew and a napkin out of the shopping bag, collected her glass from a bathroom, cleaned it, drew the cork and set the table. Today she needed some wine, no matter what the doctor said.

She appeared in the doorway with the tray and stopped in surprise when she saw the bottle. I took the tray from her and pulled her down on the chair, using force to spread a napkin on her lap.

"Napkin," she said contemptuously. "Reminds me of my mother. All that damned ritual. You think I don't know about that? I was brought up as a precious jewel soaked in loving affection, the real article, you know, no phony stuff. Plus splendid examples set by my father and mother of the right kind of behavior and the right kind of manners. They did a good job, it certainly took with me, and I had a hell of a time getting rid of them—the good behavior and the manners, I mean. They cling to one like a permanent illness. When things go wrong, you run to your good manners and you think you find solace by 'behaving well.' A drastic withdrawal cure was the only thing that saved me. After that my work began at last to buzz and to crackle."

This unexpected outburst contained more words than all the ones strung together that she had ever addressed to me since I first met her.

"Eat. It's getting cold." I sat down in the corner on my hassock.

She ate. "It takes a great effort to go to pot when you've been well brought up. At home everything was so—so right, so solid. No cheating, no flimflam, no false facades. Everything was the genuine article. My father, my mother— they were genuine too."

"Were you the only child?"

"Yes. That was the trouble."

She ate her soup in silence, drank the wine and grunted contentedly.

"Is there any more? I know, I'm not supposed to, but . . ."

I brought the bottle and she filled her glass and drained it slowly.

"And you, too, you'll never amount to anything if you don't learn to be less level-headed. You are level-headed—I can smell it, and it's death. Death to anything connected with art. And you are an artist, after all."

"I'm not sure. I have to labor for everything."

"Nothing wrong with that." She poured the rest of the wine. "Labor is always good, even if you're a genius. Genius is mostly hard labor. Did you know that? Obsessive hard labor. Are you obsessed?"

"Sometimes."

"That's not enough. You ought to be obsessed *all* the time."

The wine had taken effect quickly. All that medication had made her vulnerable.

"I'll try," I said and stood up to take her plate back to the kitchen. "Dirty plates stink."

"There you go again," she said fiercely. "What's wrong with stink? You're squeamish and orderly, like my mother. Her last request, on her deathbed, five minutes before she died, was for a toothbrush to clean her teeth."

I put the plate down and moved my hassock close to her chair. She leaned back and took off her glasses and I could see quite clearly how she must have looked when she first arrived in Paris, young, sturdy, but thin-skinned and lonely. She felt with her hand for the familiar pack of Gauloises, remembered that she wasn't allowed to smoke, fidgeted, and finally folded her hands to keep them still.

I waited until her gaze came to rest on me, then took a chance.

"How was it with you? Congenital? Didn't you like boys even when you were a child?"

"I certainly did. I liked them a lot."

"When did you change? In Paris?"

"No. Long before. In Rouen. I was still at school." Silence. After a while she spoke again, more to herself than to me. "I can't be absolutely sure, of course. Who knows how it might have turned out if it hadn't been for that?"

"For what?"

She settled even farther back into her

chair, lying rather than sitting, staring at the ceiling without moving. "For what?" I asked again. She took her time.

"I'd just been confirmed. He was sitting on a bench in the park."

"Who was?"

"He was. That was the first time I ever saw him. The day after my confirmation, on the way home from school. There was a little lake, with ducks and weeping willows. A bench. Usually empty because it was so damp there. I used to catch frogs there when I was small. He was sitting on the bench, feeding the ducks. They came waddling out of the lake and quacked around him. He was talking to them, and now and again he'd try to stroke one of them. Then they'd squawk and run away, but they soon came waddling back again. We stopped and watched, two girl friends and I— we always walked part of the way home together. Next day there he was again, feeding the ducks. He waved to us. The day after, he wasn't there, but the following week we saw him from a distance and ran up to him. He was very tall and his hair was white at the temples. At school we could talk of nothing else, and we combed our hair and tied each other's ribbons before we set out for home. He let us sit by him on the bench and talked to us, calling us 'kleines Fräulein' and using the grown-up Sie rather than the childish du. He asked about our parents, about school, wanted to know what we were studying and how old we were. I was the oldest, almost sixteen, the others a few months younger. He was particularly nice to me, and they noticed it, of course. One day they told me they weren't walking through the park anymore and I could have him all to myself. From then on I went home alone. Every day I prayed that he'd be sitting on the bench. Two or three times a week he'd be there and I did have him to myself for ten minutes—no longer or they'd have asked questions at home. He told me he was a retired army officer. He looked like one too, distinguishd, and very elegant and precise in his movements, and polite and reserved. I hadn't mentioned him to my parents, and my girl friends weren't speaking to me. I didn't care. Things went on that way for about a month and then one day I told him tomorrow would be my sixteenth birthday—a great day, I would legally be an adult then, and my parents were planning a little party for our relatives and friends. 'What time?' he asked. 'About six. Why?' Did he want to come too? No, he had something else in mind, he would like to give me a birthday party too. His mother would bake me a cake and there would be a special surprise. He wrote down his address. I knew the house, not far from ours. He lived with his mother, they'd be expecting me for coffee and birthday cake at five o'clock."

She got up abruptly, searching for her Gauloises. I didn't dare to protest, because she looked as though she needed one. She inhaled deeply, returned to her chair, stretched out and stared at the ceiling.

"What a night I spent, the night before my birthday! Only a child can get into such a state! Juliet's age. Shakespeare wrote about other lovers too, but never again about another fourteen-year-old. For good reason. Of course I wasn't an Italian girl, I was really only a child. All I dreamed of was to be allowed to sit beside him and look at him. Maybe hold his hand. Maybe—maybe kiss him. But that was going almost too far. The idea of meeting his mother, being allowed into his house, his living room—I stayed awake half the night.

"Early next morning there was a birthday celebration at home before I left for school. My father made a little speech, he had tears in his eyes as he hung my great-grandmother's pearls around my neck. My mother brought in her present, holding it carefully over her arm: a white batiste dress trimmed with lace and white satin bows, the sort of thing girls wore in those days, delicate as a soap bubble. At school, the class sang "Happy Birthday" and in honor of the occasion I made up with my two girl friends. Today, we decided, we'd all three walk through the park like old times and say hello to him—but the bench was empty. We hung around for a while, as disappointed as the ducks quacking around us. I didn't say a word about the invitation—they might have wanted to accompany me.

"At five o'clock sharp I was at his house, one of the city's seventeenth-century buildings. I was wearing my new dress, hadn't even dared to sit down at home for fear of wrinkling it. White shoes and stockings. I had told my parents some tale about a birthday party a friend was giving for me and had promised I'd be back in time for the family celebration.

"I let two minutes pass for the sake of good manners, then I rang the bell. I could hear it ringing inside the house. Silence. Good God—he couldn't have forgotten, could he? At last I heard steps and breathed again. The massive old door opened and there he stood, smiling at me, kissed my hand 'in honor of my sixteenth birthday' and led the way through the front hall and into the living room. A large, dark room full of heavy oak furniture. I couldn't see it very clearly, since the curtains were drawn, although it was still daylight outside. 'It's more festive that way,' he explained in answer to my question, pointing to the table. And there, on a white tablecloth, stood a magnificent cake with sixteen candles, the only source of light in the room.

"'How kind of your mother!' I exclaimed. 'Where is she? I must thank her.'

"'She'll be here in a minute,' he said. 'She's in the kitchen making coffee—it's the cook's day off. Come along now, make a wish and then you must blow out all sixteen candles in one breath and your wish will come true.' He took my hand and led me to the table. My head swam. What could I possibly wish for when my heart had everything it desired? Dimly my brain formulated something like an absurd wish to remain for the rest of my life as blissfully happy as I was at that moment. Then I took a deep breath and blew out all the candles. Suddenly it was pitch dark. 'Please turn the lights on!' I called out. 'Where's the switch?' 'Here,' he said in a voice I'd never heard before. 'Give me your hand.' I groped blindly in his direction and felt his hand close over mine. With one shove he threw me down on the floor. I screamed with fright, thinking it was an accident, and tried to get up. But he was already on top of me, pinning my shoulders against the floor with his full weight. My dress! I thought. My dress! On the dirty floor! 'What are you doing?' I shouted. 'Let me get up. Let go of me!' And all at once I realized what was going to happen, because I could feel his hands tearing at my skirt. 'Help!' I screamed. 'Mother! Mother!' I was calling his mother as well as mine.

"And then something frightening occurred. He relaxed his grip for a moment. I could feel his breath on my face and heard his hoarse voice quite close to my ear, tough and vicious. Nobody had ever spoken to me in such a voice before. 'Shut up, you stupid cow. There's no mother here.'

"From then on I offered no resistance, it was as if I were paralyzed. I screamed. I don't know for how long. Suddenly he was gone, but I can't remember hearing him leave. I was alone in the pitch darkness. I tried to get on my feet, but I fell down again, bumping into a piece of furniture. I didn't dare make a sound for fear he'd come back. I groped around until I found a wall, then a door. The hallway was dimly lighted. I saw a large mirror but turned my head away; I couldn't bear to see my hair in a mess and my white dress crushed and torn. All I wanted was to get away, out of the house, quickly, quickly, before he could grab me again.

"I had some trouble opening the heavy

door. There wasn't a sound from inside the house. And suddenly I was standing outside in the street in bright sunlight. Fortunately there were not many people about. I ran, pressing myself close to the buildings, until I came to the corner, when I heard someone behind me calling: 'Whatever's the matter, child?' I ran all the faster, crossed the road right in front of a street-car and head another voice: 'What on earth has happened to you?' I ran and ran and ran and finally I got to our house.

"I didn't wait for the elevator, I climbed the stairs to our apartment step by step. Every step hurt. But I made it, and I finally stood in front of our door and heard voices and laughter and the chinking of plates. I waited. Inside, a door closed and the voices grew fainter. I rang —I still had no key of my own. And then I realized that our maid would be serving the coffee and that my mother would open the door herself.

"Too late. There she was, her eyes laughing and welcoming, her mouth open and ready to say: 'Well, here you are at last, we've all been waiting for you...'

"Then she saw me and turned pale.

" 'What in God's name ...' she gasped.

"I walked past her and made it to my bedroom door, hoping to get to the bed, but the carpet came up to meet me.

"I was out for a few minutes only, because, when I came to, my mother was kneeling on the carpet beside me, holding a bowl of cold water. 'Have you been run over?' she gasped, her eyes wide open in terror. I struggled to get up. She unbuttoned my dress and gave a loud cry. She'd seen the bloodstains."

•

Her voice had grown more and more husky, and I couldn't quite catch everything she said. Suddenly she stood up, extended both arms sideways as if she were doing her morning exercises and yawned loudly.

"Are you still awake?" she asked. "I've almost talked myself to sleep."

I was wide awake, I said, and I simply had to know what happened to the man. Jail?

"Jail, hell," she said, looking for her throat spray. She opened her mouth wide and sprayed. "Grrr. I was legally of age as of that day. That's what he'd been waiting for. Grrr. Grrrrr. All the same, my father wanted to kill him. It's a good thing he wasn't to be found. Of course, the house didn't belong to him—he was the caretaker and the owners had left their keys with him while they were on vacation. Grrr . . ." She shook the spray. "Empty."

"Did it take you a long time to—to get back to normal?"

"To normal? A lot of people would tell you I'm not normal even now. My parents took me on a long trip to Italy and Greece, everybody who 'knew' spoke to me in a soft voice as if I might break apart, but by the time we got back to Rouen, I was really in pretty good shape. I could laugh again and I'd even gained some weight. Though three or four years later—my father had died in the meantime—when my girl friends were having their first love affairs or getting married, I simply couldn't go along with it all. Couldn't stand looking every day at my mother's unhappy face. So I dropped out of medical school and took off for Paris. Other people had worse things happen to them. That's my life, and that's all there is to it. Tomorrow we'll start work again, ten o'clock sharp."

15

My first portrait sitting in three weeks, and the painter was too nervous even to say hello. She sat in front of the easel like a clod, stared and stared, jumped up, put on a Mozart record, stared again, and at long last turned toward me, though her imploring eyes didn't really take *me* in, they were firmly embedded in her own and purely arbitrary guidebook to my face. She was hunting for traces of the path she'd been pursuing before her illness, and she was terrified that she might not recognize the signposts.

I sat completely still, intent on helping her by concentrating on "something definite." That was easy nowadays—so many scenes emerged, unbidden, from the past that the problem was rather to get rid of them. There appeared, for instance, a view of Jerome and me in our tiny kitchen, getting breakfast ready. I was piling plates and cups on a tray, my mind on Anabel. Since I had found her crying on the floor, everything was changed; now it was she who needed my protection and solicitude. Protection against outside interference and possible suspicion and solicitude for her state of mind.

"He's torturing her," I said, thinking aloud. "The son of a bitch has a guilty conscience toward his wife and children and he's taking it out on Anabel. I have a feeling he's the type of man who doesn't mind tormenting people."

"Maybe that's what she likes," said Jerome, carrying the tray into the studio. Since my success in *Little Ladyship*, it now boasted a table and two chairs.

"She says he's in London right now. I wouldn't mind telling him a thing or two."

"What would you say to him?" Jerome spread butter and honey on his roll.

"I'd tell him to leave her in peace. I'd tell him that he's ruining her life."

"What makes you so sure he's ruining it? Was she any happier before she met him?"

I stared deeply into my coffee cup as if it could provide the answer to this difficult question. Happier? With Bill and Nina? Jerome lighted a cigarette, watching me without his customary smile, his narrow black eyes deeper than ever under the heavy brows, and an unshaven hollow under the sharp edge of the cheekbones. That's what he'll look like when he's old, I thought to myself. Not like his father or his mother, both conspicuously and oppressively manifest, but like a nomad, inscrutable, shadowy, unsmiling.

"Well?" he insisted. "Was she happier before?"

"Probably not. All the same, I'd like a word with him. He doesn't have to make her suffer, does he? Why can't he be—well, nicer to her?"

"Like Bill, you mean?"

I piled the plates on the tray and carried them back to the kitchen, calling through the open door, "Maybe one day I'll tail her."

Jerome appeared in the doorway, cigarette in mouth, and watched me washing the dishes. He took a towel and started to dry them.

"Don't," he said calmly. "One shouldn't poke one's nose into other people's secrets."

"Even when it's a friend you love?"

"Particularly then."

•

"Break," said the painter, heaving a deep sigh. She got up and wiped her sweaty brow with her sleeve. "Not bad," she said. "Not at all bad."

I stretched. I hadn't noticed that fifteen minutes had elapsed. I was still standing in our little kitchen, handing the dripping plates to Jerome.

The painter brought in the coffee, found her Gauloises and gave me a look that was almost affectionate.

"I'm back. Right back. It's crackling again."

She poured herself a cup of coffee, held it

in front of her eyes and contemplated her shaking hand and paint-stained fingers.

"That's enough for today, or I might ruin it. But it's still all there, that's all I wanted to know. Ten o'clock tomorrow, okay?"

●

Diary, March 23:

L.'s filming during the day. In the evening she's at the theater. She's so tired that she prefers to sleep at her mother's in her old room, in what I call the nursery. She says her mother looks after her, leaves a dish of applesauce by her bed at night, gets breakfast for her at six a.m. She couldn't ask that of Jerome. True. No one can ask anything of Jerome. He gives what he thinks he should give. But that doesn't mean that he gives what one needs. L. knows this. Never demands anything of him. Wise! Whereas I demand. I demand that he make an effort to come to our apartment even when it doesn't suit him. Because *I* need it. He doesn't respond to that, remains deaf. Today, for instance. Today I needed to be with him, to lie beside him, his arms around me, my arms around him. Today's our anniversary. Two years ago today —by the boathouse in Regent's Park. Two years! The other day I added up all the hours we've spent alone together and it comes to no more than five hundred. A little over twenty days. Haven't had him to myself even for one single month. Can one live like this?

I called him up and said, "Happy birthday!" He said not to bother him with crap like that while he's working. I hung up. Nina happened to come into the room just at that moment. Didn't ask any questions, just looked at me and went out again. So what.

Tried to think of something, anything, some way to celebrate. Hit on a crazy idea. Went to see Simon.

What? I read the sentence again:

Went to see Simon.

So she did meet Simon! I had no idea. She knew Simon! That explained a lot of things.

Just dropped in. Knew he'd be home. Had to be near something that belongs to J. In any case, have been wanting to meet him for a long time. J. always refused point-blank. Knocked cautiously at the door and waited. That business with the fly. But he called out right away, "Come in!"—doesn't have a fly at the moment. Instead he has a creature called an axolotl, a kind of pink lizard with a flat head, as if somebody had stepped on it. Keeps it in a goldfish bowl.

When I introduced myself, he was first surprised and then delighted. Apparently he knew all about me. J. has told him, he said. I wonder why? J. always says Simon's not to be trusted. More likely he hasn't told him anything and Simon just put two and two together. I'd brought him a bottle of brandy and he couldn't wait to open it. I kept up with him for a couple of glasses, I needed encouraging—or company, or some sort of trampoline. Something to stop me spinning around my own axis like a top. He knew right away why I'd come, so didn't have to explain anything. He's not very fond of L. Said she's not his type, and that he's surprised at his son.

L. doesn't fit into the family. But she's useful, he said, let her keep on being useful. Her matinees are useful too—"Aren't they, Anabel? I may call you Anabel, mayn't I?" Suddenly he looked like a crocodile. "No," I said. "You may not." He laughed as innocently and naturally as a small boy, took my hand with *grandezza* and kissed it respectfully. I didn't know anymore where I stood with him. He poured us both another cognac. Fool that I am, I drank it, and much too quickly. Suddenly I banged my fist on his desk and said, "Stop making trouble between L. and Jerome, will you?" He burst out laughing again until he choked, and his eyes watered. "And what about you, dear?" he said. "What are you making?" I stood up and leaned across the desk until my face was quite close to his. I really wanted to spit in his face. But I couldn't. My mouth was too dry. Realized I was about to burst into tears. So I began to yell at the top of my voice—can't remember what exactly, very longwinded, not very coherent, something about being well aware that I meant nothing to J., that I was on the receiving end of all that was bad in him while he was the beneficiary of all that was good in me, that I felt it would soon be over, that it was two years ago today, that I had never tried to take him away from L.—on the contrary, that I knew I was exactly what J. needed in order to be happy with L., and if it weren't for me, they'd be in trouble all right. That did it. I was exhausted all of a sudden, and deflated, and sat down.

All through my screaming, that fat barrel organ of a man kept staring at me openmouthed while his double chin wobbled up and down like other people's Adam's apples. "You're the only *woman* I've ever met who knows where she stands," he said at last. "Take me, for instance. I'm a bastard; I know it and I take pleasure in it. But I'm an absolutely honest man and I decline all responsibilities that don't fit into my life style. My flies fit in, one-day flies, four- or five-day flies at most. But marriage, fatherhood, friendship, possessions—they're only impediments. They all entail obligations, and that's a dirty word in my vocabulary. Thank God, there are hordes of people around who vie with one another in order to be responsible for somebody or something. Only then do they feel grown up. Now, where would all those people be if it weren't for me? I allow them to be concerned about me, to boost their moral ego at my expense. I could furnish a *raison d'être* for an entire Salvation Army."

"You're dripping with brotherly love," I said, getting up.

"Oh, don't go, Anabel!" he exclaimed.

"Will you stop calling me Anabel!" I said.

He pretended not to have heard. "My son doesn't know what a treasure he has in you, he's still wet behind the ears, no backbone, no line of his own . . ." And all the while he was trying to push me toward the sofa, that great colossus—and me not too steady on my pins, though still faster than he was. I grabbed the table lamp and he let go of me and laughed—reminding me suddenly of J., for the first time—and retreated behind his desk. Said it was all in fun. Only then did I put the lamp down. Must have been pretty plastered, because I remember asking if he could recollect the last time he had cried. He thought very seriously but couldn't remember. Said he thought it must have been when he was about ten and lost his first watch.

I picked up my coat and stopped on my way to look at the bowl with the axolotl in it. It was floating motionless, midway between the surface and the bottom, its hands, minute human hands, spread out, ogling me out of its round eyes. On its flat, bald head was a little ring of red spikes, like a crown. "He looks as if he's been dead for a long time," I said, at which Simon hurriedly ambled over. "Doesn't he, though? That's what I love about him. He may be dead for all I know, or he may be in the pink. I feed him regularly—that is, I dangle a tiny bit of meat in front of him as if it were alive, but he never snaps at it, just lets it sink gently to the bottom. Sometimes it gets caught in his crown but he doesn't deign to notice. He never eats in my presence. He's either a snob—or he's dead."

I feel a certain resemblance to that animal.

That was the last entry until May 1939. Inexplicably, for six long months she hadn't written a word. Suddenly, on May 25:

For Christ's sake, I can't be . . .

On June 1:

I am.

●

151

So it must have been early in June that she showed up in my dressing room between the matinee and the evening performance. She would do this occasionally when I was too tired to drive to her house during the interval, for I was filming at the same time. That meant that except on matinee days, I spent the day at the studio and the evening at the theater. I raced back and forth, changing costume in the car, tearing my wigs off, nervously looking at the time, arriving everywhere at the last minute, and getting dirty looks from everyone. There was no choice, though. "Strike your neighbor while he's hot," we used to say at school. Well, at long last it looked as if my neighbor was hot and waiting to be struck. It was only a question of holding on for another month and then—vacation, Gurnemantz vacation, with Jerome and Anabel. During the last few weeks I didn't even have the time to see the people I loved. No more Sunday drives with Anabel—I spent my Sundays sleeping and got up only for an occasional dinner at her house, accompanied by Jerome. And every time I thought Anabel looked pale and thin. Bill was thin too, even Nina was thinner. Maybe it was my imagination, or something wrong with my eyesight. Like El Greco.

On that June day she sat on the visitor's chair in my dressing room and watched in silence as Maudie, my dresser, helped me out of my costume and into the old makeup bathrobe, and covered the tray of sandwiches and orange juice with a napkin. "Go to sleep," she said, significantly wagging her finger at Anabel as she left the room.

"I'm going," said Anabel. She stood up and switched off the light. I made no effort to stop her; I simply had to get some sleep before the evening performance. "Bye-bye, darling," I said with a yawn and turned my face to the wall. Silence. No sound of a door opening or closing. I turned around again and peered through the darkness. There was the outline of a limp hand hanging over the back of the visitor's chair.

"What's the matter?" I cried, sitting up and groping for the light switch. She looked green in the face, there was sweat on her forehead and her eyes were closed; her breath came convulsively through tightly compressed lips.

"Anabel! What on earth's the matter?"

"I feel sick," she whispered.

"Do you want a glass of water?"

She shook her head. "Give me a minute—I feel terribly sick—yesterday too—and the day before."

Wide awake, I knelt beside her chair.

"Something you've eaten? Think back. Do you have a pain in your stomach?"

She opened her eyes, twisted her face into a faint smile.

"For a doctor's daughter—you're pretty dense."

I understood and involuntarily drew back.

"Ferencsi?"

She didn't consider it worth the effort to answer.

"Oh, my God! What on earth—do you want to keep it?"

The raven eyes turned slowly toward me. They had never looked so diabolically black before.

"Do I want to?" The eyes searched my face, as if seeking a solution there. I met them helplessly, tried to muster a cheerful smile to make sure she knew that she had my support no matter what she was going to do. Her eyes grew dull, as if she had switched off the light.

"Do I want to?" she repeated again. "That isn't the point."

I didn't have to ask what the point was. Ferencsi was married in the Catholic church; a divorce was out of the question, she had told me that right at the start. Should she leave Bill and Nina and have Ferencsi's child somewhere in secret? And then what? As if in answer to my thoughts, she said, "Of course, he doesn't know about it. If he did, he'd never see me again. In any case I have a feeling it's only a matter of time."

"So you want to get rid of it?"

"Yesterday I went to see Mildman, our doctor. He confirmed it. He also made it clear that he has no sympathy whatever for the situation."

"How does he know—"

"That it's not Bill's? He knows I haven't slept with Bill for years. Bill once asked his advice. They went to school together."

I got up.

"Do you feel a bit better? Can you walk?"

She managed to stand up by holding onto

the dressing table, but she still looked very white.

"Come on, we're going to see *my* doctor. He's a refugee, used to practice in Berlin, where he was official doctor for the British Embassy women. He knew my father, although he's younger. I think—I can't promise—but I think he'll help you. In the first place, he doesn't know you, and I'll introduce you as Miss So and So and say you haven't got the money to bring up a child and you'd lose your job. In the second place, he has a sense of humor. I once went to see him and told him about Jerome and he asked me in a fatherly way if I was 'being careful.' 'Well, I'm trying,' I said, 'but it takes a while to get used to driving on the left.' He laughed so much he couldn't speak for a while and just patted my head. He's had a soft spot for me ever since. Come on. Let's see if he's still at his consulting room."

•

Dr. Lauter's Harley Street waiting room was full, but his receptionist said she'd "squeeze me in" since I only wanted to ask him a question and had to rush back to the theater. Anabel had remained outside in the taxi.

Lauter, washing his hands, greeted me with the usual inquiry as to how I was making out with driving on the left. I laughed heartily for Anabel's sake and came straight to the point: I had a friend, my one and only girl friend. In trouble. I'd pay all the expenses. This idea came to me spontaneously as I was speaking, and I felt sure it would sound more convincing and perhaps more appealing and noble on my part. The doctor stopped laughing. He sat down behind his desk, rested his chin on his hand and sighed.

"I never thought that *you* would come to me for that. Every day people pester me with exactly the same story. And I refuse them all. Categorically. Every time. Why should I jeopardize my existence and that of my family just because some silly kid can't—"

He broke off, so I took the risk of finishing his sentence with: ". . . can't get used to driving on the left?" And he couldn't help grinning, his anger gone.

"Unmarried, you say? And the man won't —the old story. And no money either."

"She's—a kindergarten teacher."

"That too! And you're being noble and offering to pay for it? Out of the question. You're not exactly affluent all of a sudden, are you?" I felt neither appealing nor noble anymore. "So if I do it—mind you, I'm saying *if*— it won't be at the hospital but here in my office. After six. She'll have to take a taxi home. And it won't be any fun for her, I can tell you that. Call me tomorrow evening. At home. I want to think it over."

"Dr. Lauter—thank you!"

"Nothing to thank me for yet," he snapped. "I haven't promised anything."

I walked toward the door.

"How's what's-his-name—your boy friend?"

"Jerome. He's fine."

Some time before we had happened to be

sitting next to each other at a movie and he'd had a long conversation with Jerome afterward and seemed to like him.

Anger suddenly flared again behind his glasses.

"Let me tell you one thing, so you won't ever come here to ask. You've used up all your credit with me. I'm not going to abort any child of what's-his-name's—eh, Jerome's. Let's get that clear."

•

In the evening I called Dr. Lauter from the theater. Might "Miss Shelling" come and see him after office hours? "Yes—for an examination," said a testy voice. "And then perhaps— next Friday. I'll see. And if . . . then you'll have to wait in the waiting room and take her home. She can't go alone."

"But Doctor, I have to be at the theater at seven."

"Then you'll be late," he snapped and hung up.

He knew perfectly well one couldn't be late for a performance! And yet the call "Curtain going up" was so trivial compared to an ever-looming medical disaster. As ill luck would have it, I appeared in the very opening scene— in fact, when the curtain went up I was already on stage, alone, in bed. A lucky thing that I wasn't needed at the studio on that Friday. I decided to take my stage makeup home with me the night before and to wait in Lauter's waiting room already fully made up. That would save me half an hour. The curtain went up at eight, but before that I had to take Anabel home in a taxi. Everything depended on how long "Miss Shelling" would have to spend in the doctor's consulting room.

Anabel had been strangely monosyllabic when I told her, radiantly, that Lauter had agreed to see her. She seemed neither grateful nor relieved.

"Have you changed your mind? Do tell me! Maybe you want to have it after all? Or at least talk it over with Ferencsi first?"

"No. Never."

16

Diary, June 1939:

She asked if I maybe wanted to have the child after all. "Maybe!" Never in my life have I wanted anything so much. Up to now I can't remember ever wanting a particular thing very much. (Except Jerome, and I realized right away that no one can "have" him.) It was only when I did *not* want something that I'd blow my top. "Wildcat!" my stepmother would scream, before she slapped me.

Now I want this child. At night I spread my hands on my belly, trying to persuade myself that I can feel it.

At the same time—grotesque, of course—I tell myself that it doesn't belong to me, that it's only on loan. I'm just a deputy. L.'s deputy. The other day she told me she never allows herself to look into baby carriages because it makes her feel envious. She knows there's no place for "all that" in her life, she said, not now at any rate. Maybe later. Maybe never. Said she knows J. doesn't want a child. The idea scares him. He knows he's not cut out to be a father. He once said something to the same effect to me: "What will I use for flies when I'm old?"

I lie awake at night, stroking my belly, imagining how it would be if I could have the baby and place it in L.'s arms. "It's *our* child," I'd say: "Yours and mine. From now on you'll never have to look for work anymore, I'll make all my money over to you—and to our child." I believe—I truly believe—I could then manage to live without J. I would never even need to see him again because we'd have the child, she and I together. I know, I know. Pregnant women are often quite unhinged.

At six-fifteen on Friday evening I was sitting in the waiting room. "Miss Shelling" had disappeared into the consulting room after her knock had been answered by a brusque "Come in!" Lauter hadn't even said hello to me.

That was more than twenty minutes ago. Almost a quarter of seven. I went over to the window. How long did this sort of thing take? Did they have to make all kinds of preparations? Injections? How long would the effect of the anesthetic last?

It hadn't been too easy at home either, for my mother had suddenly appeared in my room.

"Isn't that Anabel out there in the car—"

She broke off when she saw the heavy stage makeup on my face. "Why are you making up at home?"

I stared fixedly into the mirror. She'd been an actress herself; I couldn't fob her off with any pseudo-professional device. No credible explanation occurred to me however feverishly I racked my brain. My mother sat down and broke her iron rule of never interfering in her daughters' affairs unasked.

"What's going on? What are you up to?"

"Don't ask. I can't tell you."

I reached for the powder puff, upset the box, and a cloud of white powder streamed across the table, settled on the makeup mirror and hid my face.

"I have something to tell you," said my mother. "I hoped I'd get away without having to, but now I think you ought to know."

"Go ahead, go ahead," I snapped, polishing my mirror.

"The other day, when you were all in the garden drinking coffee, you went back to the house to get something. I happened to be looking out of the upstairs window ..."

"And?"

"Jerome bent forward and put his hand on Anabel's knee and said something I didn't hear ..."

"And?"

"She didn't answer, but the way she looked at him ..."

I turned and looked her straight in the eye.

"I've asked Jerome—for good reasons of my own—I've asked Jerome to take care of her."

"He's taking care of her, believe me."

"Oh, for God's sake!" I had to laugh, out of sheer despair. "You're on the wrong track altogether."

She sat there for a moment and watched while I hastily put mascara on my eyelashes and dark-red stage lipstick on mouth, then she got up without a word and left.

•

Anabel was waiting outside in a rented car with chauffeur. She didn't want to use her own. When I opened the door, she was sitting huddled in one corner.

"Are you in pain?"

She straightened up and shook her head. The car drove off. I looked out the window.

It was some time before I noticed that she was crying, soundlessly, the way she had cried among the Christmas wrappings. I took her limp, icy hand, couldn't think of anything to say. She pulled her hand away and threw her arms around my neck, holding on to me as if she were drowning. I tried to stroke her head —unsuccessfully, for she kept thrusting it in mute despair from side to side—and then her face, bathed in floods of tears. She stopped throwing her head about and allowed my hand to rest on her cheek, and then she began to kiss my hand as if she were in love with me. I tried to pull it away but she wouldn't let go, burying her face in it and kissing it over and over again.

Gradually she calmed down. The tears dried up and the wordless sobbing stopped. She sat there so rigidly, her face still buried in my hand, that I wondered if she had fallen asleep.

Harley Street. I waited in the car while she combed her hair and rummaged for powder and lipstick, then I opened the door. Remote and impassive, she walked up the steps beside me. The car waited.

That had been forty-five minutes ago. The lazy-busy tick-tock of the clock on the mantel. Seven o'clock already, only one more hour until curtain time. It was raining outside. Suppose there were complications? Suppose she didn't wake up from the anesthetic? Things like, that did happen—anesthetic shock. The door would open. Dr. Lauter would appear and say hoarsely, "Miss Shelling is dead—"

At that the door did open and the doctor appeared. "All right. You can come in and collect her. She must rest here for another ten minutes before walking down the stairs. And then get out—both of you."

In the car she lay back in the corner and slept, all the way home. No, she wasn't in any pain, she had assured me. How was I to smuggle her into her bedroom without anyone seeing? Bill might be home already. Nina certainly was. The car stopped in front of her gate.

"Anabel, listen, if we meet Bill or Nina, we'll say you suddenly got a bad migraine in my dressing room, and that's why I'm taking you home myself. Do you hear me?"

"Yes."

I rummaged in her purse and found two different keys.

"Anabel, which is your house key? This one or the other one?"

She opened her eyes, looked at me distractedly, then at the two keys I was holding out to her. She snatched one of them forcibly out of my hand and crammed it back in her purse.

"So it's the other one," I said, opening the car door. The chauffeur and I helped her across the front garden and carried her up the few stairs to the door. No light in the entrance hall. Thank God! I whispered to the chauffeur to go and keep the engine running—I'd be right back. In the darkness my watch glowed seven-thirty-five. Christ! But I couldn't just dump her on the floor. Without switching on the light, I groped my way along the wall to her bedroom, half pushing, half lifting her. From the library came the sound of a rapid radio commentary, some boxing match—Bill was home. I opened the bedroom door. She fell from my arms onto the bed. I switched on the bedside lamp—and turned at a noise. Nina was standing in the doorway. For a second she looked at her mother, then at me, questioning but indifferent.

"Look after your mother, Nina," I said hastily. "She can do with it. She was sick with an awful migraine in my dressing room. Put her to bed and bring her a hot-water bottle."

"A hot-water bottle? For a headache?"

"Yes, yes! Her feet are cold. Hurry up, Nina, I've got to get back to the theater. Why don't you help me!"

"I'm always glad to help *you*," said Nina and began to undress her mother. The last thing I saw was Anabel's white face, her eyes tightly closed, before I ran out of the house.

The car raced through the wet streets. A red light—another one—my teeth were chattering. "Please drive fast or I won't make it." Ten to eight . . . six minutes to . . . three minutes to . . . and the car stopped at the stage door. The stage manager, Maudie and the doorkeeper were all standing outside in the rain, waving excitedly.

"Thank God!" moaned the stage manager. "I thought I was going to have to make an announcement . . ."

"Thank God!" whispered Maudie, rushing along the passageway and down the stairs behind me, unzipping me as she went.

Everywhere the dressing-room doors stood open and a chorus of "Thank God!" and "Whatever happened to you?" and "Why, you're made up already!" echoed in our wake. Maudie threw the nightgown over my head, I shook off my shoes, squirmed out of my stockings and ran barefoot back the length of the passageway leading to the stage, Maudie following with brush and comb. The bed, already turned down, was waiting. I jumped in, hissed, "Get the hell away from me, Maudie darling," as the stage lights dimmed and went out. I got into position under the bedclothes. Then came a familiar, ever-new and exhilarating rushing sound. The curtain was going up.

17

Next morning at the studio, during a break in the shooting, I hurried to the telephone. I had to know how she was. I wasn't allowed to leave the set, however, and was forced to make out, over the turmoil and the hammering around me, whether she was telling me the truth when she said she was still in bed, but everything was fine.

"Well, it's all over now," I shouted, struggling to sound buoyant.

Her voice was faint as though it were coming through a sieve. "What did you say?"

"I said, it's all over now," I yelled as hard as I could.

"Yes, all over," she repeated almost inaudibly. Perhaps she was in pain after all.

"I'll drop in on my way to the theater. Just for a few minutes."

●

She was lying flat on her back when I opened her bedroom door. Everything was white, her face, her nightgown, the pillows, those forlorn hands, except her hair and her eyes, now circled by dark shadows.

Without taking off my coat I sat down on the bed, turning the clock on the bedside table toward me. Ten minutes. First the essentials. Any pain? No. Had Bill noticed anything? No. And Nina? Neither. She hadn't asked any questions, just brought a hot-water bottle and left.

Pause. What else could I ask? I couldn't think of anything. But that sudden drought in my brain came directly from her, from those vacant eyes, from that arid voice. She didn't seem to give a damn.

Then suddenly her face relaxed as if she had caught hold of a train of thought and her eyes came to life again. She clasped her hands over the sheet—white on white.

"Listen to me carefully, and don't interrupt," she said, paused, and spelled out every word of the next sentence. "I can't come with you to the Gurnemantzes'."

Although she spoke so slowly, the words came tense and inflexible. In spite of her injunction, I flared up. "Anabel—please—we've already got the tickets and the sleeping car is reserved! You need a vacation more than ever. Think of the swimming in the warm sea . . ."

The black eyes stared stonily at the covers. "The peaches—remember? Aesculapius! Our suppers on the terrace—you said yourself you'd never had such a marvelous time." I shriveled up; there was no sign of a reaction from her. One last time I tried. "But why? Why on earth can't you?"

"Because Ferencsi's coming. He'll be here for a whole month."

Oh. That, of course, was a different matter All the same, I found it hard to swallow the bitter pill. I very nearly burst out, exactly as I did when I was a child and a cherished plan of mine was thwarted, "But I was looking forward to it so much!" To which the inevitable impassive grown-up answer had been: "Then you'll just have to unlook."

I began to unlook. I got up and walked toward the door—had to flail about once more: "I hate the fellow. What does he give you except unhappiness?"

"Not all the time."

"What's the good of that? That's no way to live."

"It's better than nothing."

"Oh, for God's sake," I muttered and left.

•

Diary, June 1939:

> Just got rid of her. It wasn't easy but I was prepared for it. "Ferencsi" got me out of the jam. She said: "Oh, for God's sake!" and left.
> When I invented Ferencsi, sitting among

the Christmas wrappings, I hadn't the faintest notion that I was handing myself a marvelous defensive weapon, a permanent alibi, an ever-valid excuse, a cast-iron immunity.

Funny how he gets more real all the time. I've now invented a wife for him, French, red-haired, a bit short in the leg. Maybe that's how writers work, the fiction factory just grows and grows with a life of its own. Pity L. never asked about the children, for I was prepared for that, too. I was prepared for anything—except for J.'s child.

Last night I heard every single hour strike. One always claims that, but last night it was true. I was counting them, didn't really want to sleep. Could have taken the stuff Dr. Lauter gave me to help me "spend a decent night." Of course he saw through the whole thing, never for one moment believed in Miss Shelling, the kindergarten teacher. When I entered the consulting room, he was standing by the window, looking down at the street. "Is that your car?" he said. I nodded. "Good," he said. "At least you'll get home comfortably."

I thought I'd better say something to him—if not an explanation, at least a few words to thank him. "Doctor," I began—but he raised both hands. "Don't tell me anything. Don't make any confessions to me. I'm going to do it and it isn't the first time. But I can't stand any more confessions."

I liked him. I liked him very much. Unfortunately he clamped the ether mask over my nose and thus wiped himself out. I only have a vague memory of what happened after that. Didn't come to properly until much later. In bed. Nina. Hot-water bottle. Didn't have the strength to put it on my belly. It stayed where she placed it, burning my feet. Heard the church clóck strike eleven. Alone. Good. Silence and darkness and plenty of time to sort things out.

It was a boxing match. I was in one corner—and at the same time in the opposite one. The gong sounded and I went right in and punched myself. Right away a murderous jab on the chin: Give J. up! That was quite enough for a start, and I fell clean through the ropes. Climbed back into the ring. Went on the defensive, dancing around. Why give J. up? He doesn't know, L. doesn't know. So why give him up, what's changed? At that a terrific punch caught me on the head: Do you really believe you can continue indefinitely—waiting, waiting waiting in the apartment, listening for the sound of his key in the lock . . .?

The key! There'd been something about a key. Whatever was it? Then I saw it—in L.'s hand! Had I dreamed that? No! There she sat, next to me in the car, as large as life— holding our doorkey in her hand.

Almost a K.O. The gong saved me just in time. Rubbed myself with a towel and administered a pep talk: What's the panic? She hadn't noticed anything
nothing had happened, so shut up, for God's sake. Second round. A merciless uppercut right smack in the face: You're going to give up the apartment! No, I yelled, flailing and punching in all directions and missing every time. I grabbed hold of my opponent and hung on with all my strength so that he was

unable to hit me again. Then I fell down.
Flat on my back. The referee was bending over
me, counting: "One: Give up the
Gurnemantz vacation. Two: Give up the
apartment and take a trip around the world.
Three: Give up J. Four: Give up L."
Give up—give up! I gave up. K.O.

The next day she had written:

It's enough . . . I was about to write: It's
enough to drive anyone insane—but now
it occurs to me that perhaps it's all for the
best. It might even help. It *will* help, I know
it, though at the moment the pain makes me
breathless and I feel I'm suffocating.

He called early this morning. I was
awake, forcing myself to make plans for a
trip around the world. With Bill, of course.
Maybe with Nina too. Stay away for months
and months .After we come back, refuse to
see J. and L. Give no reason. Just refuse.
Then the telephone rang.

He doesn't know what happened
yesterday. Am certain L. hasn't told him,
she swore she wouldn't. But he senses
something's up, he feels the tension, wonders
what the hell is going on—and wants out.
Typical. That's his only method of dealing
with things: to get out. I understand only too
well. Am no hero myself. He spoke hurriedly,
in a way I'd never heard him talk before, as
if he were being chased by something. Said he
was leaving. Today. For Paris. He couldn't
stand it any longer. (What did he mean by
that?) He'd meet us there. "Us" being L.
and me. Then we could go on to the
Gurnemantzes' together. I didn't answer.

Let L. tell him I'm not coming. Maybe he'll be glad! That thought almost choked me. I could hardly speak, barely managed to answer. I feel as if the slightest breath of air could blow me to smithereens.

PART TWO

18

Already three fifteen-minute poses this morning. Even during the coffee breaks the painter didn't utter a single word because she wanted to remain "charged." She was plain stingy in that respect, for she was never quite sure how long her fuel would last and she hoarded every bit of it. "I'm getting to be short of breath," she said, and by "breath" she meant the sparks flying from her paintbrush.

For the third time that morning she returned from the kitchen with her tray, but now there was a dish on top of it containing something warm, two plates and a pair of poultry shears.

"Lunch break," she said, setting a plate in front of me. "I bought a chicken. Ready-cooked."

She cut it in half and began to eat her half neatly with her fingers. I hesitated.

"It can fly," she said with her mouth full. "For anything that flies, fingers are okay."

We ate in silence. From time to time she wiped her hands on her smock. I used my poncho. Suddenly, brandishing a chicken bone like a club, she glared at me as if she'd just remembered something disgraceful.

"How did it come to an end between your Jerome and Anabel?"

"Someone broke it up."

"Anabel's husband?"

"No. Another woman."

She replaced the bone on her plate, picked as clean as if a dog had been at it, brooded for a moment and then seized it again and tapped her teeth with it.

"Another woman?"

"Jerome met someone else. In Paris. We were about to leave for our vacation again, our Gurnemantz vacation in the south of France, to pick peaches. He'd left ahead of time for Paris, where we were going to meet. I couldn't go with him, I was in a play in London with two more weeks to run."

"And Anabel?"

"She stayed in London. She was sick."

"Sick."

She played with her chicken bone, looking covetously at my plate. I had eaten all the dark meat and left the spongy white stuff.

"Aren't you going to eat that?"

"I don't like it. It never tastes of anything."

She pushed her plate aside and took mine.

"You've never been hungry, have you?"

"Not really, but pretty close to it."

"That doesn't count."

"I know."

"It would have done you good."

"I know."

"But in other respects you seem to have been through the mill, all right. Well, come on, tell me the rest. And don't just fend me off with chapter headings. Why did your Jerome go off on his own? Was he sick of Anabel?"

"He was sick of everything. He hadn't sold a painting in two years. Just a drawing now and again. He earned his living from book jackets. The pay wasn't bad, but it was making him ill."

She wiped her mouth on her sleeve with finality, groped without looking for her Gauloises and nodded.

"I once had to paint Christmas cards."

"And so one day he blew his top. 'I'm leaving for Paris today. I've got to have a show there somehow, even if it's only at the flea market.' He took half a dozen canvases with him and showed them around. That's how he met her—the other woman."

"A painter?"

"No, her husband owned the gallery."

"A gallery owner? Who was it? I know every single one in Paris."

"Dujardin, Rue St. Honoré."

She leaned across the table, forcing me to look at her.

"Jeannine Dujardin?"

I took a deep breath. She knew Anabel—she knew everyone.

She let herself fall back in her chair, smiling to herself.

"I never met her. That sort of woman wasn't my cup of tea. But quite a number of painters in Paris were keen on her. She started out as a model, you know. I only knew her husband, Dujardin. Showed twice at his gallery. That was before he married Jeannine. He was quite a guy, that man. I never understood how he and that nitwit ever got together. So your Jerome fell for her? How did she manage that?"

"I don't know. I wasn't there."

Actually I knew very well. Babs had told me all the details.

The painter frowned; she'd obviously expected more for the price of her half-chicken. She looked at her watch.

"Can we have another go." It was a statement, not a question, and she got up, her eyes already full of colors, lines and shapes, trotted over to her stool in front of the canvas without waiting for an answer, and sat down as if she had taken root.

I held the pose. Thought of the entrance to the Dujardin Gallery in the Rue St. Honoré. I'd passed through that entrance once—later on. A heavy Spanish door with an ancient wrought-iron lock. And through that entrance door, early in the morning, Jerome had lugged his six canvases in the hope that Dujardin might see him before the rush of clients and visitors began. But Dujardin wasn't there. Out of town, said his assistant, he didn't know where. When would he be back? No idea. Jerome insisted. "Surely somebody must know. Hasn't he got a wife or

178

something?" From an adjoining room came a voice: "Yes, he's got a wife or something but she doesn't know either."

Babs had described it all exactly the way it had happened; she knew her well. Jeannine had appeared in the door to the private office and had looked Jerome up and down as he unpacked his canvases. The secretary had tried to stop him. "Madame, don't forget that we're booked solid until next spring." But Jeannine said she was always interested in new talent and told Jerome to bring his pictures into the office.

I'd been inside that office too. Later. I'd taken a good look at it, a man's office of course, a man's workroom. Wood paneling, a large desk and a black leather reclining chair. That's where she must have been sitting, I thought. Or reclining à la Récamier. Jerome had stood his pictures against the wall and then—said Babs— she had offered him a sherry. After which they'd looked at the paintings together. Jeannine had taken her time, sticking out her thumb at arm's length like an expert and closing one eye to "test the proportions." After all, she knew the trade. She'd been standing next to paintings and lying next to painters for so long that she believed she knew something about it.

Jerome was an extremely talented young painter, she said, though, unfortunately, that alone was not enough. You needed some kind of trick, some gimmick, to make your work stand out. Like the young painter she had discovered recently, she said, who simply painted one broad black stroke vertically across a plain gray canvas, or two red ones. The title of the black one was *Moses* and of the red one *Abraham Lincoln.* Now he was doing blue and green ones too and they were selling like hotcakes.

Probably Jerome had liked her at first sight—Babs said men fell like ninepins for her—or was it the possibility of an exhibition at the Dujardin gallery? He must have smelled an opportunity in spite of *Moses* and *Lincoln.* And at that point—one mustn't forget that— at that point he was prepared to do anything at all. Later on she got under his skin, more than he'd bargained for.

At any rate they had lunch together at a bistro on the Left Bank, an old haunt of Jerome's. Cheap, of course, frequented by taxi drivers, and Paris taxi drivers know where to find good food. Babs told me that as soon as she heard about that, she knew it was serious, because Jeannine avoided what she called "dirty little holes in the wall" like the plague, her past having been too full of them. And after lunch they went to the Hotel de la Muette.

•

"That's enough for today," said the painter. "No, don't go yet, I'll make coffee."

I went into the bathroom. It smelled of turpentine once more; she had fired the nice Spanish cleaning woman. I took off my poncho and hung it on the door, contemplated the greasy chicken stains.

"Ready!" came her voice from the studio.

We drank in silence, as usual. Now, after her illness, she seemed drained every time we took a break, and she would gulp the coffee down with her eyes closed, waiting for it to take effect. She obviously needed something to wind her up again, something to grease the wheels. Why not a drink? There was no liquor in the studio, not even a bottle of rum.

Slowly she opened her eyes.

"How old were you then?"

"Early twenties. But in those days when you were in your early twenties you were a lot younger."

"And Jerome?"

"A few years older."

"Mere children."

I got up and wandered over to the window. The studio was on the sixth floor, with a vast view of the city, not a pretty one, but familiar, London roofs, London chimneys. I could see the dark, blurred reflection of my face in the window, and behind and merging into it, the whitish-blue, almost sunny sky. When I first arrived in London, there had been far more sunny days, I thought. I never seemed to need a coat; children and young people hate coats and warm underwear. "Take your coat," my mother would call after me, and I would only laugh, waving to her and running for the bus. Running, always running. I could even eat while running. Cherries, for instance, spitting the stones out at tree trunks along the road as I streaked past them. The painter was right. We were mere children, Jerome and I, and whenever I stepped out of the house I felt in my bones that I was the youngest person on the street. Grown-up, though, the youngest grown-up.

"I know what you're thinking," I said, standing on tiptoe to get a better view of some tree-tops in the distance to find out if they belonged to a section of Hyde Park, our Hyde Park.

She made no answer.

"It certainly does seem strange," I said. "That is—it doesn't seem strange to me because I can't imagine it any other way, but it must seem strange to an outsider that I was so easy to cheat, and for so long. And also I imagine you're asking yourself, 'Well now, didn't *she* ever play the field a bit? And if not, why not?'"

"I don't ask myself stupid questions," she said, pouring herself a second cup and feeling for her Gauloises. "What's more, it's clear as daylight."

"It wasn't virtue. I can't stand virtue. Maudie, my dresser, used to say, 'Virtue is when there's no bid.' I remember there was of course a certain amount of bidding, but I never gave myself the chance to get interested, I simply didn't have the time. I kept one eye firmly on the clock, always on the run, always rushing . . ."

"Compulsive," she said calmly, examined her fingers, picked up the jar of lanolin cream that was always within reach and rubbed some on her hands. "Compulsive," she repeated without turning around to look at me. "And under pressure from inside and from outside, plain as plain. But don't fool yourself, you'd have found the time—had you wanted to."

"But I didn't want to. Do you mind if I open the window?" She shook her head, buttoning her smock tightly around her neck. I pushed up the window and breathed the cold, still air. The smell of greasy roast chicken and turpentine and swirls of smoke drifted past me.

"Why would I have wanted to look at other men? To prove something to myself? What, for instance? After all, I had Jerome, didn't I, and that was sufficient proof, wasn't it? At least I believed I had him, and that was all that mattered to me. For three long years I believed I had him and I'm glad I didn't know any different."

"Ostrich! A wise bird, happy as long as he keeps his head in the sand? What happened when you dug your way out of the sand? How did you find out about Jeannine?"

"I arrived in Paris—and Jerome wasn't at the station. I drove to our hotel, the Hotel de la Muette, and registered as his wife, as I always did. I was informed he already had a wife. The concierge—I knew him from way back—a bald-headed, bristly old walrus, said she wasn't staying at the hotel but she came every day. He showed me the slip: 'M. et Mme. Lorrimer.'"

The painter massaged the lanolin violently into her fingers.

"What did you do?"

"I sat down in the lobby next to my suitcase and waited. It wasn't long before he appeared. Alone. He saw me sitting there and stopped in his tracks. I could see that he'd forgotten. Forgotten I was coming, forgotten me altogether. The walrus was watching us from behind his counter. I walked over and said, 'I'd like a single room, please.' I signed with my own name. Jerome stood next to me, saying nothing, while the walrus looked at him meaningfully. I went up in the elevator alone. They sent up my suitcase. Then Jerome came up."

"Did he tell you?"

"Yes."

"How did you take it?"

Now it was getting cold. I closed the window and returned to my chair, putting out a tentative hand toward her Gauloises.

"But you don't smoke!"

"I do—occasionally. At the dentist, for instance."

She lighted it for me. I often had to smoke professionally, sometimes daily on stage, at a fixed hour, but it never took hold of me, never did anything for me. Maybe Gauloises were something special.

"I asked how you took it."

"I heard you, but I don't know how to answer properly. If I'd try to describe it—crying all night, black days, watching the river rush by from the top of the Pont d'Alexandre for hours on end—none of that brings back the way it really was. But when I think of the taxi driver, then it all comes back to me. Then I can feel it all over again."

She looked at me attentively, even stubbed out her cigarette.

"The next day I took a taxi—I can't remember why—a long ride. In front of me the taxi driver's powerful, shapeless back, a thick neck with a deep horizontal wrinkle, and neatly trimmed gray hair underneath his cap. He didn't talk to me, he just drove. Soon he would stop for lunch, maybe at his regular bistro, where he'd meet his friends—or he'd drive to his wife. All of a sudden I envied that taxi driver with such a soul-sickening intensity that I couldn't remember ever having felt anything like it before. I'd have given anything to change places with him, never mind if he had to spend ten hours a day chained to his steering wheel in the maddening turmoil of the Paris traffic, never mind if he was approaching the end of his life and I was just beginning mine. He knew where he belonged—and I didn't. He had firm ground under his feet—I was adrift. He breathed slowly and with dignity—I kept convulsively snatching deep breaths because my lungs felt empty, as if they were about to collapse. I longed so desperately to transform myself into that man that I seriously believed I might bring it off by the end of the ride, if I just concentrated hard enough. Suddenly he slowed down and stopped. I got out, paid, and held out my hand to him. He gave me his, surprised, and I hung on it as long as I dared. Then he drove off. I had failed. The pain fell upon me once again and worse than before."

The painter got up and walked over to an old desk, standing in a corner of the room, covered with dust and so oppressed by canvases piled up against it from all sides that it was almost invisible. She opened the top drawer, rummaged in it and returned with a newspaper clipping.

"I cut this out. I thought it might give me

a few guidelines when you weren't posing. But it didn't. Did you ever look like that?"

It was a reproduction of an old studio photograph, and I couldn't help laughing at the flat, smooth moon face, the helpless round eyes under thin penciled eyebrows and the sterile, professional smile on the lips.

"Yes, that's what I looked like. I even remember that photograph. I thought at the time it was marvelous."

She took it from me, studied my face and then the piece of newspaper again and shook her head.

"If your name wasn't printed underneath, I'd never have recognized you. There's absolutely no connection between your present face and this one. It's a different person. Your voice is probably different too."

"I don't know. My voice always gives me a shock when I hear it from the screen—I always imagine something quite else. My idea of myself is also quite different from what I see on the screen. That's a shock too, at the beginning of every film. Afterward you get used to it. You get used to yourself."

I leaned forward and touched my cigarette to the newspaper clipping. It flared up and the painter quickly threw it in the ashtray.

I got up. "I'd like to go home now. I'm tired."

●

I wasn't tired, but I wanted to go home. Though first I intended to make a little detour to those trees I'd glimpsed from the window. The sky was still clear; it was cold but the air was dry and there was no wind. After sitting so long, it felt good to walk along the streets. I walked fast. I didn't run anymore the way I once used to, but I still couldn't saunter or stroll or tarry.

Down Oxford Street to Marble Arch, still standing up, undamaged by the war. But Lyon's Corner House, where I'd first met Jerome, had disappeared in favor of a huge movie theater. I crossed the street, just as we'd done eleven years before, and entered Hyde Park by the same gate walking toward the same out-of-the-way corner with the deck chairs that didn't even cost sixpence. No deck chairs now, in winter.

This had been the beginning, here, under these very trees. And the end had set in on that day in Paris, at the Hotel de la Muette. The following afternoon, when we went to see Babs, it had edged a little closer.

Jerome hadn't told me "Madame Lorrimer's" name. All I knew was that her husband owned a gallery; I didn't give a damn which one. In Babs's sitting room sat a girl in a bright-yellow summer dress. "Madame Dujardin."

The girl gave me a friendly smile. To Jerome she nodded and said, *"Ça va, aujourd'hui?"*

Babs sat down next to her on the sofa and explained, "Madame Dujardin's husband is the owner of the gallery in the Rue St. Honoré."

Aha! *"Ça va, aujourd'hui?"* She didn't yet know how he was today. Yesterday she had known, though.

She was perhaps a couple of years older than I, no more. A provocative and aggressively turned-up nose, very beautiful amber eyes, fair hair. Sitting there on the sofa, she looked like a Brimstone butterfly. She studied me lazily, relaxed and not at all unfriendly, wanted to know if I'd had a good journey and if I was tired, Jerome having told her my play had just closed. No one bothered to explain to me that Jerome and this girl knew each other. Or why.

If he knew that she was going to be there, at Babs's that afternoon, he showed no sign of it, looked neither surprised nor pleased. He sat next to me, listening to Robert Siodmak talking about his new film and occasionally making monosyllabic comments. He didn't speak to Jeannine or to me.

The two women on the sofa, one in black and white, the other in lemon-yellow, did most of the talking. They were apparently good friends—at least they had plenty to talk and laugh about. In French, of course. I fancied that they were talking and laughing about me, although I heard them discussing someone else. Were they asking each other whether I "knew"? I could see that Babs "knew."

I was holding a drink with a lot of ice in it. My fingers got cold too, and the chill was slowly creeping up my hand and my arm.

"You've got goose pimples," said Robert Siodmak, examining my bare arm. "Are you cold? In this heat?"

He, obviously, didn't "know." The chill was penetrating my body, soon my teeth would start chattering. Help!

Help? Why hadn't I thought of that yesterday—why had I let a whole unbearable day go by—why had I let myself sink into this awful quicksand instead of striking out for dry land, picking up the telephone and shouting: "Anabel! Help!"

I'd been standing for too long on the exact spot under the trees where our deck chairs had once stood. Then the sun had been shining. The dogs with their masters and the nannies with their baby carriages were still there, but now they were all walking briskly homeward, because it was beginning to grow dark. I found a taxi and returned to the hotel.

19

Diary, July 2, 1939:

When I got home, I found a note on my
bedside table. L. had called. Wanted me to
call her back at once at the Hotel de la
Muette. It was late, two a.m., we'd been to a
concert and then out to supper. Just Bill and
I. First time for ages. Did my best to talk to
him. More difficult than ever. But I really
tried. Don't want to call L. What if J.
answers? He knows now I'm not coming to
the Gurnemantzes'. I write those words as if
they meant nothing—yet as I spell them out,
I'm writhing with the pain of it, writhing like
a worm. Must, *must* remain firm. *Won't* call
her back. It's only one last attempt of hers
to make me change my mind. If she only knew

190

how easy that would be! One word from J.—
and I'd be off to the station in a flash!

So that was why she hadn't called back!

I had left the Siodmaks' as soon as I decent-
ly could and returned to the hotel on the pretext
that I was about to catch a cold. Jerome stayed
on—I didn't care, help was on the way. Anabel!
She'd know what to do, she'd tell me. I laughed
on the way sitting in the taxi—I actually heard
myself laugh—because Popeye the Sailorman
had come to my mind, eating his spinach. Anabel, my spinach.

For the rest of the day I sat in my room,
waiting. Nina had answered the telephone.
"Nina, I must urgently speak to your mother."
She'd gone to a concert. All right, I'd wait up
until she came home.

I waited. Midnight and then one o'clock,
two o'clock. At three I asked the night clerk for
something to make me sleep and he brought me
a white pill. I had never taken a sleeping pill
before. It made short shrift of me, made me
quickly go under in a deep, dreamless sleep.

I woke up late and immediately reached
for the telephone. Anabel! The maid said she'd
gone out. I left another message for her to call
me. Urgent!

I waited. Probably she'd left early in the
morning to meet Ferencsi, a thought that obliged
me to try to be happy for her. I spent the entire
day in my room. Silence.

●

A note from Jerome had been slipped under the door. It said that he had lots of things to do and would be having lunch with a gallery owner. (A gallery owner? Well, sort of.) He'd be back at the hotel to pack in the afternoon, and our train would leave for Marseilles at eight that evening.

At six he poked his head around the door. I was standing at the window; I hadn't even dared to sit out on the balcony in case I missed the telephone. He didn't ask what I'd been doing all day, seemed distraught and irritable. I heard him giving the chambermaid hell—something I'd never heard him do before. We drove to the station in silence.

This time we had been extravagant and taken a two-berth second-class sleeping compartment. Last year Anabel had shared our third-class one, containing three beds. Jerome had slept on top, I'd slept in the middle, Anabel in the bottom berth. First we'd had dinner in the dining car and they had shared a bottle of red wine and then we had made our way back through car after car, endlessly it seemed, laughing and squealing and lurching and swaying with the motion of the train, until we finally reached our compartment. Blissfully exhausted, we collapsed on Anabel's bed, all three of us, until we'd recovered sufficiently to take turns at undressing discreetly in the tiny toilet compartment. Jerome, the last, climbed the ladder to his bunk and turned out the light. In the darkness we called out to each other: "Sleep well! Happy dreams! Good night! Sleep well!"

The memory assaulted me and proved so

lethal that when Jerome said he was tired and didn't want any dinner, I quickly turned out the light over my berth to hide my tears. Fully dressed, I lay on my blanket until I had calmed down enough to get up and unpack my nightgown and brush my teeth by the light that shone in from houses rushing by along the tracks. Above me Jerome was snoring gently.

20

The train wormed itself booming and moaning into the station in Marseilles at seven o'clock in the morning. Slowly it glided past hundreds of people packed on the platform despite the early hour, all craning their necks upward, everyone's eyes eagerly searching each passing train window for the object of their early-morning pilgrimage.

Jerome shoved our suitcases along the corridor while I, leaning out of the window, scanned the sea of faces for the Gurnemantz threesome. There they were—but it was only a twosome. Peter and Eva, tanned, laughing and waving, fought their way through the crowd, Peter catching the suitcases Jerome tossed out to him, while Eva stood under my window, beaming up at me and asking the questions one always asks at railway stations, expecting no answer beyond a nod of the head. Yes we'd had a good journey, yes we'd had a good breakfast, yes it was a glorious day.

"Where's Ursula?"

"At home. It's a good three hours from Grasse to Marseilles—and the car's not getting any younger, you know."

This was quite evident a few minutes later when we watched Peter patiently using the starting handle to crank the old car into action.

So Ursula still wasn't well. By now an entire year had passed since she'd told us. Could it possibly be something sinister? In the ten months between our visits to the Gurnemantzes, we never exchanged letters. "If anything's wrong, you'll hear about it soon enough," we said when we kissed each other goodbye. All the same, last Christmas I had written and asked for news about Ursula's health, but in place of information I received a card with a drawing of Aesculapius, carrying a Christmas tree on his back, with the entire family assembled in front of him, their arms full of peaches. *"Joyeux Nöel!* Peter, Ursula, Eva, Jean-Pierre," it said. Happy Xmas.

●

They were standing at the garden gate, waving, when we roared up, the boy, now ten years old, with close-cropped stubby blond hair, tanned and naked except for his swimming trunks, and his mother next to him, looking not the least bit ill—on the contrary, she had gained weight, her freckled face was fuller than it had ever been before, her strong arms were as muscular as a man's.

"Something's up again," I said to Jerome when we were alone in our room. He nodded. "Poor Peter."

It wasn't only with me that Jerome was taciturn. I watched him later through the window as he sat on the terrace wall with Gurnemantz. Neither of them spoke; both were looking into the far distance with the vacantly concentrated expression of dogs when they seem to be listening for a bell inside themselves.

During lunch we all made an effort, as if by agreement. Sometimes three people would start talking at once, trying to avoid a silence. Eva, who was sitting next to Jean-Pierre, tied his napkin around his neck for him and rearranged his fingers when they gripped a knife too close to the blade. Ursula looked on.

Peter and Eva, who had gotten up at the crack of dawn to meet us, dispensed with their coffee in order to get some sleep. Jerome, on the other hand, declared he didn't need a siesta and would go for a walk. At this, Jean-Pierre eagerly asked if he could come along—and was refused. He was sorry, said Jerome, but it would distract him, since he was on the lookout for subjects to paint. In the nick of time I remembered that I had brought an airplane kit for the child, who, quickly comforted, disappeared with it into his room. Ursula and I were left alone on the terrace, watching the wasps buzz about the remains of our lunch. "Oh, just leave it," said

Ursula when I got up to carry the plates back to the kitchen.

We stretched out side by side under an old umbrella pine. Peter had laid out the terrace in such a way that at noon half of its ground was shaded by the tree to protect one from the burning rays of sun, though it was powerless against the heat, which only Aesculapius, gray and invulnerable, could withstand without having to lie down. All the dogs were stretched out against the cool terrace wall, panting in short, convulsive gasps, unable to bark, wag their tails or show any other sign of life.

I, too, would have liked to collapse and close my eyes, but Ursula, lying right next to me, was humming the same song again and again, and off key to boot. I sat up and looked at her, stretched out in her old kitchen apron, freckled arms crossed behind her head, her excessively long legs with the schoolboy knees and angular feet in sandals. She always wore sandals because she didn't want to appear taller than Peter.

"You're well again, aren't you?"

"I could uproot a tree—preferably a peach tree," she said and laughed noisily upward into the dark parasol of the pine tree. Turning her mop of short, curly brown hair toward me, she added, "But *you* don't look too good to me. Was your play exhausting?"

"Eight performances a week."

"Go and sleep," she said. "I'll wake you up at six when we start picking."

I wasn't sorry to go, nor did I want to know why her laughter had sounded so joyless. Could

be that she sensed it wasn't only the eight performances a week that had made me look 'not
too good'—and could be that she, too, wasn't
up to sharing other people's troubles.

●

At six o'clock we assembled at the orchard gate,
each arriving from a different direction though
all with the same expression of determinedly
eager, slightly forced cheerfulness on our faces,
all except perhaps Eva, who yawned unasham-
edly while helping Jean-Pierre strap the baskets
on Aesculapius. Jerome appeared from nowhere
and went ahead with Peter. I hung back as we
passed the water cistern to splash cold water on
my face.

Everyone chose his own row of trees. Jerome selected the bottom one and set off down
the steep grassy terraces with his baskets; two
rows below me Ursula hummed her tuneless
song; I could hear Eva's bursts of laughter and
from time to time Peter's deep bass voice. Occasionally somebody whistled for Aesculapius.
The smell of the hot pine bark, foliage and fruit
was soothing as ever—everything was as it had
always been, yet everything was quite different.

I wasn't working properly; my arms seemed
to be aching. I kept moving around, trying to
keep an eye on Jerome, who was picking five
hundred yards or so below me. Sometimes I
caught sight of his hand or a tuft of his black
mane, but mostly I could only tell which tree
he was working on from the movement of the
branches.

Then, suddenly, I couldn't see either head or hand any longer, and the trees in the bottom rows stood motionless. I climbed laboriously up on the strongest branch—it bent under my weight—and balanced perilously on one knee, just in time to see Jerome's blue shirt disappearing among the olive trees that covered the lower slope of the hillside.

The branch began to creak ominously. I hastily jumped down and inspected the damage: a crack in the cleft! Full of remorse, I shamelessly clamped a leaf into it—Peter made a tour of inspection every evening—and sneaked to the next tree. Where had Jerome gone? The lower gate of the orchard led only to the olive grove which served as boundary to the neighboring farm—one couldn't get to the street that way. Was he tired of picking? Was he again looking for subjects to paint? At seven o'clock in the evening? My basket was filling up with peaches—until I suddenly realized I hadn't checked a single one for quality. I discovered I'd picked a lot of hard ones, which I hastily threw into the bushes. One rolled downhill and landed at the feet of Ursula, who picked it up in surprise.

"This one's still green!"

"It broke off by accident. Sorry!"

She looked up at me for a moment, then went on picking.

I didn't take my eye off the olive grove. For a full half-hour there was no sign of life, then the blue shirt emerged again, and a few minutes later the branches in the bottom row of trees began to shake as if a tornado were passing through or as if the picker was fighting a duel with the recalcitrant fruit. And all this to the accompaniment of loud and cheerful whistling from that direction. What could have happened to put him in such an exuberant mood that he was giving Aesculapius a kiss on the nose?

•

Supper on the terrace, then Pernod and almonds —as usual. Memories of last year and of Anabel got stuck in my head. Why hadn't she called back?

Suddenly I knew why: Something had happened with Ferencsi! That was the reason. I'd have to call her immediately.

"Did you get your telephone installed?"

"No," said Peter, "and we never will. I've given up. We can manage without one, and if there's something urgent we go next door to Madame Raquin's. She has one."

Tomorrow morning then: Madame Raquin.

•

Later that evening the old routine: The girls lay down, dressed, on their beds and slept, were called at three o'clock and staggered in the darkness, still half asleep, to the truck.

Suddenly a wide-awake little voice called through an open window, "I can hear you! Next year I'll be coming with you."

Ursula, who was walking a few steps ahead of me, stopped.

"Who told you that?"

"Eva promised me."

I can't be certain of what happened next because I was groping my way along the wall with the others, but there was a sudden scuffle of feet, then something that sounded like a slap, and a half-smothered cry from Eva: "Are you crazy?" Then silence, except for the sound of our footsteps. A moment later the lights of the car went on and we climbed in, Eva beside Peter, who was driving, then Jerome, then I. Ursula was the last to jump in, after slamming the garden gate shut.

•

When I woke up, the other bed was empty. Jerome must have dressed without making a sound, or I had been too deeply asleep to hear him, for we hadn't gotten home from our early-morning swim in Nice until six o'clock. For the sake of everybody's safety, I had had to decline my fifteen-minute stint at the wheel and had slept shamelessly all the way home, either on Jerome's shoulder or on Ursula's. I couldn't remember how I'd ended up in my nightgown and in bed.

Already one o'clock. Madame Raquin! I threw on my clothes and ducked out the front door to avoid Jean-Pierre. On the days following our market excursions he would keep himself quietly occupied all morning so that we could sleep, but around noon he would be tired of his toys and ready for company. I saw his cropped blond head bent over the airplane kit outside the garage and tiptoed toward the orchard gate—in vain; children have keen ears. "Wait! I'm coming with you," he yelled, catching up with me in a couple of leaps.

"I'm only going to Madame Raquin's to make a phone call."

"You too? Jerome's just gone there. He wouldn't take me with him."

I stood with my hand on the open orchard gate, pressing the latch up and down, and looked into the blue eyes looking up at me expectantly. So Jerome had gone to make a phone call—to the "gallery owner" in Paris . . .

"But I can come with *you*, can't I?" He must have noticed that I wasn't listening because he boldly put his hand on my arm and shook it. Then—instinctively?—he spoke the magic words: "I know a short cut, but you'll have to wade the stream."

Barefooted, he ran along the first row of trees without looking back, certain that I would follow, then jumped down to the next terrace like a rabbit. I slithered after him, clutching at boughs and branches, and saw him crawling under some bushes before leaping down a couple more terraces. I blessed my espadrilles, which kept me from slipping until the herd instinct and the instantaneous coordination acquired in my girl-scout days shifted into gear, and I made it.

Swerving suddenly sideways and downward, he reached the foot of the hill and stopped at a certain place in the tall wire fence which surrounded the orchard. I panted up. He knelt on the ground and triumphantly showed me a spot where the wire was slack enough for someone to slip underneath it, lifted it a few inches and wriggled through like a dog. From the other side he looked at me with contempt as I leaned against the fence, trying to catch my breath. He didn't know why I wanted to get to Madame Raquin's as quickly as possible, but he didn't care—the whole thing was a game, a race, we were going to beat Jerome! And there stood this stupid woman who gasped for air, wasting valuable time!

"Come on!"

Obediently I flung myself flat on my stomach and wormed my feet through the eight-inch gap. Jean-Pierre grabbed them, pulling and twisting mercilessly and with all his strength until he had my stomach, chest and shoulders safely on the other side. But what about my head? The aluminum links dug into my neck—like the blade of the guillotine, I thought, as I ground my nose in the dirt.

"Shut your eyes and take a deep breath. Now!" he commanded, pressing down on the back of my head with both hands. I was just about to suffocate—he grabbed my hair and pulled me through in the nick of time. As I got up, spitting dirt out of my mouth and blindly trying to get the sand and grit out of my nose and eyes, he burst out laughing. "You've certainly got a thick head!" he said. "The stream's just down there, you can wash your face in it."

He jumped up and disappeared under oleander bushes. I hobbled painfully after him, drained and parched, longing for a drink of cold spring water. He was waiting for me, up to his knees in the stream, kindly offering to splash me.

"Don't you dare!"

Whereupon he climbed up the bank on the other side and disappeared over the hill. I held my face under the water as long as I could, then proceeded to rinse amazing quantities of sand out of my ears while discovering some sizable scratches on my neck. Suddenly I couldn't keep on my feet any longer and collapsed on the nearest rock. After all, what was the hurry? I knew now why Jerome was from time to time off looking for "subjects to paint." What was the point of getting to Madame Raquin's before him?

Jean-Pierre reappeared on the far bank.

"You've lost," he shouted across the water. "Jerome's there already. Do you give in?"

"Yes. But I still have to use the phone."

"I'll show you the way," he cried magnanimously. "And I'll wait for you or you won't find your way back."

I stopped in midstream.

"Do you think I'm going to crawl back through that hole?"

"Sure!" He caught sight of my face. "Uh— you haven't got any guts."

Two bends farther up the stream stood Madame Raquin's house, shaded by tall willow trees. Jean-Pierre ran ahead, for even though the race was over, he couldn't slow his pace down to mine. He was soon back, however, with the news that Madame Raquin had invited me to a glass of wine—her own, of course, "the best in the entire region."

The last few hundred yards took me through a carefully manicured vineyard, its grapes and leaves sprayed a mottled green-white. Twice more Jean-Pierre ran back and forth to the house. He had told Madame Raquin I was an actress, he confided in whispers, and it turned out that she'd never seen an actress before in her life. He tilted his head sideways, gave me a critical look, and added, "But she'll be disappointed—the way you look now." He fished a handkerchief out of his shorts. "Spit!" he said. I spat and with a surprisingly gentle touch he rubbed the last bits of dirt out of my hair line.

The house was a two-story cube, painted yellow with brown shutters. It had no balcony and no terrace, but right next to the front door was another, smaller cube, a grape arbor. The six posts erected years ago around which the climbing tendrils of the vine had cautiously wound themselves were now completely covered up. Branches as thick as an arm had intertwined affectionately and braided themselves like pigtails into a square roof, whose green leaves and still-unripe grapes cast a gentle greenish sheen on the people and objects below.

Hand in hand we entered the arbor. If Madame Raquin was disappointed at the sight of me, she didn't show it, but lifted herself an inch or two from her chair to greet me. She was enthroned in lonely stateliness behind a garden table, a bottle of wine and a half-filled glass within reach. Her broad face was framed by white hair—light-green in the glare that filtered through the vine leaves—like tangled knitting wool. Her sly little foxy eyes encased in little cushions of fat smiled at me amiably. A set of yellow teeth, grandly bared in welcome, added to the impression of benevolent neighborliness.

"*Bonjour*, Mademoiselle."

"*Bonjour*, Madame Raquin. I hope I'm not disturbing you."

"Not at all, I'm always glad to see visitors. Jean-Pierre, bring two glasses."

"Two?" His blue eyes opened wide and stared at her incredulously, not daring to hope.

"Yes, one for you too." He was gone in a flash. "If you teach children early enough to appreciate good wine, they'll never be drunks later on."

I thought of Monsieur Raquin, who was said to have drunk himself into an early grave on his own wine. He'd obviously been taught too late to appreciate it. I wondered if Jerome was still on the phone to Paris. Right through my misery, I was suddenly struck by the prosaic thought that we really couldn't afford any of this.

"Madame—may I use your telephone?"

"*Mais oui*, as soon as the young man has finished. He always talks for a long time. Do you know him? I believe he's staying up at the Gurnemantz house too." (She pronounced it "*Gürman*.")

Jean-Pierre reappeared with two glasses.

"You pour," said Madame. "If you're going to drink, you must be able to pour. Hold the bottle at the top—careful! Don't spill a single drop."

The child clutched the bottle with both hands, biting his lips in concentration and effort as the wine gurgled slowly into the glasses. Breathing heavily, he set the bottle down.

"Bravo!" said Madame. "Well then—your good health."

We clinked glasses and drank.

"Wonderful!" I said. Jean-Pierre wanted to say something too but he was fighting for breath and his eyes were streaming. His first taste of wine. (Peter had always vetoed it.) He must have been expecting something quite else than this pungent, slightly sour beverage.

"Madame?" That was Jerome's voice from inside the house.

"Won't you join us, Monsieur?" called the old woman over her shoulder. "Come and have a glass of wine—I have a visitor."

I sat there like a piece of stone. I couldn't imagine what he'd say—or what I would say, or why I had come charging over here at all. What on earth had I intended to do? Snatch the receiver out of his hand?

"I really haven't time, Madame." Through the arbor's wall of leaves I could vaguely make him out as he was standing in the doorway. "They're expecting me for lunch. I'll be back this evening, though, and then we'll have one together. Would you find out what I owe you?"

"Coming." She heaved herself out of the chair and waddled on huge shapeless legs out of the arbor and through the open door of the house.

Saved.

Jean-Pierre raised his glass and clinked it once more against mine.

"Cheers!" Again the blue eyes filled at once with tears but he swallowed bravely. "She's fat, isn't she?" He leaned forward and whispered in my ear. "But she's not going to have a baby."

"Are you sure?"

He nodded reassuringly.

"She's always this fat. Once, long ago, she had some children, two at a time—"

"Twins?"

"One of them takes care of the vines here. The other is . . ." He tapped his forehead.

"Crazy?"

"He can't eat by himself, she has to feed him. You know something? Maybe she has another one in her stomach. I asked her, but she says no. I think she doesn't want to admit it, because it's probably like that too"—he tapped his forehead again—"if it's been sitting inside there for so long, don't you think?"

"Could be."

"Do you know why she wheezes like that?" He whispered again. "She has amsta."

"Amsta? What's that?"

He puffed and gasped like a locomotive. "That's called amsta, don't you know that?"

"Amsta? You mean asthma!"

He stared at me, puzzled and vexed—but was rescued from the dilemma by the return of Madame.

"You can have the phone now. Did you like your wine?"

I hurriedly drank up but prevented the child from following suit.

"Run on home and tell your mother I'll be right back. And say thank you for the wine."

"*Merci*, Madame." He made his little bow, adding, with the expression of a connoisseur, "An excellent wine."

Madame Raquin laughed and shuffled ahead of me into the house. The telephone, an old-fashioned box with a handle to crank it up, hung on the wall in the dining room. Through a window in the hallway I had seen Jerome's blue shirt making for the olive grove, while Jean-Pierre's blond crew-cut bobbed along on the other side through the vineyard.

It was nice and cool in the dining room because the shutters were closed, and Madame showed no intention of switching on the ceiling light. She groped her way along the wall, lifted off the receiver and cranked the machine vigorously.

"What number do you want?"

"I want to make a call to England."

"Person to person?"

"Not necessary."

She cranked again.

"She's having lunch, that lazy good-for-nothing operator, so it may take a while. For the young man I always make it person-to-person. Always to the same number in Saint-Tropez. He has a girl friend there, a married woman—*Allo*, Mademoiselle—ah, there you are at last."

She handed me the receiver and groped

her way out of the room, closing the door behind her.

Mechanically I gave Anabel's number. I'd have known that number in my sleep, and just as well, for my brain was completely emptied by what Madame had just said. Jeannine Dujardin in Saint-Tropez! Practically next door! So that's why he'd said he wanted to ride the Michelin electric train along the coast and maybe spend a few days looking for subjects to paint . . .

I leaned against the wall, pressing my forehead against the cool stone, wishing desperately that I hadn't drunk the wine, trying to sort out the jumble of thoughts that came racing back into my head. Saint-Tropez . . . next door . . . therefore cheaper telephone calls . . . soon he'll go there by train and never come back . . . and then, suddenly, Anabel's voice.

"Hello?"

"Anabel?"

I knew I was screaming. I couldn't speak, all I could do was to howl into the receiver without restraint.

It was a while before I could hear anything except my own sobbing. She had probably made several attempts to interrupt me or calm me down, because now she called out severely, "Pull yourself together and tell me what's happened."

I told her. Starting with the single room at the Hotel de la Muette, then the afternoon at the Siodmaks', Jerome's solitary walks in search of subjects to paint, and now Saint-Tropez and the Michelin electric train. I didn't know whether she'd got it all or even whether she was still on the line, because, when I finally stopped speaking, there was nothing but a dead silence.

"Anabel? Are you there? Did you hear what I said?"

"Yes, I heard."

"Anabel, what am I to do? Anabel! Say something!"

"I'll come."

"What?"

I had shouted so loudly that I clapped my hand over my mouth.

"Stop crying. Don't let him notice anything—don't tell him anything—don't tell anybody anything. I'll be there."

She had hung up.

I called her name again several times, but there was no sound from the black box. I hung up the receiver and leaned my head against the wall. She was coming. She was leaving Ferencsi, the man she loved—leaving him in the lurch—to come to me. Was there anyone else like her in the whole world? Was there ever such a friend? I rolled my temples, my forehead and my burning face back and forth against the cold, damp wall, as if I could drink the soothing coolness. Anabel was coming. Anabel knew. Everything was all right again.

The black box squawked and buzzed like a swarm of bees, bringing Madame back into the room. Just as well that it was too dark for her to see my face. She took the receiver from my hand. "*Merci*, Mademoiselle, I'll see to it." Neighborly friendship was one thing—but the exact amount of how much my call had cost was another. After all, this was a call to London. A pretty penny!

No, I thought, as I counted out the money, cheap! Dirt cheap! Money? How could money come into it when all of my life was at stake?

21

I made my way back through the olive grove, taking my time, thinking, sorting things out, planning, giving my red, swollen eyes time to recover. Late for lunch? Never mind, let them wait or eat without me. All the same I took in the fact that the garden gate was open. Jerome, usually so meticulous, must have charged through, as absorbed as I was in plans and deliberations. Aesculapius might easily have escaped!

I closed the big gate and slowly climbed the orchard terraces. "Don't tell him anything." Of course I wouldn't. God knows if he'd even be here when she arrived. The Michelin train! Which hotel would "she" be staying at? Maybe I could find out from Madame Raquin, who set up the person-to-person calls for him. "Don't tell anybody anything." That one was more difficult, since I'd invented convincing reasons for Anabel's sudden cancellation, a long and complicated story about some sort of mysterious malady. The whole family had been genuinely disappointed that she hadn't come with us; her room had been prepared for her, flowers on the bedside table . . .

I climbed the last steps—and found myself facing Ursula, watching for me at the upper gate of the orchard.

"The spaghetti's being kept warm on the stove. Jean-Pierre told me where you were. By the way, he smelled of wine. Did Madame Raquin—?"

"Yes, she did."

She laughed.

"She's been trying for ages—the old witch! She's obsessed with the idea that the child needs to be 'immunized.' Do you know what time it is? After three! What's going on today? Everybody dribbling in, first Jean-Pierre, then Jerome—and now you. Eva's about to blow her top in the kitchen."

"Ursula, I'm not hungry—please!"

She looked at me for a moment, nodded, turned and went back to the house, calling something through the open kitchen window.

I wanted to continue my "sorting out" and looked forward to the cool silence of our bedroom. Alone! I made sure that Jerome was out on the terrace, under the pine tree, reading a small booklet. Perhaps a railway guide.

214

I closed the shutters and crept into my unmade bed. In London Anabel's travel arrangements would be well under way by now, reservations for the Dover-Calais boat and for a berth in the Paris-Marseilles sleeping car. What would she tell Bill and Nina? Above all, what would she tell Ferencsi? Suddenly deeply ashamed of my wild, selfish screaming for help, I pressed my face into the pillow—at the same time hugging it gratefully as if it were Anabel.

How soon could she get here? When would I get news from her saying, "I'm in Paris," or, better still, "I'm at the station in Marseilles"? Three or four days at the earliest. I would have to live through them calmly and quietly.

But—oh God! Suppose she couldn't get reservations? After all, it was the holiday season!

•

In the late afternoon, freshly bathed, I made my appearance on the terrace. No one in sight. I climbed up on the wall and looked around, eager to try out my newly acquired equanimity. Not a living soul. Only Aesculapius, on his day off, grazing way down at the bottom of the slope.

Silence. An unnatural, desolate silence, most unusual in the Gurnemantz ménage. Last year they'd all been members of the same orchestra, but now everybody seemed to be a soloist. They still "played" together but each simmered and stewed somewhere on his own. Earlier on, on my way to my siesta in the "thigh," I had quickly glanced around: Peter was tinkering with the truck, Ursula had started to take down the washing from the clothesline, Eva was banging around in the kitchen, no one was paying attention to anyone else or lending a hand or boosting morale by just standing close by, chatting and laughing. There was no life left in the team, although the individual limbs were still twitching like those of a galvanized frog.

I sat on the wall and looked down. Everybody who stepped out onto the terrace and sat on the wall looked down. Way down below, willow branches breaking through the olive trees marked the course of the stream—and somewhere down there, among those very willows, was Madame Raquin's little yellow cube with the old black telephone box. In the green arbor Jerome would be taking a glass of wine with Madame . . .

How had Jerome reacted to the news that Anabel had decided not to come? How very strange that I had to make an effort to pin down the exact moment when I'd told him! He must have suspected it the instant he saw me sitting alone in the lobby of the hotel. But we'd hardly said a word to each other there, for my appearance as the second Madame Lorrimer had eclipsed everything else. So I must have told him later, upstairs in my "single." Yes, that's how it had come about—he had asked and I naturally told him the truth: that Ferencsi was in London. I remember his looking surprised for a moment—and then definitely relieved. He still didn't like Anabel! But only because he didn't really know her. Now, when she suddenly showed up here, at least he'd be forced to realize what sort of a person she truly was, a woman who was capable of jeopardizing her love in order to help her friend! For he would of course immediately realize that Anabel was coming to help me stand up to the "gallery owner." He would have to respect her for it—and hate her all the more. But Anabel wouldn't give a damn about that. She didn't really like him either.

●

During supper Jerome remarked casually that he would be leaving by the Michelin train tomorrow. I managed to continue winding my warmed-up spaghetti around my fork. Tomorrow!

"When will you be back?" asked Ursula, the housewife.

"In two or three days. I'm going to stop off in Saint-Tropez. There's a gallery there."

"The Nouveaux Artistes Gallery," said Peter. "I know it. Not bad. But they take one-third of the sales price."

"They can take half as far as I'm concerned. All I want is to see the damn things hanging on a wall—and people looking at them."

He pushed his chair back, got up and sat on the terrace wall. Peter turned his wary, slanting eyes toward him.

"It's about time, too. By the way, if they want a deposit to cover expenses—catalogue and all that—we can advance you something."

Ursula nodded, although she hadn't been asked.

Jerome didn't answer, just stared down the slope.

"I'll drive you to the station," Eva piped up. "What time does your train leave?"

"One-thirty."

"I'll make you a sandwich," said Ursula.

"I'll write you a note to the Nouveaux Artistes," said Peter.

They're playing chamber music together again, I thought.

•

Jerome was up early the next morning. He had slept badly. Once I had waked up to see him standing by the window looking out into the night before creeping noiselessly back to bed. A little while later it sounded as though he was sitting up, bending over me. I kept my eyes tightly closed, but I felt that he was watching me. Then he lay down again.

While he was packing, I dressed. I was making for the door when he grabbed my arm and forced me to look him in the face.

"Let me go—it's only for a few days."

"I'm not stopping you."

"You're spoiling it for me, your face is spoiling it."

I had promised myself not to probe, not to demand an explanation, to wait quietly until Anabel arrived. But in spite of my firm resolutions, I heard myself asking him the question that had been haunting me ever since the Hotel de la Muette. "Could you—could you live without me?"

He immediately let go of me and turned away. I'd ruined it.

He went to the closet, took out a shirt, folded it and said matter-of-factly, "I can live without anyone—if I have to. You know that."

No, I didn't know that. I'd thought I had a special place in his life. "But I don't have to, do I?" he added—and there was that old defensive smile again. "I'll be back in a few days."

He placed the shirt carefully in the suitcase. I left the room.

It was only eight o'clock, but the hot breath of the sirocco hit me in the face. What was I to do now? Eat, drink, pick peaches, sleep —until Anabel arrived. In three days at the earliest . . .

I remained standing in the guest-room doorway, trying to get up enough energy to walk across to the terrace. Something bright-red was catching the light over there. Ursula and Eva were surely still asleep. A visitor? For a moment I was tempted to go back into our room and throw myself down on the bed—but Jerome was in there, packing.

I set myself in motion, took a step forward, then another . . the red spot grew bigger . . . my sandals grated on the sand . . . the spot took shape and turned around . . . Anabel.

She called—and I ran, collapsed sobbing beside her on the terrace wall.

How was it possible? How had she managed it? Yesterday noon she'd still been in London. Had she taken a plane?

"I simply got into the car, the little Alfa—there it is, by the garage—and drove off. Direction: south. Got to Dover at six, got a place on the eight-o'clock ferry. And kept driving."

"You didn't stop over in Paris?"

"I wouldn't be here if I had."

Of course she wouldn't, stupid question.

"So you drove all night?"

"Yes. Just got here."

I searched her face for signs of exhaustion and found none. On the contrary she looked wide-awake, full of energy, almost electrified.

"But I wouldn't mind some breakfast. I haven't eaten anything since lunchtime yesterday."

I shook myself like a wet dog to get some coherent thoughts into my brain.

"Stay here and relax. I'll get it for you."

She laughed and got to her feet.

"I know what kind of a cook you are! But you can get the tray ready."

She followed me into the kitchen. No word, no sign, no questioning glance. She behaved as if she had planned her visit this way all along, because she enjoyed driving fast and nonstop in her Alfa.

She put water on to boil, sliced some bread, stuffing a dry piece in her mouth, found the coffee, milk and sugar while I watched, holding the empty tray. I couldn't think of a single word to say.

Bending over the stove and absorbed in the gradual heating of the water in the pot, she asked casually over her shoulder, "Is he still here?"

I pointed to the window: Jerome was walking slowly toward the terrace. He jumped up on the wall and looked down into the valley. My heart began to pound. I sat on a kitchen chair while Anabel walked over to the window and looked at him, standing there with his back to us, a lonely silhouette on the long wall. Then she said calmly, "Watch the water, don't let it boil over. Pour it over the coffee—there, in the glass filter. I'm going out on the terrace to speak to him. Get the tray ready, breakfast for three—but don't bring it out until I call."

At the door, she turned around to add, "And don't forget to turn off the gas."

I went over to the window, following her with my eyes. Jerome heard her footsteps, looked over his shoulder—and remained motionless. She walked slowly toward him, picking up a chair on her way, turned it around, and sat down facing him. I could see nothing but his face and her back, once again only a spot of red.

I didn't dare make a noise by opening the window, but I watched his face like a hawk, trying to guess what she was saying to him. He turned toward her, put his hands on his hips, remained standing on the wall in this posture, challenging—and dangerous. She made a gesture as if asking him to sit down, but he stayed where he was.

As far as I could tell, he still hadn't spoken a word. His head was lowered; he reminded me of a young black bull I had seen in the arena in Madrid. Was Anabel still speaking? He seemed to be listening to something.

From behind me came a hissing sound—the water was boiling over. I ran and looked for a potholder—I'd never been any good at handling hot pans—finally grabbed the hand towel, picked up the pot with both hands and carried it over to the coffee machine as if I were holding the Holy Grail. I poured the water on the coffee. It splashed over and I jumped aside, swore, wiped the floor with the hand towel, gave up and rushed back to the window.

Anabel turned her head and called out, "How's breakfast coming along?"

Frantically I threw open one cabinet after another in search of cups and plates, savagely pulled all the drawers out to look for knives and spoons, and piled everything on the tray. No room for that coffee-filter thing—oh well, I'd get that later. Opening the door with my elbow, I stepped out on the terrace.

Jerome jumped down from the wall and took the tray from my hands without so much as a look at me. Anabel's face gave nothing away.

"The coffee," I stammered. "Just a moment . . ."

I turned and raced back to the kitchen, grabbed the coffee machine—and set it down again. What was going on out on the terrace? What had she said to him?

The door opened and Eva's sleepy face appeared. She looked around, stunned.

"What's happened? Have we had vandals in here? Good Lord—it stinks of gas!" She ran to the stove and turned off the gas. Only then did she see my face. "Don't you feel well? Why didn't you wake me up if you're hungry?"

I shook my head and pointed to the window.

"No!" she shouted in amazement. "Anabel! Is she all right again?"

Picking up the coffee machine in her strong, capable hands, she walked out on the terrace, laughing and calling. Through the window I saw Peter and Jean-Pierre approaching, then Ursula—greetings, embraces—nothing to be afraid of anymore, the tornado had passed. But I stayed in the kitchen for a little while before I joined them on the terrace.

22

What had she said to him out there on the terrace when she sat on the chair with her back to me? I leafed through the diary, although I knew she never took it with her to Grasse, but perhaps she'd written about it later.

Nothing.

There weren't that many entries left, and those I skipped for the time being. I didn't feel up to them as yet, I was too caught up in my own journey through the past. Right now I was on the point of reliving those days in Grasse with such detailed precision it was as if I had myself written a diary at that time, and was now reading it again. Every face, every word, even the light and the time of day—morning, noon or night—everything had been faithfully recorded and came flooding back. Not hectically and randomly, as it had at first, but more systematically, and more thoroughly.

I now actively enjoyed posing in the studio, getting lost in my thoughts. The familiar room with its smell of paint, the music, the presence of the silent, shapeless form in front of the easel —all created a balmy emptiness in my mind, so that the bygone course of events could unfold at leisure. I was so absorbed and far away that it often came as a shock when the fifteen minutes were over.

The painter praised me. "You sit there now as if you really belong. Almost like a professional model. I can't work properly unless my model cooperates, and you're so lost in your memories that your face now matches my poncho. Indians sit for hours like that, chewing coca, or not even chewing, just thinking about something that feeds them inside. Exactly like you, now. Anabel's a hard nut to crack, isn't she?"

She laughed. She had given up asking me questions.

One day, out of the blue, I said, "You mentioned some time ago that you knew Dujardin. What kind of man was he? What did he look like? Tell me about him."

She gave me a puzzled look, surprised at the urgency in my voice, leaned her head back to stare at the ceiling, took off her glasses and thought.

"Dujardin? When I knew him he was about forty. Short, but well put together. He held himself very erect but not stiff. He had a definite

—presence, authority. Thinning hair—dark. Dark eyes too. A strong face—good face—large. Eyes, nose, mouth—all large. Very decisive. Good voice. Hands—yes, good hands too. Actually he wasn't much interested in the gallery, he only bought it to give himself something to do. His father had plenty of money and let him do what he wanted. Once he showed me his Sanskrit manuscripts and medieval illuminated books. That was more than just a hobby; he was an expert, the Louvre used to consult him at times. What you want to know is, of course, how Jeannine fitted into all this. Nobody could understand it. She was his second wife—the first one had died. He was said to have been happy in his first marriage and—well, you know the old story, one tries again and can't repeat the trick. While I was having my second show with him, he suddenly disappeared from one day to the next. No one had any idea where he was. Clients came—people like Leger or Van Dongen —wanting to speak to him, and I was particularly angry because I couldn't very well do the dealing and haggling over my pictures myself and his secretary was a half-wit. One day she told me all the dirt—he fired her later when he found out. Jeannine, she said, was in Barcelona with a bullfighter, living quite openly with him in his apartment, sitting in the president's box whenever he appeared in the arena. One afternoon he was awarded both ears and the tail, and the French newsreels picked it up. I didn't see it but I heard about it. Apparently you could recognize Jeannine quite clearly in the box, bending down to embrace him, while the audience cheered. That was the day before Dujardin disappeared. A week later—the last week of my exhibition—he showed up again. Without Jeannine, said the secretary. I must say, he looked as if he'd been crucified. All kinds of wild rumors were going around—he had beaten Jeannine up or she had beaten him up. It finally turned out that he had beaten up the bullfighter, who wasn't able to fight for a while. Apparently Jeannine nursed him, and I suppose that gave them time to get to know and bore each other. Anyhow all of a sudden she was back, though she didn't show her face in the gallery. Now then—if you're ready . . ."

I was ready. I had a lot of new material to work on, new angles had just evolved: Dujardin. According to Anabel, he had been the key.

Now then—take it easy, don't rush, go back to the scene on the terrace, at breakfast, the day Anabel fell out of the sky. Extraordinary, the aplomb with which she caught on to Eva's cry: "Are you well again?" and the innocuous explanation of her "miraculous recovery." She took care, of course, not to go into details—after all, she still didn't know what was supposed to have been wrong with her—but changed the subject elegantly and nonchalantly to the effect that one didn't bore one's friends with one's ailments.

Did Jerome believe her? His face seemed to me pale under his tan, his narrow eyes unfathomable, though he ate with concentration and appetite. Suddenly he looked up and said to Eva, and apparently to no one else, "You needn't drive me to the station. I'm staying here." Astonishment and consternation among the entire Gurnemantz clan.

Peter protested. "But you must go! It's important for you. Here's the note for the gallery. Anabel won't mind if you're away for a few days, we'll take good care of her, won't we, Anabel?"

She smiled disarmingly and nodded, noncommittally. The others didn't notice anything, kept urging Jerome to go, wanted me to persuade him—I remained neutral and silent—and didn't give up until he said, "After all, it doesn't have to be today. I can go another time."

Soon after that Anabel excused herself and went off to the second guest room. She wanted to "rest a little." She hadn't mentioned that she'd been driving all night—it wouldn't have made sense and would have sounded suspicious, coming on top of all those stories about her illness and quick recovery.

Wise Anabel, equal to anything. She would now take the reins, take over, teach me.

The terrace gradually emptied as the Gurnemantz family dissolved in all directions to go about their individual business. Jerome and I remained. I, because I didn't know what else to do, he, because he had something to say to me.

"Well? Are you satisfied?"

He took my hand and stroked it, almost the way he used to.

"Yes."

It was true. I certainly ought to be "satisfied" now that he'd given up Saint-Tropez—for the time being at least. That I owed to Anabel.

He seemed to be thinking along the same lines.

"Quite a coincidence that she should arrive this morning, isn't it?"

He knew, then. Had she told him? Not that it mattered. Better—and simpler—to tell him the truth.

"She's here because I asked her to come." He didn't answer, but since he did not relinquish my hand, I felt this might be a good moment to tell him the truth. "She dropped everything, imagine! She dropped her lover, left him high and dry in London, sitting there all by himself."

He let go of my hand as if it had burned him, and jumped up on the wall, turning his back on me. I watched him, feeling relieved and gratified. Without a doubt, my story had considerably impressed him. A flood of love and gratitude for Anabel overwhelmed me—but he suddenly turned to face me and rudely cut off any further account of her self-sacrifice.

"So you think she's helping you?"

"Well, you're not going to see—you're not going to Saint-Tropez today. That's a help."

I looked up at him. He squatted down, stretched out his hands and cradled my face in them, looking urgently, almost beseechingly, into my eyes.

"You should let things take their course. Unfinished business rots and torments. Do you understand what I mean?"

I shook my head. To me the only thing

229

that mattered was that this "business" had been nipped in the bud. Out of sight, out of mind.

Jerome let go of me, said he was going to Madame Raquin's to call Saint-Tropez and cancel his visit.

He left and I remained alone on the terrace, alone and suddenly assailed by gnawing doubts. "Let things take their course . . ." What had he meant by that?

•

Market day. Peach-picking day. I was glad to have something to do, since Anabel hadn't reappeared as yet.

"The journey must have been very tiring for her," said Ursula, who was working next to me to make sure I didn't pick any more unripe peaches. No danger of that, I was on my toes today. "She mustn't come with us to Nice tonight."

That was quite all right with Anabel. She didn't show up until we were out on the terrace by candlelight, drinking our Pernod and eating almonds. Leaning against the pine tree in something long and white, she said she wasn't hungry but she'd like some coffee. Shortly afterward, when I looked back at the pine tree, she was gone.

I felt somehow let down. I had hardly exchanged a word with her, yet there was so much to tell, so many questions to ask, especially about what Jerome had said that morning about letting things take their course. How long would she be staying? Probably only a few days; she'd want to get back to Ferencsi, surely.

Peter and Jerome were changing a tire on the truck, Eva offered to put Jean-Pierre to bed, Ursula and I were left alone in the dark.

"How do you like Madame Raquin?"

"I like her."

"Could you imagine her as my mother-in-law?"

Mother-in-law? I didn't know what to reply, and Ursula wasn't expecting me to.

"She knows what's going on here," she continued. "Probably the whole neighborhood knows. You've seen for yourself how Eva's acting. Any moment now she'll be claiming that Jean-Pierre's really *her* child. Madame Raquin has a son who's a widower—no, not the retarded one, the other one. She'd like us to get married. I think it's really Jean-Pierre she's after—she's taken a great fancy to him. She has visions of him taking care of our peaches and her vineyards. Not a bad idea at that."

"Ursula, I don't know what's going on here. I can see that something's wrong, but—"

"Remember our council meeting last year? I've been completely well again for months, but Eva says that Peter is her whole life. *Basta.*"

"And what does Peter say?"

"Why don't you ask what *I* say?"

"I think I know."

"Do you?"

"You wish that council meeting had never been held."

231

She walked across the terrace and sat down on the wall. "I was sitting right here, wasn't I, exactly a year ago. Well, if I could turn back the clock . . ." She broke off.

"What would you do?"

"The same thing. There was no other solution. And now you can ask me what Peter says. Peter says nothing at all. He hopes we can keep everything flexible—adaptable. He still sees people the way a sculptor sees them. As long as we're still clay, still malleable, there's hope. What he'd really like to do is wrap us in wet cloth at night to keep us soft until the next day."

"You mean he can't decide between the two of you?"

She didn't answer.

•

When we got home at five o'clock the next morning, I found a note on my bedside table. "Slept enough. Gone to Cannes to visit friends. Plaza Hotel. Back this evening. Anabel."

Not a word of it was true, I knew that even before I'd finished reading it. But where was she?

In spite of my disappointment and a feeling of having been abandoned, I fell into bed, dead tired as usual. Toward noon a rustling sound at the door woke me up. Someone—probably Jean-Pierre—was trying to slip a piece of paper under the door.

Jerome was still asleep. I got up without making a sound. A telegram. For me. "Call me Hotel Albi Saint-Tropez Anabel."

This time I was lucky, for Jean-Pierre and his fishing gear were immersed in the water cistern and I was able to escape into the orchard without his seeing me. Downhill I went once again, through the lower gate and the olive grove to the square little yellow house. An old Renault was standing at the door and a young man with fair hair was carrying crates of empty bottles out of the house. Probably the widower; the fine curly hair reminded me of his mother. He nodded and glanced at me curiously. The actress! His mother was in the kitchen, he'd fetch her. A glass of wine? No, thank you, no time!

Madame Raquin waddled up, arms spread wide, yellow teeth bared, and kissed me on both cheeks. Another telephone call to England? No, this time to the Hotel Albi in Saint-Tropez, please.

"The Albi? Oh, yes, I have that number," said Madame. "That's the one the young man always calls. Person to person?"

Anabel at Jeannine Dujardin's hotel! What could she possibly be doing there? While Madame turned the crank, shouted and laboriously spelled out "Maclean," I thought about the Brimstone butterfly sitting on Babs's sofa, gently flicking her toes in her sandals, as befits a butterfly. . . .

"*Voilà*, Mademoiselle."

She handed me the receiver and wheezed out of the room.

"Anabel? What in God's name . . ."

"Listen. I've been waiting for hours for you to call. I'd like to get back tonight, but I don't know if I'll make it. If I'm not back by eight, don't worry, it means I'll be staying here and I'll be back tomorrow morning. Tell the others I'm visiting friends at the Plaza Hotel in Cannes. Jerome mustn't know I'm here. Okay?"

"What are you doing there? Are you talking to Jeannine?"

"No, to her husband. He's the key."

She hung up, as abruptly as usual. She never said goodbye. When she was through, she simply hung up, leaving you holding the receiver. A tiny protest pimple sprouted on the so far unblemished skin of my gratitude. She was turning me into a child. Deliberately.

Outside, Madame was waiting. She insisted that I take a glass of wine in the arbor. While she waited for the operator to tell her the charge, I racked my brains over Anabel's puzzling words: "He's the key." Monsieur Dujardin. What was he doing in Saint-Tropez? Had he returned to Paris unexpectedly, found his wife gone, and set off to find her?

Madame came snorting through the leafy arbor entrance, her forehead and upper lip covered with drops of sweat. She plucked a vine leaf and wiped her face, but it crumpled up and little scraps of it stuck to her chin.

"Clean," she said collapsing into her chair. "Nothing's as clean as wine. Even its leaves. Your good health!"

But before I could raise my glass, the foliage parted for the second time and Ursula's head appeared, with Jean-Pierre's yellow crewcut a foot or so below it.

"Come in, come in," called Madame, over-joyed. "Jean-Pierre, bring some glasses—and let my son know!"

She made several unsuccessful efforts to get to her feet, in order to embrace that long beanstalk which was Ursula, gave up, wheezed, thumped her chest and turned a bluish color.

"The sirocco," said Ursula. "Shall I bring your drops?"

Madame gasped for air like a codfish on dry land, shook her head, grabbed Ursula's hand in place of a cold compress and held it to the top of her heaving chest. Ursula, embarrassed and bent double, drew her hand away and stood up straight.

"Here," she said, picking up Madame's glass. "The cure-all."

The old lady pushed it aside. Her eyes were still popping out of her head but her breathing was easier.

"It's not the sirocco," she gasped in my direction as if asking me to be her witness. "It's the constant worry. I'm not going to last much longer and what's going to happen here then?"

Ursula frowned; she knew this was directed at her.

Jean-Pierre returned, followed by Marcel Raquin, whom Madame formally introduced. Four glasses were cermoniously filled. Jean-Pierre glanced at his mother—the fifth remained empty.

"To the boy's health!" wheezed Madame, who had intercepted the glance. We all drank and looked at the blushing towhead, who reached up to Madame Raquin to hide his embarrassment.

"You've got something on your chin," he said, carefully scratching off the specks of green while Madame closed her eyes in bliss.

Suddenly she opened them again and said firmly, "Marcel, show Madame Gürman the new irrigation system. She could do with something like that at her place."

Marcel, who was considerably shorter than Ursula, looked up at her yearningly. Ursula's lips trembled, and she abruptly turned to me, ignoring the others.

"When we bought the hill five years ago, we had no money for that kind of thing, you know. Peter racked his brains and finally came up with a crazy idea. He'd read in the papers that the fleet had docked at Toulon, so he went there and inspected their old pipes. He guessed they would have no use for them, and sure enough, they were just lying around, so they practically gave them away, glad to get rid of them. He hauled them up here—poor old Aesculapius had a hard time, I can tell you— and for months on end it looked as if giant worms were wriggling around the house. One by one, he patched them together, and that's still the only irrigation system we have. It works pretty well though, doesn't it? Anyway, we're proud of it, but maybe it's time to make some changes. So, I'd be interested to see yours, Monsieur Marcel."

"So would I," exclaimed Jean-Pierre, running after them—much to Madame's displeasure.

"A fine young couple!" she declared emphatically, parting the vine to gaze after them. Marcel's head reached just to Ursula's shoulder. "I'm against divorce, I'm a Catholic," she added severely, raising her voice as though her father confessor were in hearing distance. "But in this case . . ."

She pounded the table with her fist, gave me a challenging look, bent forward and hissed, "It's not true that I used to beat up my late husband, people only say that because he was puny and I'm fat. I'd have liked to but I couldn't, he had the strength of a giant when he was drunk. I hated him, all right, because I had one stillbirth after another—all full-term, *that* was the reason, Mademoiselle! They'd lay them down on the sheet, not breathing, all of them full of alcohol—or that's what they looked like to me. And that's why I was happy to see him buried. I didn't shed a tear at his funeral, and people never forgave me, for you're supposed to cry at the funeral, that's the custom here. But when the priest said, 'And now our beloved brother is gone from us forever,' I said aloud, 'Amen!' Just look at the two that survived, Mademoiselle! Upstairs there's one who can't even speak, and out there in the vineyard, Marcel—well, he's all right, thank God, and he's a good son, but the doctor says he can't have any children. Now you see . . ." Her voice grew faint, as if she were repeating something she said to herself a hundred times a day, sitting here in the green arbor. "You see—if we could have Jean-Pierre, there would be no problem. Do you understand me, Mademoiselle?"

I understood but I didn't feel like admitting it, so I got up.

"Nobody but the child's on my side!" exclaimed Madame in despair.

"Jean-Pierre? You mean to say he'd like to change fathers?"

Madame made a slapping gesture, as if my question had been a mosquito.

"*Mais non, mais non!* He wouldn't have to change fathers. His father's right next door and he could go and visit him every day." She drew a deep breath and her voice took on a threatening tone. "But he'd only have one mother—his own mother, Madame Gürman!" She looked at me significantly, bared her teeth in a flash and added, "*And* a grandmother."

•

"That's it for today," exclaimed the painter, grinning. "Do you realize you've been posing for half an hour? You were so wrapped up in yourself that I didn't stop. Didn't you notice?"

I hadn't noticed anything, I was still in the green arbor.

As I opened the studio door to leave, she called after me, "I've just remembered something else about Dujardin. He's supposed to have lived for a long time in India, before the war. He was keen on yogi or yoga—or whatever you call it."

23

When Anabel finally returned from Saint-Tropez at lunchtime the next day, she revealed
only what my urgent questioning managed to
dig out of her. I had to be patient until after
lunch, when she at last beckoned to me and we
wandered toward the olive grove in order to
avoid the others.

But it was too hot to walk, even under the
shade of the trees. We marched side by side
in silence until we found some large flat rocks
down by the stream where we could sit and
dangle our feet in the water.

"Well?" All I knew so far was that she had
spent the first night sitting on the beach—while
we were at the market in Nice just a few miles
away—and that the next morning she had made

the rounds of the hotels until she had finally found Madame Dujardin registered at the Albi.

"And then—what?" The water was cooling my feet but not my impatience.

She was sitting very straight, dressed in a blouse and shorts, letting her long white legs float in the water. She never exposed herself to the sun if she could help it, never got a tan.

"Then the desk clerk called her room. No answer." She broke off a willow branch and waved away the gnats.

"But—what was it that you wanted from her?"

"I wanted to look at her, maybe—speak to her, maybe not. I had no particular plan in mind, I was playing it by ear. You wouldn't understand, you have no ear for that kind of thing."

Another protest pimple was about to sprout —but I decided not to stand up for my ear.

"And then?"

She put down the willow branch and smiled.

"The desk clerk said Madame Dujardin had a friend with her. Perhaps she would know."

"Who's the friend?"

"A Madame Siodmak."

She picked up the willow branch again and swished it methodically in a semicircle around her head. Long slender willow leaves fluttered anxiously through the air, landing hesitantly on the surface of the water as if they knew what was in store for them: the swirling, tossing rush downstream and the final drowning.

So Babs had accompanied Jeannine to

Saint-Tropez—or the other way around. Did Anabel know about Babs's earlier connection with Jerome? Had I ever told her about it? I couldn't remember.

She threw the naked willow branch after its departed leaves and watched them, absorbed, on their course downstream, getting stuck here and there—until they finally disappeared around the riverbend.

I put my hand on her arm to call her attention back to me, to my anguish, to my ordeal—to *me*! After all, she'd come all this way to help me, hadn't she? Yet, since her return from Saint-Tropez I had the extraordinary feeling that she'd forgotten me.

"Anabel—did I ever mention to you that I know Mrs. Siodmak?"

"She told me. She told me about Jerome too." She looked at me and laughed. What was so funny about that? Puzzled and unamused, I watched her in silence, but she paid no attention to me, stared again into the water, thinking aloud.

"I liked her—she seems to have a lot of fun —does only what she likes—or maybe she makes herself like what she does. Anyway, I can't imagine her worrying about anything as long as there's a deck of cards at hand."

"It looks as if you've become fast friends."

"At first sight. She told the desk clerk to ask me to come up—maybe she thought it was you, using a false name! I opened the door and there she was, in bed, her hair tied on top, looking like a black-and-white Easter egg, playing solitaire on her breakfast tray. Those hands!

I've never seen such useless hands. The cards stuck to her fingers like postage stamps. Can she ever really take hold of anything? She was amazed that I knew Jeannine was there, and asked what I wanted of her. I said I was visiting the Gurnemantzes with you and Jerome—and at that she almost upset the tray."

Anabel stopped for a moment, lifted her feet out of the water, let them drop back in, dipped them in and out, smiling to herself. The splashing got on my nerves.

"And then?"

"We talked about you and about you and Jerome—and then, luckily, before I was forced to explain my visit, the telephone rang. The desk clerk. Had Jeannine come back? When was she expected? There was a gentleman downstairs asking for her. Mrs. Siodmak put her hand over the receiver and whispered excitedly, 'Jerome's here.' But, to make sure, she said into the telephone, 'Ask the gentleman's name.' And then ..."

Anabel stopped smiling, drew her legs out of the water and, hugging her knees, frowned and stared ahead. She spoke so quietly that I could hardly hear her above the babbling of the stream.

"And then—her face just fell apart, and I was afraid her jaw would drop on the lace of her bed jacket. I thought, who on earth is she speaking to? What's happening? Why is she so flabbergasted? It couldn't be Jerome, so who could it be? She made a visible effort, gained control of her chin and said to the desk clerk with studied calm, 'Monsieur Dujardin? Yes, of

course I'll speak to him.' She'd completely forgotten me, stared at the cards on the tray, obviously waiting for this man to get on the telephone. I watched her preparing herself, considering possibilities, rejecting them again—and
then she said horasely and all in one breath,
"Jean? Well, well, how are you? What are you
doing here?' She listened for a moment, then
went on with a slightly forced laugh. 'Oh, I see,
Robert told you! How nice! Of course. Why not?
After all, it's no secret. Jeannine's down on the
beach already, I'll tell her as soon as she gets
back. What's your room number? 52? Let me
write it down.' She quickly added that she hoped
they could get together for a drink, but I knew
from the sound of the telephone that he had
hung up. All the same she said, 'Well, goodbye,
Jean,' into thin air before replacing the receiver."

●

Six years later, after the war, Babs told me her
version of the scene. Once again I was sitting by
the water, but this time not on rocks under a
willow tree but in a padded lounge chair beside
a bright-blue Hollywood swimming pool. Robert
Siodmak had made it in Hollywood, directing
first-class films which everyone except Babs admired. "I can't stand your pictures," she used to
say, which made him laugh, but she now ran an
imposing establishment, a combination of Amer-
icanized comfort and European coziness, and a
permanent haven for European refugees, suc-
cessful ones as well as lame ducks.

But in spite of her new mink coat and a garden full of orange trees, Babs missed her stronghold, the café. Cafés didn't exist in Hollywood, because there were no pedestrians—everyone rode around in cars—and you can't have a café without passersby to comment on. "Where's my Paradise?" she would sigh. "My café! The place where you can get away from home without having to be in the fresh air!"

Glumly, she would sit beside her pool, lower herself reluctantly down the ladder into the water and "swim," not horizontally, but standing erect, her head held high, hair piled on top.

I can't remember how the subject of Saint-Tropez came up. Perhaps we'd been talking about Jerome . . .

"God, what a day that was! It started early in the morning when that girl friend of yours suddenly burst in on me! When the desk clerk said a lady was asking for Jeannine, I thought of course it was you! And then that woman showed up—with those eyes! She gave me such a shock that I laid out my solitaire all wrong and of course it didn't come out and messed up the entire day. I knew at once she was there to spy on us for some reason—and just at that moment Jean Dujardin called. He was an old friend of mine, he'd just come back from India and wanted to join Jeannine and me for a few days. So touching! He always was such a very warm, loving person. While I was talking to him, I noticed that that woman—what's her name again?"

"Anabel Maclean."

"Yes—that she ate me up with those black

eyes of hers. What on earth is she after, I asked myself, what's she doing here? I bet she's up to something! So I said to her, 'Maybe we'll come over to visit you all, Jeannine and I. After all, I knew the Gurnemantzes from way back in Paris!' At that she had the nerve to say, 'Don't you do anything of the sort—you've caused enough trouble already!' And she flounced out of the room. I wanted to run after her and ask her what she meant by 'making trouble.' I'd only come to Saint-Tropez with Jeannine so she wouldn't be alone—she and I often used to spend a few days there together—but my cards had got all mixed up and I had to straighten them out first. I looked for her all day in the hotel but she'd gone. Was she really a friend of yours?"

●

But Anabel wasn't gone. She stayed in the hotel, that day and the following night too. As Babs suspected, she was up to something. Something in Room 52.

"I knocked. No one called 'Come in!' but the door wasn't locked. As I walked in, an extraordinary feeling came over me. The huge living room was empty—the door to the balcony stood open. I crossed the room on tiptoe—I don't know why. Did I want to catch him unawares? He was sitting on a chair in the shade, facing me, and he didn't look at all surprised to see me standing at the balcony door. He was waiting for Jeannine, of course, yet I felt certain he was waiting for me."

She thought a while before continuing.

"I can't describe the way I felt. I'd known plenty of men before I met Bill, and I thought I was pretty good at classifying them at first sight. I always knew right away who was a possibility and who wasn't and which ones might become dangerous. But this man was something else again, much more disturbing than anybody I'd ever met, he was a magnet—and at the same time unapproachable, and right there in the balcony doorway I'd blundered into his magnetic field. I can't even describe to you what he looked like, although I sat opposite him for several hours. His arms were resting on the arms of the chair, his hands hanging loose—that much I remember. He gave you the impression of having no life in him—and yet some kind of current was crackling around him or passing back and forth between us, as if I were hooked up to some electrical machine.

"'Welcome!' he said, without moving. I stepped outside into the sun and sat down on the other chair. Everything I did required an effort and yet I was compelled to do it. Something commanded me. 'My name's Anabel Maclean,' I said. He nodded. 'I've come to speak to your wife.' He nodded again. And that was all I had to say, my head was empty. I remember thinking, it's a good thing I told him my name because right now I don't even know it anymore. What am I called? Who am I? I couldn't for the life of me remember. I sat up straight in my chair, I saw him without really taking him in, I saw the sea without seeing it. Have you ever been given an anesthetic? It was like the last few seconds before you're extinguished—you know everything that's happening, you can still feel everything, but you can't make use of it. No, that's not quite correct, for there *was* one thing I did know, one thing I did feel: I wanted to hear his voice! He had only spoken that one word: 'Welcome!' I have no idea how long I sat there or how long the silence lasted."

She turned and looked at me as though I had just said something uncanny. "Hypnosis? Have you ever been hypnotized?"

"No. I'm scared of that sort of thing. Once at the house of some friends I met a man who was hypnotizing people. But I stayed out of it, I was afraid I might fall asleep forever."

She turned away and stared into the stream again. I stared too. The tangled reflection of willows and sky, constantly moving yet remaining the same, had a slightly hypnotic effect of its own. One couldn't sit there and look at something else, one's eyes were irresistibly drawn to the water, held by it.

"Then he spoke, but I can't tell you exactly what he said. I'm not keeping things back, I simply don't know. Ever since, I've been trying to nail down exactly what it was. Something to the effect that he wanted to talk to me but not right then. Later. I said that it was imperative for him to know that Jeannine—that Jerome—that you—but I stuttered and lost track of what I was saying, and in the end I didn't even know what I'd come for anymore. Something made me get up, walk through the balcony door across the big living room and out into the hallway. I'd already reserved a room. I lay down on the bed. There was only one clear thought in my mind: He wants to see me again this afternoon at five, on the balcony. That is, he'd commanded me to be there. Until then I could sleep."

•

Beside the pool in Hollywood, six years later, Babs leaned back against the white cushions and filled me in about Jeannine's return from the beach that morning, while Anabel was sleeping. Jeannine's bedroom was next to Babs's, the door between the two rooms was ajar, and there was the Brimstone butterfly, laughing, sweaty, with sand sticking to her legs, her yellow hair like wet straw.

"Jean's here," said Babs. Jeannine stopped laughing and leaned against the door, looking cross.

"That's all I needed," she muttered. "Couldn't he have stayed a few days longer in— in wherever the hell he was? He's been gone three months, I was beginning to wonder if something had happened to him. Now, who let the cat out of the bag about Jerome? Probably Roger, that sneaky secretary of his, the dirty little swine!" She laughed again. "Maybe there'll be another cockfight like that time in Madrid. You'd better warn Jerome, Jean's left-handed, with a mean uppercut. He gave Rodriguez a cauliflower ear to remember him by. Oh well, I'd better go and see him. Let's get it over with."

Babs could hear her in the bathroom whistling the "Toreador" song from *Carmen*.

Half an hour later she reappeared in the doorway, bathed and her hair done.

"Room 52? Okay. I think I'll tell him to go to hell. What does he mean, showing up like this out of the blue, making trouble—"

"Be careful," said Babs. "My solitaire didn't come out."

"*Merde* on your solitaire!" said Jeannine, and Babs could hear her whistling as she walked down the hallway. Only then did it occur to her that she ought to have told Jeannine about the visit of that extraordinary woman. . . .

Sighing, she had put the cards away for the day, had dressed and had gone to the hotel beauty shop to have her hair washed. When she came back, Jeannine was in her room.

"Well—how did it go?" Babs asked.

Jeannine turned a white, fragile little face toward her, her mouth open, her eyes terror-sticken. Instead of the radiant Brimstone butterfly, there hovered a plain cabbage white, utterly defeated, facing the end of its short life span.

"What happened?" exclaimed Babs, aghast. "Did he hit you?"

Jeannine shook her head.

"That would have been better," she whispered. "Even a cauliflower ear would have been better—you can hide that under your hair."

"For God's sake—what did he do?"

"He didn't *do* anything." She went over to the bed and collapsed on top of it as if she had just run several miles. "You know Jean, don't

249

you? But you'd never recognize him, he's completely changed, he's . . ." Her voice trailed away.

Babs, wide-eyed, sat down beside her on the bed.

"I know what you mean. This morning on the telephone, it was Jean—and it wasn't Jean. He sounded most peculiar."

Jeannine was slowly recovering, and the color was coming back to her cheeks. She clutched Babs's hand, the Botticelli hand, as if it were made of steel.

She had marched into Room 52, Jeannine said, whistling away. There was no one in the living room—but something had caught her by the throat, made her cough and choke, and snuffed out the whistling. At first she thought she'd swum out too far that morning, because her legs suddenly seemed to be made of lead. It took all her strength to walk across to the balcony door. Jean was sitting there in the shade, and the shade was so deep that she hardly recognized him and yet it was broad daylight, noontime. He hadn't uttered a word of greeting, although he hadn't seen her for three months, nor did he invite her to sit down, but she managed to make it as far as the empty chair in the sun. It was probably the heat that made her breathless and parched, so much so that it cost her a real effort to say, "Hello, Jean." She had intended to add, "What are you doing here?" but the words stuck in her throat.

At this point in her story Babs stood up and paced back and forth beside the swimming pool.

The very memory was too disturbing for her to sit still. At last she came to a stop in front of me.

"Do you believe in that sort of thing?"

"What sort of thing?"

"You know—extrasensory perception or whatever it's called."

"No. Even bona-fide, old-established ghosts take off when I enter a haunted house."

"I'm not talking about ghosts! I'm talking about those powers, powers one is supposed to be able to acquire—"

"Like voodoo in Haiti?"

"Or Indian fakirs."

"Well, that's different, you have to believe in them because you can see them with your own eyes, sitting there for weeks at a time with their arms raised up like withered branches—"

"Exactly," said Babs. "It seems, out there, on that balcony, there was the same sort of atmosphere as looking at a fakir—although Jeannine knew all the time it was only Jean and nobody else and she even remembered how he'd always bored her—and she couldn't understand herself, because he was really quite fascinating —at least that's what she thought for a moment. She wanted to say something nice to him, but she never got the chance. He spoke, apparently only a few sentences, she couldn't remember the exact words, but she got the message all right: He never wanted to see her again except once—that very evening, and only for a few minutes. She was to say yes or no. In any case she was to take the early-morning train back to Paris, pack her things and leave the apartment.

Roger would be there. Divorce. If she accepted his one condition, she could take her jewelry out of the safe. She would receive three thousand francs a month, enough to live on. No more. If she didn't agree to the condition, she would have no claim to anything."

"What was the condition?"

Jeannine had sat up, said Babs, staring ahead with eyes full of hatred.

"I don't understand it," she kept repeating. "If he never wants to see me again, then what does it matter to him?"

"What does what matter to him?" Babs had cried and freed her hand from Jeannine's iron grip. Jeannine didn't need support anymore, she looked perfectly all right, she was even laughing—full of hatred and a bit mad—but she was laughing.

"He's only a little man, after all. However much he may have learned in India, he hasn't grown an inch! He always was a humorless son of a bitch." She buried her hands in her hair, shaking with laughter. "His one condition—the little man's revenge—his one condition—"

Now she was screaming, couldn't stop. Babs ran into the bathroom, got a glass of water and threw it in her face. She made no protest, stopped screaming, dried her face, giggling to herself.

"His condition: that I never see Jerome again!" Babs had remained silent, she had expected worse. "It's okay with me!" shouted Jeannine, as though Dujardin could still hear her. "I don't give a damn. Jerome's not that important to me. It's a pity, of course—there's something about him that I like very much. Oh well, I'll get over it. However, come to think of it, I can only speak for myself in this business. After all, Jerome has some say in this too, hasn't he? Jean can't order *him* around, can he? Maybe Jerome doesn't want to give me up—I can't help that, can I? And Jerome doesn't care whether I have any money or not. *I* care though, I must admit! I was poor too long."

•

The shade was growing deeper inside the stream, the water was almost too cold. Only the rocks we were sitting on still glowed with heat. Anabel had her eyes closed as if she were lying on her bed at the Hotel Albi, sleeping, as Monsieur Dujardin had ordered her to do.

"Just before five I woke up and went to Room 52. Now the living room and the entire balcony were in the shade. He was still sitting in the same place—in fact, I had the impression that he hadn't moved since I'd left that morning. Again that strange feeling of something tugging at me and propelling me forward—I felt it as soon as I entered the room, and on the balcony it was even stronger, as if I were being pulled forward by the hair, though it didn't hurt, in fact it was rather pleasant, like letting yourself be blown along by the wind on the seashore. The chair I'd sat on that morning was now standing next to his, and something steered me irresistibly toward that chair. I sat down and he smiled. How can I describe that smile to you? I felt more secure, more tranquil, than I've felt for a long, long time."

She stopped, lifted her head as if somebody had just called her name. "It's still with me— not quite the velvety feeling I had at the time, but I still know exactly what it was like. I was twelve when my mother died, that's how far back I have to go to remember anything similar. Then he made me speak. I say 'made me speak' because that's just the way it was. Like in the Bible. The Lord said: 'Speak!' and whoever had the honor—spoke.

"I told him about Jerome—but he raised his hand. Again I was reminded of the Bible: He knew! There was no need to tell him anything. I believed him, although I couldn't explain it to myself. Perhaps he'd seen Jeannine in between! He guessed what I was thinking and nodded, yes, he'd seen her. Aha, that explains it, I thought and was at the same time surprised that I still needed explanations! He looked at me and smiled again. This time it was as if someone were gently massaging my back, stroking my spine until every nerve responded. That's why I was able to tell him about you. He listened. I've never seen anyone listen like that—everything I said seemed to drop into a deep well, sending an echo to the surface. Things came to my mind that I really knew nothing about and yet I heard myself telling them. A lot of things became clear, others were confused—and remained confused. He never said a word, didn't even nod, but I knew he understood everything."

"Did you tell him about Ferencsi?"

Had she heard me?

"Ferencsi!" I repeated. "Did you tell him?"

Her face, up to now wide open, vulnerable, became guarded. "Yes, I told him."

"What did he say?"

She let her straight eyelashes descend over her eyes the way a jeweler drops his iron shutter to protect his property from burglars. She was about to lie and I had no wish to listen.

"He made no comment, no suggestions. Then he talked about Jerome." I hung on her lips once again. "He's had a look at the three pictures Jerome left at the gallery in Paris and he thinks they're good. He's willing to give him a show."

I jumped to my feet, grabbed her by her shoulders, forgot everything she had said, took in one thing alone: Jerome would have a show at Dujardin's! I shook her furiously, ecstatically. "Why didn't you tell me at once? Don't you understand, this is going to be—"

"Wait. There's a snag."

She freed herself from my grip, turned her face away.

"What? What?"

"Jerome can have a show at Dujardin's—quite soon, too, in October—if he undertakes never to see Jeannine again and not to get in touch with her."

That was what she called a snag? An exhibition—*and* Jeannine out of the way! I threw myself at her, shouted, cried, sobbed—suddenly felt apprehensive. Had I misunderstood anything? Or was she holding something back?

"Anabel—what's the snag?"

"What—do you think—is Jerome going to say?"

I sat down again, thought it over, putting the question to him in my mind.

"He'll—accept."

"And—you are willing to tell him?"

I didn't answer. So that was the snag.

"Can't Dujardin tell him?"

She shook her head.

I got up again, walked a few steps, stared into the water, saw nothing but the snag.

Then I heard her voice, her arid voice: *"I'll tell him."*

24

The question was: When was she going to tell him? How long was she going to keep me on tenterhooks?

I didn't dare to ask. Our easy, volatile intimacy of old was now extinct. Difficult to remember that only a few weeks ago in London I'd been sitting opposite that yellow wing chair, unloading my troubles without having to think twice, without the smallest doubt that she would understand, sympathize and help. She was still "on my side"—but surrounded by an atmosphere of silence, or rather of withdrawal, far away from me, from all of us.

•

When we emerged from the olive grove and walked up the hill in the late afternoon we found Jerome and the three Gurnemantzes on the terrace, sitting stiffly on chairs in a semi-circle. Opposite them sat a young man with glasses and a receding chin and next to him a woman, also with glasses and a receding chin, in skirt and stockings despite the heat, a Monsieur Vallé and his sister, partners in an art gallery in Nice whom Peter had invited to show Jerome's work. As we approached, however, there was no mention of his canvases; the topic was "political commitment in the visual arts." No opening there for olive trees, gypsies and foreign legionnaires.

Eva was talking eagerly, Peter was doing his best, Ursula wasn't, Jerome never said a word, kept staring at his three neglected "children" propped against the pine tree. Just you wait, I thought, those three are going to hang in one of the biggest galleries in Paris, beautifully framed and lighted, and people will stand in front of them, lost in admiration—just you wait!

The chinless couple were by now holding forth about the sociological impact of painting while we all sat speechless and halfwitted, wondering how we'd survive supper in their company.

Eva disappeared into the kitchen, and Aesculapius and Jean-Pierre were introduced as conversational reinforcements. On the pretext of helping Eva, I went after her and piled plates and glasses on the tray, never taking my eyes off the terrace. Anabel was sitting next to Jerome —but they weren't talking. Nor did they when the meal was over. The Gurnemantz trio accompanied the guests down to the road to make sure they really left. I went along so that Jerome and Anabel were left alone on the terrace. In vain. Looking back from the garden gate I thought I saw a white silhouette entering the house, and when we returned, Jerome was alone.

One last glass of Pernod for the men. We lay on the mattresses, exhausted.

"Perhaps I should give up," said Jerome. "Start something else, the way you did. Aesculapius is getting old. I could carry the baskets back and forth."

"Aesculapius is in the prime of life. You don't know the first thing about donkeys, though you may be one yourself. You must never give up. Your work's good. I've sent off that note to the Nouveaux Artistes. Get on with it, go to Saint-Tropez, they'll be expecting you."

Saint-Tropez! It wasn't only the gallery that was expecting Jerome. The Hotel Albi was expecting him too—Jeannine in her room, and Dujardin on his balcony . . .

"Anabel!" I screamed soundlessly. "For God sake, hurry!"

●

Next morning Jerome left our bedroom very early and without explanation. From the window I watched him walk to the terrace and sit down on the wall, waiting. Before long, somebody was bound to see him there and get breakfast.

I made the beds, hung up clothes and

cleaned up the bathroom. When I looked out again, a female figure was approaching the terrace. Anabel. She stopped in front of him, evidently saying something, whereupon he nodded and stood up. At last! Relieved and cowardly, I remained behind my window, watching. Anabel knew what to do, Anabel would pull it off. This was the right moment to tell him—though surely not on the terrace! Surely they would go somewhere where they'd be undisturbed! Correct. They were leaving. I retreated hastily from the window, because they were walking in my direction—was she going to talk to him in her own room? No, they walked past the guest rooms, looking straight ahead, not speaking, past the house, toward the orchard gate and along the straight shady path, several hundred yards long, framed by olive trees.

By now they were obviously talking. Jerome stopped and said something while Anabel walked on. He caught up with her—she stopped, turned toward him and spoke. I only knew she was talking from the movements of her hands, because, already halfway to the gate, they had turned into small figures without face or features. Now it looked as if she was asking him to go on further, but Jerome leaned against an olive tree—I could hardly make him out in its deep shade—while Anabel, in her light blouse, remained standing in the middle of the path, clearly recognizable in the light filtering through the branches. She was still speaking—urgently, it seemed to me. Now she took a step backward, as if fending off what he was saying. He stepped out of the shadows, walked up to her, raised his hand and slapped her in the face. She fell sideways to one knee and collapsed on the ground.

I ran out of the room. Halfway along the path, Jerome was coming toward me. He grabbed me by the arm.

"Let go of me!" I screamed, pushing him away, but he held me tight by the wrists. I tried to break free but he held on, his face and his burning, stricken eyes close to mine.

"Don't listen to what she's saying," he whispered. "Don't listen to her—she's trying to break us up—don't listen—don't believe her—"

He couldn't hold me any longer. I tore myself free—or perhaps he let me go—and I ran toward Anabel, was was still lying on the ground, though not in the way she had fallen. She had put herself on her back, her arms extended sideways, as if crucified. I bent over her, but she made no move, just lay there, eyes open, staring up into the branches. I looked for marks on her face but there weren't any. There were tears, though, running sideways past her temples into her hair.

I knelt down beside her, begging her to get up, to tell me why Jerome had hit her.

"You know why," she said quietly.

I jumped up and ran back to the house. When I opened the door to our room, he was lying on the bed, hands clasped behind his head. I closed the door and leaned against it, didn't want to get any closer to him.

"You've hit her in the face—I saw you. How could you hit her? You can't do that—"

"Do what?"

"Hit a woman—a woman who has nothing to do with you—"

"Anabel hasn't anything to do with me?"

"Of course she hasn't. You can hit your own wife if you have to, but—"

"If you have to, you can also hit a woman who has nothing to do with you." He spoke quite quietly. A different person.

"Why did you have to? She hasn't done you any harm. She only told you about Dujardin's offer. You know very well that she only went to Saint-Tropez to help me."

He gave me a long, sad, searching look.

"Yes, I know. I'm sorry. I shouldn't have done it."

"You should tell *her* that, not me." He nodded slowly. "Will you tell her?" He nodded again and smiled. "Well then—come."

He sat up, put his feet on the floor, rested his elbows on his knees and let his head fall on his hands. I waited at the door. I should have felt relieved, the "snag" was now a thing of the past. She had told him—and so he'd hit her. Understandable enough. What was worrying me then?

What was worrying me was that it *wasn't* understandable that he should have hit her. He was still sitting on the bed, his face buried in his hands. And what about the exhibition at Dujardin's? Maybe he hadn't taken it in—or was he more involved with Jeannine than I wanted to admit? Was that what was worrying me? No. It was a weird feeling, as if I didn't know him at all. Or Anabel either.

He raised his head and got up. Together, we left the house and walked along the path. She was sitting in the grass under an olive tree, calmly watching us approach and stop beside her. She didn't look at me, only at Jerome. He repeated the words he had spoken in the bedroom as though he had learned them by heart: "I'm sorry. I shouldn't have done that."

She made no answer, just kept looking at him. He gave her a little nod as if to say, "Okay?" And I thought for a second, but they're playing a game! There was no need for him to apologize —she's not a woman who has nothing to do with him, she's an ally, she's Jerome's ally, not mine!

He gave the same little nod to me as though asking, "Will that do?" Then he left.

I sat down on the ground beside Anabel, tearing up blades of grass around me.

She followed Jerome with her eyes until he disappeared on the terrace. Then she leaned back against the tree trunk.

"I haven't told you why I stayed over in Saint-Tropez last night."

I had never even given it a thought! Of course. Hadn't she said she was going to see Dujardin again at five?

"That was again an extraordinary thing." She was relaxed and spoke slowly and thoughtfully, as though nothing had happened on this beautiful morning to disturb her peace of mind. Jerome hadn't hit her, Jerome didn't exist, I didn't exist, she had erased us. She wasn't talking to anyone in particular; I had the uncomfortable feeling that if I hadn't been sitting beside her, she would have spoken aloud in exactly the same way. "That afternoon, when I was sitting on the balcony with him, I saw him close his eyes, as though his eyelids had suddenly become too heavy. Before I had time to stand up, he said, with his eyes closed and without the least attempt at an apology, 'Please go now, I'll expect you at ten o'clock.' And I left. It didn't seem at all impolite that he didn't get up to see me out. I had the feeling that he couldn't because he wasn't on the balcony anymore, he was somewhere else, somewhere far away. I slept until shortly before ten. Very soundly.

"This time he was standing by the balcony railing, looking out at the dark sea. The table was laid. There was a bottle of wine in a cooler but only one wine glass. For me. He drank only water. We ate, almost without talking. There was only a lantern on the table—one could hardly see one's plate. The waiter went to and fro without a sound, like a shadow, as if he were barefooted. Later I noticed that he *was* barefooted. His face was dark above his white jacket —an Indian. The concierge told me afterward that Monsieur Dujardin had brought him and installed him in an adjoining room. Only the Indian was allowed to wait on him.

"The night air was completely still. Somehow the food disappeared and then the table. Only the lantern was left on the floor between our two chairs. Later on he extinguished it and we sat in the dark, but I had no trouble seeing him, perhaps because I could hear his voice so clearly."

She chewed thoughtfully at her upper lip.

"Now, in broad daylight, it's hard to describe what they were like, those hours up there on the balcony. He would talk for a long time, then remain silent for a long time. I said very little. I had the feeling that he knew all about me. He told me what it was that had originally taken him to India: copies of Sanskrit manuscripts in the Delhi museum. And there, in Delhi, he had met the guru, the man who had opened the door to a new existence by teaching him that it's possible to gain complete mastery of the body and the mind. Right at the start, he said, he was amazed and fascinated by one of the guru's teachings: 'It's a mistake to believe that we've achieved everything when we've learned to love our fellow men. The most important thing is to understand our enemy. Our friends have nothing to teach us. We *learn* only from our enemies.' Jeannine, his wife, was his enemy. For the first time in his married life he gave up all attempts to change her or dominate her; instead he tried to understand her—and learn from her. And so, after spending two months in India, he believed he was already well on the way to salvation and inviolable harmony, but when he returned to Paris, his peace of mind slowly ebbed away and he found himself more vulnerable and more emasculated than ever before. At the same time some sort of calamity occurred—I didn't quite understand what it was and didn't want to ask, something physical, a fight or perhaps a duel—anyway, it had to do with his wife, that much I understood. It made him decide to go back to India and study seriously and for as long as it would take to extricate and redeem himself once and for all. Soon he would go back there again, he said; one needed the landscape and the "brothers" from time to time, and the austere life in the cool, low, rambling house. 'How does one learn?' I asked. 'How do you go about it?' 'There are lots of ways,' he said, 'but they all lead to the same goal. Every teacher has his own methods. Mine was a young man, the only young man among many old ones. I chose him because I thought his mind might still be flexible, more tolerant in dealing with my European foolishness. I was wrong there. He was the most uncompromising one of them all.'

"I interrupted him. 'How did you start?' I had to know that, I absolutely had to know the point of departure.

" 'He led me into a white room, empty except for a table and a chair. The table was covered with a green cloth, completely smoothed out, not a wrinkle or a seam to catch the eye or divert the brain. For that's the whole point: The brain has to be starved into surrender. Only then does it learn to obey and become subordinate to the will. I sat down on the chair and he placed a matchstick on the green cloth. "Look at the match on the cloth. Think only of it, the match, the cloth, nothing else. *Think*: the match. *Think*: the cloth." That's all. The moment your thoughts wander, the moment you begin to think: "I'm sitting uncomfortably" or "I'm bored" or "What am I doing here?" the exercise is over. Then you start all over again.'

" 'How long did you manage it?'

" 'Seven seconds the first time. Later ten minutes. Now as long as I like.'

"The matchstick, the cloth, the white room, the brothers, the landscape—seven seconds—I wondered if I could do it too.

" 'Of course you can,' he said, and it no longer surprised me that he always knew what I was thinking. Then he began to speak again, for the first and only time in an urgent tone—and at once his shape and his face darkened and seemed to melt away until I couldn't see him anymore. Even his voice came from far away and I couldn't understand everything, however hard I tried. I mustn't go back to London, he said, that would be dangerous for me, I must stay here or go to Paris—or to India. There I'd be safe. I said—or perhaps I only thought—'But I must go back to London! Bill— Nina—'

"He said, 'Your husband and your daughter are better off without you than with you,' and those words I heard again quite clearly because I knew he was right. They were singing in my ear, those words, as though he were repeating them over and over: 'Your husband and your daughter are better off without you than with you.'

"I made no attempt to contradict him. Why should I? I'd always known it—but always accompanied by hatred. Now I saw it without hatred, crystal-clear. That's what made it so awful.

"Again he said something about danger in London, repeated that I mustn't go back there on any account. But I could hear no echo inside myself, I was empty, the connection had been cut off. The matchstick on the green cloth . . ." She turned her face toward me and laughed. "It's funny—wherever I look now, right at this moment for instance, there's his face and there's the matchstick on the green cloth. Over there is the terrace—and in front of it I see the matchstick and the cloth—"

I followed her glance and saw figures moving, waving, then a shout: "Where are you? Come and get it!"

We got up.

•

Breakfast. The huge coffee pot was passed from hand to hand, milk, sugar, the long, thin, golden-brown loaf of French bread from which everyone tore off a hunk, honey to spread on it, yogurt for Jean-Pierre, a bucket of carrots for Aesculapius, an egg for me—"because you're a spoiled brat."

"I'm going to Saint-Tropez today," said Jerome to Eva. "Can you drive me to the station?"

"I'll take you," said Peter.

Anabel broke off a piece of bread and smiled at me. Had she heard what Jerome had just said?

"If you pack fast, you can catch the eleven-twenty," said Peter.

"I don't need to pack," said Jerome. "I'm not staying over. Today is market day, isn't it? I'll take a late train back and meet you all at the market."

They got up. Jerome bent down, kissed me quickly on the cheek, waved to the others and followed Peter to the garage.

I ate my egg, drank my coffee and sat on for a while. Even after the table had been cleared, I still couldn't move.

"It's a good thing he's going," said Anabel. "In fact, it's necessary."

Was she still my friend? Jerome had gone and here she was using words like "good" and "necessary." I gave her a hostile look. She smiled.

"You've forgotten. Jeannine's left by now."

I closed my eyes. What was the matter with me? Of course, Dujardin had ordered her to leave. Still, just in case: "Are you sure she's gone?"

"I was standing yesterday morning by the desk in the lobby when I heard the doorman say, 'A taxi for Madame Dujardin.' Then came a lot of luggage and then came Jeannine. Alone. The doorman said, 'I hope we'll see you again soon, Madame,' and she walked right past him. Bellboys jumped to attention, the porter loaded her luggage—the taxi driver had to help him—she got in, no tips, not a word of thanks, and banged the door. The doorman, the bellboys and the porter stood outside watching the taxi drive away."

Exit the Brimstone butterfly. Beautiful, bright-yellow, sporting in the sunshine—but short-lived.

"What will Jerome do when he gets to the Albi and they tell him she's left? Will he go on to the Nouveaux Artistes?"

"Perhaps. But there are other possibilities at the Albi."

●

"At first I was really happy to hear Jerome's voice when he called," said Babs, reliving those fateful days at Saint-Tropez as she swam the prescribed ten lengths slowly and with dignity in her Hollywood pool. Every one of her movements was an order to the water: "You to the right—and you to the left." Everybody in Hollywood swam, some full of vigor and body-building ambition, spanking and flogging the water, others, like Babs, because in California it was the thing to do. "He (or she) swims every day" was a solid character reference.

"I thought of returning to Paris with Jeannine, but Robert said on the telephone it was so hot there that the asphalt had started to melt and people's shoes got stuck in it, so I decided to stay on for a few days. And the very next day, out of the clear blue sky—Jerome."

Babs grabbed the ladder, declined a helping hand, climbed panting out of the pool, gave the gleaming blue water a last dirty look and sighed.

"When I think how well I felt in the old unhealthy days ..."

She stretched out on the cushioned chaise lounge, covered her face with Nivea cream and closed her eyes.

"You know, Jerome and I had always been able to laugh together—but not this time. I had to tell him the whole story, about Dujardin and Jeannine, every detail of it. He wanted to call Paris immediately and talk to her. I said, 'Do you want to ruin her life? Can you keep her?' Whereupon he sat at my desk and started to write her a letter. I said, 'Jerome, *no one* writes to Jeannine, don't you know that? One takes her out, one goes to bed with her—but one doesn't *write* to her!' And so he just sat there, his head in his hands—I'd never known him like that before. And yet I don't think it was anything to do with love, that's not Jerome's cup of tea at all—though half-finished affairs can be dangerous, but that wasn't it, either. He was in a fix, he was at Dujardin's mercy twice over. That was it. Finally he said—and I believed him —'I could kill that man!' "

●

Nonetheless he went to see him. That very day. For when he came down to the lobby after seeing Babs, the Indian was waiting for him. Jerome told me about it later. The man had suddenly appeared, blocking Jerome's way. "What do you want?" Instead of an answer, the Indian pointed to the elevator. The bell captain intervened.

"This is Monsieur Dujardin's valet."

Jerome's stored-up hatred exploded into the dark face. "You can tell your master to go to hell."

But the man didn't move.

"He doesn't understand French, or English either, Monsieur," said the bell captain.

Jerome had the feeling that the Indian

understood every word, although the dark liquid eyes stared blankly ahead. The man turned and walked toward the elevator. Jerome followed.

The elevator was crowded; Jerome and the dark-skinned man stood chest to chest. Jerome's narrow nomad's eyes glared malevolently into the shiny black ones close to him, but they were met and deflected by an impenetrable wall of tranquillity. The Indian just stood there, calm and gentle, his shoulders relaxed. Silently he glided along the hallway in front of Jerome, stopped outside a door and opened it without knocking.

Dujardin was sitting at the desk in the living room as if he were in his office. Brochures, weighty tomes and catalogues were stacked neatly in front of him. Dark suit, white shirt, glasses, the French businessman. He stood up courteously and held out his hand across the desk.

"Dujardin."

Jerome thought it unnecessary to introduce himself. This man had sent his servant to fetch him. All right then. He ignored Dujardin's hand and his gesture to sit down, and remained standing in front of the desk.

Dujardin sat down and began to speak, curtly, in short spasms. He had a pen in his hand with which he checked off items on a sheet of paper. Not that he exactly avoided looking at Jerome, but it was the paper that claimed his attention.

"Mr. Lorrimer—I saw three of your paintings in Paris. Unfortunately only three."

"I have three more here," said Jerome involuntarily—and bit his lip.

"Good. Send them to me in Paris. I already appreciated their quality from the first three. I like your themes too. I need a figural exhibition after the last abstract ones. At the moment I'm showing primitive Asiatic art, Persian and Indian miniatures. I can offer you October first, that is, the first three weeks of October, a good date for sales."

Jerome listened quietly.

"My proposal: The gallery will retain twenty-five percent of the proceeds and will assume all costs, including framing. How many paintings would you have available?"

Jerome opened his mouth—but remained silent. Dujardin continued as if he had received an answer.

"Twenty-five is a good number. No sense in hanging them too close. In my gallery every painting has room to breathe and is individually lighted by a wall spotlight."

Jerome moistened his dry lips with his tongue.

"I think you'll be satisfied with the frames —our man works for the Louvre. Of course it would do no harm to let us have another five canvases to hold in reserve, because we may easily sell out. Now, about the catalogue: a color reproduction on the cover and four black-and-whites inside. I'd like you to leave the choice to me; I know my clients and their taste. We'll send out over two thousand catalogues. I hope you will attend the vernissage. That is always important."

Jerome stared at him, bracing himself against the desk with both hands, leaning forward, trying to force Dujardin to look at him. Dujardin lifted his face, the eyes behind the glasses questioning, neutral, courteously interested.

"What about Jeannine?" snarled Jerome.

Dujardin took off his glasses and polished them carefully with his handkerchief.

I've got you! thought Jerome.

Durjardin put his glasses back on.

"I also need a short curriculum vitae and a photograph. For the back of the catalogue."

Jerome leaned over the desk and grabbed at his collar, at his neck, shaking him, choking him. Dujardin offered no resistance. His glasses fell off, revealing myopic eyes which looked at him unseeingly. Jerome let go, stood still for a moment, shaking. Then he bent down and picked up the glasses. The bridge was broken. Someone took them out of his hand; the Indian was standing behind him.

Jerome walked slowly toward the door. As he reached it, he heard Dujardin's voice: "Mr. Lorrimer, I'll expect your three paintings in Paris toward the end of the week. Our transport agent will collect the others in London. Please leave your address with the desk clerk."

•

Jerome took off his shoes, rolled up his trousers and walked slowly along the beach, letting the water wash over his feet. At this time of day, siesta time, Saint-Tropez was dead.

He wasn't hungry. Nobody is hungry after losing a battle. He kicked at the water with his feet. His troops were decimated, his ammunition spent. Bound hand and foot, he had accepted the victor's terms—the fulfillment of all his, Jerome's, dreams. The irony of it! *Vae victis*.

He sat down under a deserted beach umbrella and watched a couple of fishing boats riding at anchor, their green paint, striped with red, reflected in the rippling water. Van Gogh, he thought. He'd have liked that. Automatically he felt in his pocket for a pencil. No sketchbook, damn it.

Jeannine. He forced himself to think of her. She was in a mess and it was all because of him. My fault, as usual, he thought without bitterness or remorse. On second thought he decided that for once it *wasn't* his fault if she was left high and dry; after all, he hadn't exactly found her in church, she knew what she was doing! Nor would she remain on her own for long; Jeannine was a born survivor. And as far as her connection with the man upstairs at the Albi was concerned, that had been ruptured long ago. He had ignored Jerome's question—"What about Jeannine?"—not because he was bleeding from a wound too painful to touch upon but because he didn't seem to remember who it was Jerome was talking about. That was what had enraged Jerome to the point of knocking his glasses off his nose, and the man had sat there, naked, at his mercy —if only for a moment. But that moment was worth it.

He stood up and looked at his watch. Soon

the shops would be raising their shutters and reopening their doors. He waded through the sand back to the sea wall.

When he entered the Nouveaux Artistes gallery, his trousers were still rolled up and he was carrying his shoes.

The gallery was empty.

"My paintings, please."

The man in the office, who looked like an Italian, heavyset, sturdy, hair parted in the middle, looked at him in surprise. Wasn't this the young man who had knocked so modestly at his door in the morning?

"I haven't had time to look at them yet. Why don't you come back in a few days' time—"

"No, thanks, I'll take them along now."

"Just a moment, please—"

The heavy man was unexpectedly quick on his feet and went over to the canvases, still standing with their faces to the wall, where the young man had respectfully placed them that morning. What had happened in the meantime? Had his competitors, the Saint-Tropez Artists Gallery, shown signs of interest?

"Wait a minute—I might have time right now—let's take a look at them."

But the young man shook his head and marched to the door, his canvases under his arm. "Bye," he muttered, closing the door gently behind him.

One has one's little triumphs, thought Jerome, stopping outside on the pavement to tie the string around his three "children."

•

Nice. Four o'clock in the morning on the marketplace. Still too hot to wait in the truck. Ursula, Eva, Anabel and I got out and sat down on the running board.

"There's Marcel," cried Ursula suddenly and got up.

"Marcel?" Anabel followed her with her eyes as she pushed her way past the stalls and through the hammering, shouting crowd to the Renault, from which a young man was unloading crates and large glass balloons encased in wickerwork.

"Our neighbor's son," Eva yelled in her ear. "Marcel Raquin. He grows wine."

We all watched as Ursula greeted the young man, who looked up at her in surprise and adoration. He didn't even stop to close the doors of his car, but escorted her a few steps away to a café, where empty tables and chairs stood waiting for the market to end. They sat down. We made no comment, just watched them in silence. Eva smiled.

A dark figure carrying a large package planted itself in front of us, saluted and stowed the canvases inside the truck. "Where's Peter?" asked Jerome.

We pointed vaguely to the heart of the turmoil and he plunged into it.

The canvases! So the Nouveaux Artistes hadn't kept his paintings! And—had he seen Dujardin? Dark as it was, I had tried to read something in his face, but it told me nothing. I wanted to jump up and run after him—but I caught a look from Anabel in time. She nodded reassuringly. She seemed satisfied.

•

Later, in the sea, I watched her swim farther out than usual, turn on her back and drift with the current, which carried her slowly away from us. I swam over to her. Her white face rested on the water like a lotus blossom.

"I'm leaving tomorrow. Or maybe right away, as soon as we get home."

I had no right to plead and implore. Ferencsi's arms were waiting for her in London.

"Won't you sleep for a few hours first?"

"I'm not tired. On the contrary. But don't tell the others. Don't tell anyone. I'll leave a note for Ursula, thanking her and all that. And —don't be unhappy, everything is going to be all right. You'll see."

•

When I woke up at midday and saw a note slipped under the door, I felt orphaned and cried.

25

The painter telephoned.

"No sitting tomorrow. I'm going to Paris."
Astonishment on my part. "I've been offered a
show." Congratulations on my part. "But I
want to take a look at the place first. All new
people since the war. I'll be back on Friday. I'm
under pressure now—I'd like to include your
portrait. Twelve o'clock on Saturday as usual."

Three days without work and without
compass.

I reached for the diary. I hadn't opened it
for an entire week. I knew it was of no use to
me at this moment, for it wouldn't have contained any reference to those July days in 1939
in Grasse, those days that I had decided to relive
once again on my own, in slow motion, hour by

hour, up to the morning when Anabel left for London. That accomplished, she could take over again.

Diary, July 1939:

> Drove home, slowly this time. Spent two nights on the way—but not in Paris. Made a detour around. Had the feeling that Jean would find me in town wherever I'd be staying. Jean. I now think of him as Jean. Perhaps he was still in Saint-Tropez. More likely, in fact. First, because he wanted to talk to Jerome about his exhibition—he'd already done that, though, I could tell by Jerome's face that night at the market in Nice. Second, and more important, he would want to wait for Jeannine to get out of the Paris apartment. "I'll have to air the place," he'd said. "Thoroughly. Chatterjii"—the servant—"will melt aromatic candlewax to a thick paste, dip his naked feet in it and walk through all the rooms, climbing over the chairs, the sofas and the beds, leaving his footprints behind. When the wax hardens, he'll scratch it off and the air will be clean again." He was standing at the balcony railing as he spoke, and he laughed. It suddenly occurred to me to tell him about the footprints Edmonde had left on me. To tell him, for instance, that even now I can't smell turpentine without getting sick.

I laid the book down on the table. Edmonde! So that was the painter's name, her Christian name. No one knew her real name. She signed her work "E.T." and had become famous under her nickname, "Madame Eté."

That was the first time I'd ever been able
to talk about it. No one listens the way Jean
does. I had hardly mentioned my dear
stepmother—and he already knew what
Edmonde had meant to me. When I told
him that even today I can't have my clothes
dry-cleaned, that they either have to be
washed or given away when there's a spot
on them because the very thought of
turpentine turns my stomach, he interrupted
me. "It will never make you sick again. As of
now you'll actually enjoy the smell of
turpentine or benzine. Like fresh pine
needles."

It's true! On the way home I had to stop
three times to fill up. Usually I have to get out
of the car and move a considerable distance
away, but I forgot all about that, sat where I
was, paid, drove off again—suddenly
remembered and actually thought I noticed a
smell of treebark or resin or pine needles
inside the car. How easily one can fool
oneself if one trusts somebody! A tricky
thing . . .

He told me, quite casually, that he
knew Edmonde, that she'd had two shows at
his gallery. No further comment.

We stood side by side on the balcony for
a long time. Most of the lights were out.
Only a lighthouse in the far distance turned
slowly around, and for a split second one
could distinguish the sea from the sky and
remember where one was standing. I would
have liked to stop that beacon. Only in
complete darkness, without horizon, without
familiar shapes, could I tell him everything.
Everything. Even about the apartment in St.
James's Street. That was the only time he

reacted. He reached for my hand and pressed it so hard that it hurt. He said I must give up the apartment at once, in fact never set foot there again, give notice by telephone and mail them a check. He was so insistent that I think I promised. Of course I can't keep my promise, I still have my things there. So does Jerome. Have to pay Mrs. Cook too.

At twelve o'clock on Saturday I was sitting in the studio holding my old pose. The portrait was finished, but when I said so, the painter just muttered, mixing her paints.

During our coffee break she chortled into her cup.

"I've got a bit of news for you."

"About your exhibition? Have you accepted?"

"It's all arranged. Decent people. A bit young but well mannered. No, I mean a bit of news for *you*. I went to the Dujardin Gallery. It isn't there anymore—that is, Dujardin isn't there anymore. He's gone off to India or Tibet or somewhere for good. Nobody knows where he is. It's now run by other people, mediocrities, uninteresting. But I made some inquiries. Jeannine's still around. Do you know what she did during the war? Joined the resistance fighters!"

"There's an old Jewish saying, 'Before I'm surprised—I don't believe it.'"

She laughed. "She really fought. In her way, of course. She had a couple of German army officers for lovers. Pure patriotism. And so, during the occupation she had plenty of nylons and champagne for herself and plenty of military information for a fine young chap in the resistance. After the war she married him. The people at the gallery had her address, and I didn't want to pass up the opportunity— for your sake." She grinned. "Now you're sitting there with your ears pricked up like a dog's. Well, her husband is an instructor at the local driving school. He's younger than she is. They live in Neuilly, in a little house with a garden. God-awful! Roses around the door, a swing for the kiddies. Two of them. A fat woman opened the door—I wasn't sure at first whether this could be Jeannine or not. A living room with crocheted mats all over the place, and a mother-in-law who lives with them. Didn't leave us alone for a minute, either, but Jeannine didn't seem to mind. She showed me a print in their bedroom—abstract—the only souvenir of her Dujardin days. Mother-in-law stood in the door-way watching us suspiciously, an old dragon with her mouth turned down and a mustache like a hussar. Jeannine remembered my name. I pretended I'd come for Jean Dujardin's ad-dress, but of course she didn't know it. Then I left. The children were playing in the sandbox in the garden. Pretty funny, eh? Hold it! There's an expression on your face just now—I'd like to get that on the canvas! Keep thinking the same thing. Let's get back to work."

It was easy to keep thinking the same thing, to run the film backward, back from the fat wife of the driving instructor to the German army officer and to the Hotel Albi in Saint-Tropez.

•

At the Gurnemantzes' the hot days had dragged on after Anabel's departure. Outwardly everything was just the same. Only Jerome was now excused from picking, for he would set out with his easel in the morning and return only when the light began to fade. He painted doggedly, joylessly. Even in the evening, when we stood the wet canvases against the trunk of the pine tree and admired them, the corners of his mouth turned up into the old defensive smile. He wasn't fooling himself. He didn't allow himself to forget the reason why on October 1 posters would appear all over Paris saying: LORRIMER. FIRST EXHIBITION. DUJARDIN GALLERY.

Ursula spent some time every day at Madame Raquin's—on account of the asthma. She always took Jean-Pierre with her. Peter didn't say anything, Eva did three people's work and could be heard singing in the kitchen. Aesculapius showed up on the terrace more frequently, as if he sensed something, trotting from one person to another, nodding his head vigorously, and was paid off in carrots. Once, when I was drying dishes, he poked his big donkey's head through the kitchen window. I had the feeling I could lift off his head—and there would be Bottom standing outside like in *A Midsummer Night's Dream.*

Once, while I was filling his baskets in the orchard, Peter appeared with a bottle of disinfectant to get rid of the ticks which liked to settle in the long donkey ears. I held on to the wildly twitching gray felt tubes while Peter painted away.

"Peter," I finally said into the silence, "why

don't you talk to me? Nobody talks to anybody anymore. Everyone's stewing in his own juice. Couldn't we have another council meeting?"

He shook his head and kept on painting.

"The weather's changed. We're all frozen. The great ice age is coming."

"Don't you mind Ursula spending so much time at the Raquins'?"

"I have no right to mind. If she's going to marry Raquin, the boy has to make friends with him."

"And suppose she comes back to you?"

"Then Eva will kill herself. That's what she says."

I released Aesculapius's ear and he made his escape, protesting loudly.

"Take the chance! I don't think she'd do it, she's always singing so happily in the kitchen—"

Peter packed up his pharmacy, took out his pipe, filled it, and thought it over.

"I have an idea that the ones who sing in the kitchen are apt to cave in when the going is rough."

•

When I got back to the house, a telegram was waiting for me. From my agent. "Return soonest stop Leading role excellent script *Captain's Lamp* with Oskar Homolka stop Rehearsals begin July 20." I ran to Eva, to Ursula, explained to Jean-Pierre, kissed Aesculapius, whirling in ecstasy like a spinning top. All the pressure of the last weeks had lifted—at least for a few glorious minutes.

Where was Jerome? Somewhere under the umbrella pines on the adjoining hillside. Clutching my telegram and trying to stay in the shade, I raced down our hillside and up the next one. I could see him in the distance, crouched on his folding chair, absorbed and paying no attention to my shouts announcing my arrival.

"Jerome!" I waved the telegram under his nose. He disengaged himself from something a long way off and made an effort to focus on the piece of blue paper.

"Well, what are you going to do?"

"How can you ask?" I cried. "There's a train at eight-thirty for Paris. If we can't get a sleeper, we'll simply have to sit up."

He stuck his brush in the jam jar dug next to him into the sandy ground. Then he said with slow deliberation, pointing to the half-finished canvas on the easel, "I can't come with you. You can see for yourself why I can't."

I sat down in the sand. Why was I always charging ahead like a horse with blinkers thinking only of myself? To hell with my London job—it was Jerome's turn now at long last. Of course he couldn't come with me, he now had to look after his own interests. My excitement and ecstasy melted away. Ahead of me lay nothing but the long railway trip back to London, rehearsals—alone.

Not completely alone, though. Anabell But could I impose on her again? I'd really have to let her spend all her time with Ferencsi—if he was still in London.

Jerome would stand on the platform tonight and wave to me. Separation. Weeks and weeks of separation. And just at the time when it was so important to reconstruct our life together again. We were rid of Jeannine, root and branch, but that didn't mean that we two had grown back together again. We'd have to go about that slowly and cautiously—and casually. No demands, no searching looks, no "proving our love," just being together . . .

All *kaput* for the time being. Should I turn down the part? Could I afford to?

Jerome too had been staring thoughtfully into the pine trees. Perhaps he had been thinking along the same lines. I hoped so. Now he started squeezing paint out of tubes and picking up his brushes again.

"You could do me a favor though: Take my finished paintings with you and deliver them to the Dujardin Gallery, rue Faubourg St. Honoré."

•

I sat up all night, slept for a few hours, and when I woke up we were at the Gare de Lyons. Taxi to the Hotel de la Muette, and in answer to the porter's fond inquiry, "No, Monsieur's not with me this time," a quick shower and off to the Dujardin Gallery with the paintings.

The secretary had been duly briefed and took charge of the package; Monsieur Dujardin wasn't around. Disappointment! I had looked forward to meeting him. The secretary showed me into the office, unpacked the canvases and stood them against the wall—just as Jerome must have done when he came for the first time while Jeannine was lying on that leather sofa over there! The secretary nodded approvingly; Monsieur Dujardin would be pleased . . .

I took the bus back to the hotel. Economize! Who knew whether the new play would be a success? The heat wave was finally over and it was pouring rain. Paris in a summer rain. The pavement glistened, the Arc de Triomphe was reflected on the Champs-Elysées. My bus took me past the Café Colisée. Babs! Should I call her up? Certainly not.

After sleeping for a couple of hours at the hotel, I called her and we met at the Colisée. Her faithful followers didn't bother us; most of them had left Paris, if possible for America, and she herself, she told me, would be leaving soon for Hollywood. Robert had had a couple of offers.

I looked around and thought that Paris smelled of war. People were hurrying through the street, nobody strolled about windowshopping, the cafés were half-empty. I had never seen the Champs-Elysées so hushed. Only Babs doggedly radiated high spirits in her usual black-and-white elegance. Obviously, the little mishap at the Hotel Albi lay way behind her.

"Why isn't Jerome here?"

I explained. She stared at me open-mouthed.

"An exhibition at Dujardin's? How did he manage that?"

I shrugged my shoulders, looking ignorant and clean. She sensed something, couldn't puzzle it out.

"And where's your girl friend—what's her name?"

"Maclean. In London."

"And Jerome's staying on in Grasse?"

I nodded, managed to keep up the innocuous expression on my face. She gave me a thoughtful look.

"You know, you're not quite so germ-free and wholesome as you used to be. You're catching up!"

"I'm learning. Soon I'll be allowed to stay up late and talk to the grown-ups," I said, paying for my own coffee and for hers.

Back to the hotel. There was still some time left before my train. I stood by the window, looking at the trees, whipped by the rain. The Calais-Dover crossing would be awful. Telephone. A voice I didn't recognize.

"Jean Dujardin."

"Yes?"

"I'd like to talk to you about Anabel."

"Yes?"

"Tell her I'm waiting for her here in Paris. But not for long. I'm going back to India."

"But she can't just drop everything and—"

"Before long, millions of people are going to have to drop everything."

He seemed to be speaking of a *fait accompli*. War. An alarm bell started ringing in my brain: What would become of *The Captain's Lamp?*

"Very soon individual destinies won't count anymore," said the voice. "Your friend has only a few weeks' time. She must hurry. I'm waiting."

He hung up. I remained sitting on the bed, trying to find my way out of this labyrinth. What did this man want of Anabel? He knew all about Bill and Nina—and about Ferencsi. Why was he interfering? And so authoritatively, as if he had a right to, as if he were her guardian or guardian angel. He hadn't mentioned the "danger" that was supposed to be threatening her in London. All the same, his voice left me resentful and troubled.

●

Diary, July 1939:

L. back from Grasse. Quite unexpectedly. Alone! Rehearsals for a new play. Jean called her in Paris—
No echo inside me. Every day pushes him farther away. On the balcony at the Albi I seriously considered—only for a second but quite seriously—going to India. Getting away, making my escape, stripping off my life like an old dress and burning it. Putting on another one, start again. Absurd. I'm Bill's so-called wife, Nina' bad mother, I run the house, I'm brailling a new book for the blind. From morning to night I have only one thought in my head: When will J. be back?

●

Rehearsals had started. A good part, an insolent young woman who goes through "terrible sufferings," grows up and is "purified" in the process, the way these things happen in scripts.

A telegram from Jerome: "Tomorrow Simon's sixtieth birthday stop Take bottle red wine stop Four canvases finished stop Love Jerome."

Dilemma. Tomorrow I would have rehearsals all day and an evening script session at the director's home. I called Anabel, although I felt guilty, having seen her only once and very briefly since I had gotten back. On top of it I had actually forgotten to ask her if Ferencsi was still in London or whether her trip to Grasse had ruined everything. What kind of a friend was I? One couldn't excuse everything on the grounds of pressure of rehearsals.

But on the telephone Anabel was her usual self, didn't seem to feel at all neglected. Yes, of course she'd get the wine and take it to Simon. In case he wasn't home—there was no *r* in August—she'd leave the package at the door.

She called me that evening. Simon, she reported, hadn't been home.

●

Diary, August 1939:

> Visited Simon. His birthday. Brought him wine from J. and L. and cognac from me. Received an appropriate welcome. Had firmly resolved not to drink with him. Refused the first glass but kept him company on the next four. Felt wonderful. Told him—I'm afraid— all about my trip to Grasse. Except for Jean. I didn't leave him out on purpose—after the fourth drink I didn't have any control over my purposes—but because Jean just didn't

show up. He remained invisible, out of reach.

Simon enjoyed it all immensely. He needed cheering up just as much as I did: His axolotl is dead. Assassinated. He left his cleaning woman to look after it while he went to the seaside on vacation. She fell ill and sent her sister over to clean up. The sister had never seen an axolotol and when she saw it floating there motionless, she thought it was dead and flushed it down the toilet.

We were both in mourning. He for his love, I for mine. Simon, whom I hate, is the only person I can drink with. And only then can I stand him. What's more—it almost doesn't stop there! I don't fool myself. Ever since Edmonde I've tried my damnedest to suppress it but it's still there. Edmonde couldn't take alcohol, she'd fall into a kind of stupor, sitting or lying on the floor, her eyes and mouth wide open, looking surprised and moronic. I used to die laughing at her. Once—strange, now I actually feel ashamed, whereas I used to get a kind of kick out of this memory—once we were drinking in the studio when what's his name, that pianist, knocked at the door. Can't even remember his name, only that he was crazy about me. Edmonde was half gone already, so I poured another whiskey down her throat and she passed out, stiff as a ramrod. And then I made the pianist—what the devil was his name? Richard something—I made him sleep with her instead of with me. I remember we both thought it was terribly funny. Between us, we carried her into the bedroom—and then I went back to the studio and kept on drinking until Richard came back from the bedroom. Suddenly, the whole thing seemed to me extremely squalid and I threw him out. Never saw him again. Edmonde didn't wake up until the next morning. She knew nothing, thought she'd had a nightmare. After that she never touched another drop of alcohol—although I never told her! I was afraid she might kill me. And today, twenty years later, I got really drunk again. And with Simon, who's responsible for the whole mess, for Jerome's his work after all. He'll never be able to shake his father off, for Simon's the stronger of the two. There's no chink in his armor. The more I insulted him, the more happily he agreed with me.

When I began to flag, he went over to the attack. Said he hoped I wasn't trying to kid myself that I wanted to save J. for L.'s sake. Nothing but my own vanity and my own jealousy had made me race across France all night like an avenging angel, he said. The hell with L.! I, Anabel, was the one who had lost J., I'd been beaten with my own weapons.

What is truth anyhow? Everyone has his own. I denied it, told him I'd broken off with J. beforehand, swore a sacred oath on "my daughter's life"—at this he nearly choked with laughter inside his wobbly double chin and congratulated me on my sense of humor. When it was all over, I found myself at a dead end, disarmed. I staggered down the five flights of stairs, holding on to the handrail. Never in my life have I felt such hatred, such impotent hatred. Sat at the wheel for ages before I drove away. Wasn't sure I could find my way home.

●

After an interval of one week there was another entry, the last one. August 1939:

> Jean's trying to reach me. Person-to-person calls from Paris. I always pick up the receiver —after all, it might be J.—and tell the operator that I don't know where to get in touch with Mrs. Maclean. Which happens to be true. I'm not in touch with her.
>
> I had a letter from him today—where did he get my address?—he was sailing this week, I must hurry, he had reserved two cabins—
>
> None of this concerns me. I'm not reachable. I'm on another ship, traveling in another direction.
>
> J.'s been back in London for several days, so L. told me. Not a word from him. I didn't expect anything else and yet I'm incapable of taking any action. I sit at my desk and look at the telephone. In front of me is the brailling machine and the book I'm working on, in case Nina comes into the room. She does so quite often nowadays, unfortunately. Tells me about her exams. As though she were trying to include me in her life. Too late. No interest. My loss. But—how can a child replace the man you love?
>
> L. senses something, although I do my damnedest to keep her from suspecting anything. She calls me from rehearsals, driving me crazy because I think each time: J. at last! She wants to know how I am, apologizes for the hundredth time for not coming to see me. I'm glad she can't come. How could I explain the way I look? My clothes are flapping about me, I look like a scarecrow. I'd have to resurrect Ferencsi and

blame it all on him—and that thought makes me puke now.

Jean wrote that war would break out within the next three weeks. As if I cared. Other people care, though; it's the only subject of conversation all around. Total strangers babble away at each other on the street, seeking reassurance. Bill's organizing a branch office in Scotland—he's expecting his call-up any moment because he's a reserve officer. He's in high spirits, as if he were looking forward to it.

L.'s rehearsals are in hot water. Yesterday on the telephone she said in a shaky voice, "We may not even open."

J. would have remained in Grasse if war were not just around the corner. I wonder if his exhibition will still take place? L. says J.'s not very hopeful but is neither disappointed nor depressed. I know why. He's probably even relieved. He's rid of Jeannine, of the Dujardin "charity" exhibition, and he's rid of me. In fact, he's rid of all the counterfeit currency in his life.

Those were her last words. Except for the letter—still unopened.

26

"Where were you in the autumn of 1939?" I asked the painter.

"In Paris. Where else?"

She was giving the canvas a coat of temporary varnish. She learned back and narrowed her eyes. "The raw umber on the shoulders has sunk right into the canvas. English paints! French umber never does that. I'll have to go over it again. Pose, please."

I pulled the poncho over my head, sat down in my chair and submerged myself into the nightmare days of those last few weeks of peace in 1939.

In the middle of August they had called a meeting on stage. The director, looking pale, remained standing in the wings, staring at the floor. We knew what was coming. For the last week *The Captain's Lamp* had been barely flickering—two members of the cast had already been called up—and today it would be extinguished.

The producer saw to that. Rehearsals were suspended as of today, he said, that is—well, they would be temporarily interrupted. He hadn't given up hope but in the present political situation—one could only pray that things would soon settle down—one never knew—anyway, for the present there was nothing one could do except listen to the radio, read the papers and wait.

We melted away. Everyone silently picked up an envelope containing half a week's rehearsal pay at the stage door. The doorkeeper waved to us, knocked at his wooden leg. "Got that the last time around. Only have one more to give."

I found my little car at the parking lot and caressed the wheel. It would have to be sold at once. Misery. How about ambulance driving? Good idea, I'd sign on today.

But my mother was waiting by the window with a huge smile on her face: My film company had called! Could I come to the studio immediately; an American actress had preferred to go home while the going was still good, and the film had to be finished, with retakes of all her scenes. Hallelujah! That very afternoon I stood in front of the camera and worked every day—until the morning of September 3.

"That's it," said the painter. "I'll have to wait and see how it looks when it's dry."

While she was making coffee—for the last time?—I wandered about the studio, saying goodbye. Of course I'd be back sometime, but only as a guest; I wouldn't belong anymore. I came to a stop in front of the bookcase. There, exactly at eye level, stood the little bronze head.

I picked it up and placed it on the table. Throughout those long weeks, while I had relived my life with Anabel, I had to make the same effort every time I entered the studio, to remind myself that she had once led another existence, a ragtag, dunghill one, with Edmonde, the painter.

She entered with the tray from the kitchen, sat down, poured the coffee. Anabel's head stood exactly midway between us. We drank in silence, our eyes meeting on Anabel's profile.

September 3! An easy date to remember. I raised my eyes to the painter's blunt face.

"Do you remember what you were doing on September 3, when the declaration of war was broadcast? Here in London it was eleven o'clock in the morning."

"I was in Paris, sitting in my bathtub. And you?"

"I was in a film studio, lying on a few square yards of artificial grass."

She stretched out her hand and pulled the little bronze closer, taking off her glasses. "And Anabel? What was she doing?"

"I don't know."

She gave me a severe look, had one last go at cross-examining me.

"Weren't you friends anymore?"

"Oh yes, we were friends."

She looked at me for a long time, sighed, gave up, pushed the head aside.

"Pose, please. Just a last check. I think we can finish today."

I picked up the little sculpture, carried it over to the mantelpiece and put it down where I had first seen it, half hidden by the vase.

Took up the pose. Looked in the direction of Anabel's head.

●

I knew very well what Anabel had been doing on September 3. I had been told. In detail. By two eyewitnesses, Nina and Mrs. Cook.

Nina had had lunch with her mother and heard her say she was going to the library for the blind. She wanted to find out what they were going to do with all those books, she had said. There might soon be a great many more blind people . . .

She had put on her red coat and left. But she didn't go to the library for the blind. She went to St. James's Street.

Mrs. Cook was working in the living room when she heard a sound at the front door. She switched off the vacuum cleaner and called, "Anyone there?"

"It's me, Mrs. Cook."

"Oh, Madam!"

Anabel was hugged and kissed. Thank God she was back! Just in time, too—Mrs. Cook had been so worried—and where's the young gentleman? Called up already? Not yet. Oh well, there was plenty of time for that, after all, one still wasn't quite sure . . . perhaps Mr. Chamberlain hadn't really meant what he'd said that morning, perhaps he was just trying to show old Hitler . . . what did Madam think?

Anabel was not given time to answer. She was stripped of her coat and forced to accompany Mrs. Cook on a tour of inspection. Big summer housecleaning, everything neat and shiny.

The old girl thought Anabel looked a bit thin. And pale! What about a nice cup of tea with lemon? Mrs. Cook shuffled off to the kitchen, leaving the door open, talking away while the kettle boiled.

Receiving no answer from the living room, she stuck her head around the door and saw Anabel sitting very straight on the sofa, like a visitor, looking around the room as if she were seeing it for the first time.

Mrs. Cook ambled into the room with the tray, collapsed into a chair, poured out two cups, murmuring a belated "If Madam doesn't mind . . ."

Anabel stirred her tea.

"Mrs. Cook, I—we'll have to give up the apartment."

Oh Lord, oh Lord! That was just what Mrs. Cook had been afraid of, everybody was giving everything up! She made one last try: "But Madame, the apartment's so convenient! When the young gentleman comes on leave . . ."

Anabel didn't answer, kept on stirring her tea.

Something began to dawn on Mrs. Cook.

She hesitated, then took the plunge. Really, the young gentleman was—if Madam would excuse her—he was a bit too young. That never worked out, she could tell her a thing or two herself, her own late lamented had been too young too, six months younger than she was, that made quite a difference, a man ought to be older, ought to be able to protect one . . .

Anabel nodded absently. Encouraged, the old woman laid a hard, wrinkled hand on her arm. Madam was still young, there were other fish in the sea! She herself hadn't believed it in her first grief, but later on . . .

Anabel gently freed her hand in order to open her handbag, took out her purse and laid some pound notes on the table. Three months' wages.

Mrs. Cook made a half-hearted protest, pocketed the money and staggered to her swollen feet. She must finish vacuuming, she said, or she wouldn't be able to sleep that night. Just five minutes more, if Anabel didn't mind.

Anabel didn't mind. She remained sitting, even with the machine buzzing around the sofa, lifting her feet obligingly so that nothing should be overlooked. The roar didn't seem to bother her.

Later, she got up and sat down at the desk, took a pad of notepaper and an envelope out of the drawer, rummaged in her purse but couldn't find what she was looking for. Turning to Mrs. Cook, she made a writing movement with her hand. Mrs. Cook understood, took a pencil out of her apron pocket and held it up questioningly. Anabel nodded and Mrs. Cook vacuumed over to the desk and handed it to her.

She wrote very briefly—just a few lines, as far as Mrs. Cook could tell—tore the sheet roughly off the pad, put it in the envelope and sealed it.

"Shall I post it for you, Madam?"

Not necessary, thank you. She put the letter in her handbag. Tore off another half-sheet and wrote something on it. Without putting it in an envelope, she stuffed that in her purse too.

"I've almost finished, Madam."

She smiled at Mrs. Cook. No hurry.

At last the vacuum cleaner stopped raging and was wheeled back to the kitchen. Anabel remained sitting at the desk, her head resting on her hand, waiting patiently. Probably for the young gentleman! Oh well, this wasn't the first time Mrs. Cook had seen her sitting about, waiting, though all the other times she'd been restless, impatient to get rid of her. This time she was quite different. Mrs. Cook untied her apron and hung it on the kitchen door. Then she returned to the living room.

"The key, Madam."

No reply.

"Madam?"

"Oh, yes. Thank you, Mrs. Cook."

The old woman looked at the motionless figure at the desk and realized that Anabel wasn't even aware of her presence anymore. She felt hurt.

"Well then—goodbye, Madam. Many thanks . . ."

"Goodbye, Mrs. Cook."

A few minutes later she put on her red coat, slipped the long strap of her handbag over her shoulder and stepped out on the balcony.

27

On the late afternoon of the same day a police car stopped outside No. 104A, Cheyne Walk. Two officers got out, looked up at the sky for a moment—the first drops of rain were beginning to fall—and disappeared inside the house.

Shortly afterward they knocked at Simon's door.

Simon got up, distinctly annoyed at the disturbance. He had just set up a new sheet of graph paper and was waiting for Jerome; the refrigerator was empty. This morning the declaration of war—and already the authorities were knocking at his door! Why did they want? Gas masks? Ration cards? No? Well, what then?

They'd like him to come along. Out of the

question! What was this all about? Alien registration?

The men in uniform hesitated.

"Sir—it's a question of identifying a body—"

Simon stared at them in bewilderment. "There must be a mistake somewhere—"

One of the men took a piece of paper out of his pocket and spelled out, " 'Contact Mr. Simon Lorrimer, 104A Cheyne Walk.' Is that you, sir?" And since the fat man made no move, just stared at him with wide-open eyes, he held the piece of paper in front of his face. "Recognize the handwriting, sir?"

Simon, with shaking hands, put his glasses on. "No."

The policemen looked as if they didn't believe him. The body was that of a woman, they explained. Thrown herself from the balcony. In St. James's Street. Nobody knew her—that is, nobody knew her name.

For a split second Simon thought it was me, as he later confided to Jerome, but when the policeman spoke of black hair and a red coat—

"Anabel!" he whispered hoarsely.

"Sir? Then you do know her, don't you? What is her name, please?"

Simon silently cursed his bad memory, his lack of interest. Jerome had in fact mentioned her name—some Scottish-sounding name. "Macmillan or Maclaren or something like that . . ."

"Sir, you'd better come with us, please."

Simon retreated hastily behind his desk. Absolutely not! The whole thing had nothing whatever to do with him!

The policemen were full of solicitude. "It's only a question of a few minutes, sir—the City morgue isn't that far from here, we'll take you in our car."

"No!" Simon yelled at the top of his lungs. "I mustn't leave the flat!"

"Why not, sir? You'll be back in a jiffy—"

They advanced a step. Simon barricaded himself, picking up his chair threateningly.

"Impossible! I can't—there's an *r* in the month—"

"How's that again?"

"An *r!* September has an *r* in it—I can't go out in the street—"

The officers exchanged glances, then moved to encircle him, one of them closing in from the left, the other from the right.

"And it's raining!" Simon screamed. "I haven't got a raincoat—"

A few minutes later they were dragging him toward the police car, a woolen blanket thrown over his head.

•

They drove him rapidly to the City of London morgue. Although it was still pouring rain, a few people stopped under their umbrellas to watch a fat elderly man being forcibly hustled out of a police car and through the entrance.

In the outer office Simon regained his composure. He broke away from the policeman's grip with a surprisingly deft movement, wiped his wet forehead and said imperiously, "Where's my blanket?"

It was brought in from the car while he stood erect, like a bear about to pounce. He snatched the blanket from the policeman's hand and began to fold it, matching the corners with extreme care, taking his time. His guards did not interfere.

"And now?" he asked curtly.

The two policemen beckoned to him to follow them down the long dark corridor. There was a strong smell of Lysol and of something else—Simon didn't know what it was but he had to stand still for a minute, gasping for breath.

The policemen stopped outside a door, waited politely for him to catch up with them, and opened it. The room was no bigger than a large waiting room. Tiled floor, tiled walls, about a dozen stone slabs, some empty, some occupied and covered with sheets.

One of the policemen remained at the door. The other walked across and raised one of the sheets, dropped it again, went on to the next slab, raised the sheet, and beckoned to Simon.

Simon took a step forward, turned and retreated to the man at the door, whispering hoarsely, "I can't do it—don't you understand—"

The policeman took off his helmet, passed his hand over his sparse hair, and looked at the figure in front of him, at the limp shoulders and the helpless, gaping mouth.

"Come on, man," he said slowly. "Show some guts."

"Come on!" called the other one.

Simon took a deep breath. Just a few steps—

Her head was turned to one side. All he could see was the black hair, matted with blood, and part of the forehead. He fled back to the door, sweating profusely. "Anabel," he groaned, leaning against the door frame.

Outside in the hall was a bench, probably placed there for good reason. Simon just made it. He put his head down between his knees. When he was able to sit up again, one of the policemen was holding a glass of brandy out to him. He gulped it down—suddenly clutched his forehead.

"My son! My son knows her name."

"Where is your son? What's his name?"

"Jerome. Jerome Lorrimer. He may be at his apartment."

They helped him walk down the long corridor to the office. He knew the telephone number by heart; he'd always been able to remember figures. The policeman dialed and handed him the receiver. It rang and rang. No answer. No one at home.

"Is there anyone who would know where your son might be?"

Yes, I might. But Simon didn't know where I lived, in fact he may only have known my first name.

"Wait outside," said the policeman. "We'll call the number every ten minutes and let you know."

There were more benches in the corridor. Simon chose one under the window and managed to open it, but the rain came streaming in. He shivered and wrapped himself in the blanket.

Gradually it grew dark. At one time, one of the policemen came out of the office and looked at the motionless figure under the blanket, then returned, closing the door. A short time later they called him in. The number had answered.

"Jerome?" whispered Simon. "It's me—Simon. No, I'm not sick. Jerome, what's Anabel's last name? Quick, Jerome, tell me, what was her name? Maclean?" He turned to the watching faces. "Maclean! Anabel Maclean. I told you it was a Scottish name."

A policeman took the receiver from him.

"Excuse me, sir, but do you perhaps know the address too? Yes, sir, something has happened. Sorry, sir—she fell from a balcony. No. Killed instantly. Do you happen to know whether there are any relatives? Hello? Are you there?" He reached for a pencil. "William Maclean, 32 Queen's Gate, S.W.2. Is that her husband or her father? Aha. Thank you, sir. Just a moment, please—" He turned to Simon. "Your son wants to come and pick you up here—is that all right? Yes, sir, City of London morgue."

•

Simon went back to his bench. The policemen left for Anabel's house to inform her husband. A good thing they hadn't tried to saddle him with that too. What the hell did it have to do with him, anyhow? Why had Anabel asked that he be notified and not her husband? And if she was trying to get her own back on somebody, why not on Jerome?

The last time she had been to see him—

how long ago was it? A week at the most—she had stood by the door, holding on to the handle because she'd had too much to drink, reciting poetry, a passage from John Donne, the famous one, which even he had recognized: "No man is an island, entire of itself . . . Any man's death diminishes me . . . Therefore never send to know for whom the bell tolls—" At that point he had joined in and they had declaimed in unison, "It tolls for thee!" And they had burst out laughing. She had been laughing too, he could swear to that, she had laughed just as loudly as he had, repeating, "It tolls for thee!" and pointing at him.

Had she said anything after that? Simon racked his brain. No. She had left. He had heard her going downstairs, still laughing.

He pulled his head in like a snail and wrapped himself up in the blanket as if it could make him invisible.

•

The next time he looked up, Jerome was standing in front of him. Behind him, an official.

"This gentleman would like to see the body of Mrs. Maclean—"

"No!"

Simon shook off the blanket, jumped up and grabbed his son.

"No, you mustn't! Out of the question."

Jerome was pale under his tan, haggard, his lips pressed tightly together, the dark eyes flickering dangerously.

"I must see her."

310

But Simon held him firmly, pressing him against his great chest, feeling his son's body against his own—for the first time.

The official watched with neutral eyes.

"Is the gentleman a relative?"

"No!" shouted Simon.

"Only the family may give permission for the body to be viewed."

Jerome pushed against Simon's shoulders with his fists and broke loose.

"I'm a friend—an intimate friend—"

"Sorry, sir," said the official. "But why don't you wait here? They'll be here before long. They've already been notified."

Jerome clasped and unclasped his hands.

"Come," said Simon quietly. "Come. Or do you want to meet them?"

Jerome looked along the dimly lit corridor and considered for a moment if he shouldn't simply run down the length of it and throw open every one of the doors—but the official intercepted his glance and lifted a warning hand without saying a word.

Simon folded up his blanket again.

"Come on," he repeated calmly.

It was dark outside. The rain was falling less heavily, a steady warm late-summer rain.

"Let's go to my place," said Simon.

Jerome shook his head.

"I can't. I've got to go back to our apartment. She might be there already, waiting for me. She's been on her feet at the studio all day. I always get our supper ready."

They were still standing in the shelter of the portico. Simon looked uneasily around, but there was as yet no car in sight bringing "the family."

"Let's walk a few steps until you find a taxi." They wandered down the dark street in silence. Tonight, the evening after the declaration of war, most people were staying at home, listening to the radio, arguing, speculating, making plans.

Jerome paused.

"What were you doing there? How did you know?"

"She had a note in her purse asking that I be notified."

"You? Why you?"

Simon lowered his head, hesitated.

"She wanted to punish me."

"Punish you? She didn't even know you."

"Yes, she did, she came to see me. Twice. I never told you. I liked her, I liked her a lot. That's why it was so terrible to see her lying there—"

Jerome stepped up very close to his father, peering through the darkness into a face that involuntarily drew back.

"What did you do to her?"

"Nothing."

"What did you say to her?"

"Nothing except the sort of thing you and I always say. Nothing else. You must believe me. I was just joking—"

Jerome raised his trembling fists and held them close to his father's eyes. "I know your jokes!"

Horrified, Simon watched the tears rolling down his son's cheeks, watched him shiver in the warm air, turn and run blindly across the street.

"Jerome!" shouted Simon. But he didn't turn around.

•

When I opened our apartment door that evening, he was sitting on the bed.

"Good Lord!" I cried. "You're all wet."

He ran his hand over his wet hair, his dripping coat.

Only then did I see his face. He made an effort to stand up, but I quickly sat down beside him and took his hand. Ice-cold.

"Jerome, what is it?"

He looked at me with stricken eyes, looked away, tore his hand out of mine and sat motionless for a moment. When he turned back to me, the eyes were guarded, and his voice was firm.

"Anabel's dead. She jumped from the balcony."

He gave me time, waited until I could speak.

"Where?" The Macleans' house had no balcony.

Without taking his eyes off me, Jerome said in a quiet, steady voice, "In St. James's Street. She had an apartment there. *We* had an apartment there, she and I."

He's lying, I thought. I don't know why he does it, but he's lying.

"Ferencsi? Did she have an apartment with Ferencsi?"

"I am Ferencsi."

His eyes held mine until I was able to stand up and walk over to the window. I felt an acute pain in my stomach and remember opening the window and noticing that it had stopped raining. There was a pleasant smell of wet leaves. War had been declared that morning. Anabel was dead. What Jerome had just said was thrown out by my mind with extraordinary rapidity, was not allowed to register. Not yet. First the other hurdles. Don't rush me, Jerome, or I'll collapse.

"When did it happen?"

"This afternoon."

"Does Bill know?" No answer. I turned toward him, saw him nod slowly. My feet took me to the telephone at the other side of the bed. I sat down beside it, picked up the receiver, put it down again.

"Why did she do it?"

"I didn't want to see her anymore."

"Because of Jeannine?"

"No. I just didn't want to anymore. Hadn't for a long time."

We sat there on the bed, our bed, each on his own side, back to back. He got up, walked around the bed and stood in front of me.

"I told her that I'd like to die in your arms."

"That's easy," I said. "The hard part's living together *until* you die."

"Don't you want to anymore?"

I took his hand, still cold as ice.

"I don't think so. If I still feel tomorrow morning the way I feel now—then no."

●

That was the last time I saw him.

I heard later that he had been drafted soon afterward.

●

I spent the whole of the next day filming. Got through it somehow. That evening I went straight from the studio to the Macleans'. Saw Bill. Saw Nina.

Bill very pale, his lips pressed tightly together. Already in uniform, with a black armband. He was sitting stiffly in a chair in his library, looking at the empty fireplace. I took another chair and sat down next to him. He gave me a hostile look.

"Did you know?" he asked in a dry voice.

"No."

A long silence. I think he believed me.

"How can one live for twenty years next to a woman and know nothing about her?"

"You knew she wasn't happy."

"But all the rest! I had no idea. Why didn't *you* know? Women are supposed to have a better instinct for that sort of thing."

"I was too busy."

He turned his head and looked at me out of somber eyes.

"I asked you a serious question."

"I gave you a serious answer."

●

Nina was waiting for me in her room. She wasn't wearing black. I put my arms around her and we stood holding each other. Now, for the first time, I was able to cry. She wasn't. She did not cry. She whispered into my neck, "Do you know now—about St. James's Street?"

"Yes."

"I've known for more than a year. I saw her coming out of the house—him too. At times I wanted to tell you, then I'd think: better not. I'd suspected something for a long time. Hadn't you?"

"No."

"I don't understand that."

"I was too busy."

She pulled back to look at my face, wiping away my tears with her hard little hand.

"What will you do now?"

"Go on living."

She disengaged herself from my arms and stood in front of me, very straight, her shoulders no longer hunched, her face serious, not sad, grown up.

"I'm going to volunteer for the Land Army. It said on the radio that they need sturdy girls. I'm sturdy."

●

Bill called me after the funeral. He said he had something to give me. I drove over, parked at my usual spot next to the garden gate. Every step I took reminded me that this was the last time.

Bill was waiting for me in the library. I took my time crossing the living room, but I never paused, not even by the yellow wing chair.

He was sitting at his desk with a cardboard box in front of him.

"This is for you," he said. "It has your name on it. I found it in her safe." He hesitated, smoothed his fair, wavy hair. "And—the police gave me this letter. It's marked 'For L.' It was in her purse. They opened it but it contains nothing of any interest to them. I resealed it but—I read it too. Sorry. But I thought, perhaps —anyway, it's for you."

He pushed the box and the letter over to me and got up.

"I'm glad about the war," he said. "I hope they'll send me over to France."

Some ten months later, he was there, trapped at Calais with his regiment. He fought his way out, survived Dunkirk and D-day plus 3, went through a campaign in the Vosges as major in a commando unit. Survived.

Simon didn't. A bomb got him in his apartment in December 1941. He never went to the air-raid shelter during the months with an *r* in them.

Peter Gurnemantz also died in the war. He had volunteered for the foreign infantry regiment and was among the first to be killed. After the liberation of France in the autumn of 1944, I had a letter from Grasse. Ursula wrote that Eva had had a breakdown after Peter's death and had spent several years in a sanatorium. She was better now, however, and the two sisters were living once again together on the Gurnemantz farm—Jean-Pierre was now sixteen! New peach trees had been planted and were doing fine. But Aesculapius was dead. ....

●

All that was left was the letter. The diary, locked up again with its golden key, had returned to its old cardboard box. There was really no need to carry it around with me anymore. Perhaps I ought to get rid of it, throw it in the Thames.

I opened the envelope.

One page crudely torn off. No salutation.

I feel an enormous relief. I'm completely free. No one has any power over me anymore. I don't love anybody—or else I love you all equally. It amounts to the same thing.

Do you remember the last time we went swimming at Nice? The current was carrying me out to sea, I was very happy letting myself drift along—but then you came swimming up, looking at me so anxiously—

Now you don't need to worry about me anymore.

A.

28

The painter was on the telephone.

"I'm just packing my canvases for Paris. Maybe you'd like to see your portrait before the crates are nailed up."

In the studio was a huge shipping crate, six feet high and almost as wide. The canvases were stacked one on top of the other, separated by slabs of cork. On the very top was my portrait.

She took it out, put it into a plain, make-shift frame and stood it against the wall, looked back at me and scrutinized my face once again.

"I can still see a couple of things I'd like to change, but I suppose I'd better leave it as it is. A portrait's never finished, anyway. You know, you look quite different now from the way you looked at our first sitting."

I felt quite different too. It's not true that one grows up slowly but surely; one marks time for years—and then one suddenly takes a leap forward.

The painter knelt in front of the canvas, took off her glasses and peered closely at it.

"What do *you* see when you look at yourself in this picture?"

"A half-finished woman."

She nodded slowly.

"That's what I was after. Your face still has quite a few possibilities."

She got up and passed her hand over my forehead, my cheeks, my chin, as if she were blind and wanted to "see" me. "Don't ruin it," she growled, almost threateningly.

Ruin what? My face? No, she meant my entire keyboard, the white as well as the black keys. So that I wouldn't wind up in the end looking like a double-crossed clown . . .

That was her goodbye. Suddenly she was in a hurry to get rid of me, as if she could hardly wait to be off, bag and baggage. For Peru. For how long? A few years, perhaps forever. She flew off like a bird, free as a bird.

One day somebody would find her, all shriveled and rolled up in a ball like one of Simon's flies, and dried out like her Indian mummy, the Doge's cap still on top of her head.